MW01384156

The Vagrants of the Barren

and

Other Stories

The Vagrants of the Barren and Other Stories of Charles G.D. Roberts

Edited with an Introduction
by
Martin Ware

The Tecumseh Press
Ottawa, Canada
1992

2nd printing, 1997

Tecumseh Press Limited
7 Mohawk Crescent
Ottawa, Ontario, Canada K2H 7G6

CIP data

Canadian Cataloguing in Publication Data
Roberts, Charles G. D., 1860-1943
The vagrants of the barren and other stories

Includes bibliographical references.
ISBN 0-919662-34-X (bound) - ISBN 0-919662-35-8 (pbk.)

I. Ware, Martin II. Title.

PS8485.024V28 1991 C813'.54 C91-090565-7
PR9199.2.R6V34 1991

Cover photograph courtesy John Coldwell Adams, taken by Elsie Pomeroy

Cover design by Aerographics, Ottawa

Printed and bound in Canada.

Content

Introduction ix

Mothers of the North 1
A Master of Supply 8
Keepers of the Nest 17
By the Winter Tide 29

The Little Homeless One 33
The Lord of the Air 47
The Keeper of the Water Gate 63
The King of the Mamozekel 73

The Little Wolf of the Pool 100
Little Silk Wing 104
Queen Bomba of the Honey-pots 113

Mrs. Gammit and the Porcupines 127
The Vagrants of the Barren 146
The Ledge on Bald Face 159

Textual Note 169
Bibliography 171

Introduction

This selection presents the reader with a small sampling of the best of the more than two hundred and thirty animal stories written by Charles G.D. Roberts over a span of almost fifty years (1886-1935). Recently readers have been more and more drawn to the best of his animal stories—for their story-telling and artistic power, for the modest precision of their representation of animals, and for the challenge offered by their interpretation of animal psychology. It would be fair, I think, to say that there has been a growing consensus that his animal stories represent his most valuable contribution to the literature of Canada and of the English-speaking world. This is not to suggest that the reader should overlook his poetry, his translations, and his prose idylls. It is simply to recognize that his main writing energies went into his animal stories, and that in the best of these (perhaps about five dozen[1]), we recognize a distinctive voice and a distinctive achievement.

The task of making a representative selection of these stories is a daunting one. Beginning in 1892, Roberts started to publish them in Canadian, British and American periodicals and magazines, and for most of the next thirty years, new stories were constantly appearing, sometimes as many as sixteen in a single year. He adopted the practice of periodically making collections in book form of recent work, and tried as best he could to link the stories in each single volume according to a principle of thematic unity: the stories of *Earth's Enigmas* (1896), for example, are almost all concerned with the mysterious cruelty of fate, and *The Kindred of the Wild* (1902) pieces centre on the strange parallels between the lives of animals and lives of humans. Indeed each of the more than ten U.S. published collections of his work has a distinctive focus, and so the thematic concerns of his work are remarkably diverse. As well, there is considerable variety in the tone and form of the stories that he wrote over the years. This inevitably means that it would be very difficult to bring together a relatively brief selection of his stories which would adequately represent his overall achievement. And no guidance is to be had from Roberts himself, because, perhaps for copyright reasons, he never issued a representative selection of his animal stories in his own lifetime.

This selection of fourteen stories cannot be said to be significantly more rounded than the seven or more selections published since his death.[2] Each of these has had a thematic, or a geographical, or an aesthetic focus, and none makes any claim to offer a selection based on comprehensive principles. In my selection, which I have entitled *The Vagrants of the Barren*, the first three stories are Arctic stories; and the title story, which comes second last, places man within the pattern of wintry imperatives of an essentially Arctic world. The Arctic, it seems to me, represented a kind of absolute zero of Roberts' imagination, a place where, as he writes in "The Master of Supply," it often seems as if "the incalculable cold of outer space were invading the outpost of the world" (*infra*, p. 8). His Arctic animal stories are closely linked with the long poem of his old age, "The Iceberg," which depicts "the immeasurable desolation" of the primeval Arctic where "Forever no life stirred."[3] Yet just as in the poem, the bulk of the iceberg will outrage "the silence" of the Arctic sea "with mountainous surge and thunder," so in the animal stories, Roberts emphasizes again and again the suddenness of Arctic happenings. As he writes in "The Keepers of the Nest," the coming of the Arctic spring was so sudden that "all the forces of the cold were routed in one night" (*infra*, p. 21). The "implacable savagery, the deathly cold of the Arctic winter" is a constant symbol in these stories for the life-extinguishing and life-threatening forces which call forth all the capacities and energies of those they threaten. The first three Arctic stories offer an appropriate point of departure for this selection by providing a backdrop to Roberts' celebration in his stories of the life instinct which not only drives individual animals to preserve life either for themselves or their tribe, but also makes them, in Fred Cogswell's words, "glory in the activity of the moment."[4] The locales of the stories range from the Arctic tundra to the Tantramar Marshes, and from these to the backwoods of the Saint John River Valley and to the mythical Ottanoonsis country (probably a fictionalized version of the highlands not far from the Restigouche River). The diversity of the chosen stories is as wide-ranging as possible—in terms of the animal protagonists, of the forms of the stories and their date of composition, and of their prevailing tone. But in virtually all of them, we see that the workings of inexorable necessity, so immediately apprehensible in the Arctic stories, can sometimes be averted by chance aberrations or by an animal's sudden adoption of a course of action which defies expected patterns. In Roberts' fictional animal world, the principle of indeterminacy is at work.

One of the main values of Roberts' animal stories lies in the way they give powerful imaginative expression to the lonely struggle for life in the Canadian wilderness. In a recent documentary Irving Layton has referred to Canadians' confrontation from the beginning of their history with a nature "raw in tooth and claw" which is "one vast warring turbulence."[5] The isolated villages and settlements often seemed to be no more than mere dots, surrounded by vast tracts of tundra or bushland, more the domain of the wild beasts than of man, and the settlers never enjoyed the feeling of nature mastered, which Americans have with the triumphant movement of their pioneering "frontier" from East to West. Canadians, it has been said, have always felt that their settlements and now their cities are mere specks "beleaguered by darkness"; and critics have added that the country's outstanding writers have ventured into the threatening circle, and made their peace with the wild beasts literally or symbolically associated with it. To borrow Irving Layton's words, we cannot escape the apparent "nothingness of the cosmos," its marvellous fertility and ceaseless savagery. From the first, the best Canadian artists have been imbued with an awareness of "the double hook of beauty and terror" and a restless metaphysical questioning. Roberts, in his animal stories, was surely one of the first and remains one of the most gifted writers to have articulated this outlook. We find in his work numerous variants of the universal metaphysical symbols of the life-giving cup of blood, or the eagle clutching the dove in its talons, as a glance at the conclusion of "By the Winter Tide" or of the title story will indicate.

The realistic animal story as developed by Roberts and his fellow Canadian and contemporary, Ernest Thompson Seton, has its place in the literature of the English-speaking world as the ultimate development of the romantic lyric of nature. Roberts himself was very much an heir of nineteenth-century romanticism. He himself edited a volume of Wordsworth's poetry, and he would have heartily endorsed the latter's exclamation "How exquisitely... / The external world is fitted to the mind."[6] As a writer, he aspired to be a "dawn-clear" reflector of the life of nature.[7] With Wordsworth, he might well have said that nature was "all in all," but his was not the benign nature "which never did betray / The heart which loved her."[8] Joseph Gold has pointed out in a seminal article that the Wordsworthian sentiment with which Roberts had most affinity was that of the "Mutability Sonnet": "Truth fails not, but her outward forms that bear / The longest date do melt like frosty rime."[9] For both Roberts and Wordsworth the metaphysical symbol of the snake with its tail in its mouth had decisive significance. Plants and animals are constantly dying that another generation may live: life is continually dissolving and renewing itself in unexpected ways. It was the role of the Canadian backwoods boy, far closer than the English dreamer to the raw reality of the natural struggle, to chronicle the often violent and painful but sometimes noble and reassuring process by which life is sacrificed that life may be sustained.

Roberts wrote the stories selected for this volume out of deep familiarity and personal knowledge of the animals, birds and fish that provide his subjects. In response to a reader who found it difficult to believe that a first-rate writer could also be a woodsman, Roberts wrote:

> It is right that I should tell you that I, for my part, am perhaps more than an 'amateur' woodsman—having spent my childhood and boyhood on a backwoods farm, shared in all the work of the woodsman and never been to school til I was fourteen. Then til the age of twenty-five, I managed to spend a good deal of time in the woods—the real backwoods, and ever since I have been making frequent returns to the life to which I am native.[10]

For the first thirteen years of his life (1860-1873), Roberts spent endless hours exploring the glebe farm and surrounding woods attached to his father's Westcock parsonage, and roaming the "miles on miles" of the long salty reaches of the Tantramar Marches which join New Brunswick to Nova Scotia. Then after his father's move to St. Anne's Church in Fredericton, he devoted weeks each year to long camping and canoeing trips into the back country; and after his appointment in 1885 as a Professor at King's College, Windsor, his main release from academic and domestic routine was provided by wilderness expeditions, often enough in pleasant female company. For years he had innumerable opportunities not only to study, but to know as a fellow creature the moose, bear, lynx, cougar, porcupine, fox, beaver, muskrat, eagle, goose, duck, deer, otter, weasel, hare and bat which he was later to depict with such skill.

In turning to the animal story, Roberts had innumerable memories on which to draw. He also had some knowledge of the range of animal stories available in the world's literature. His prefatory essay "The Animal Story" to his first widely acclaimed collection *The Kindred of the Wild* (1902) makes it evident that he thought carefully about his own adaptation of the animal story, and its place in the evolution of the genre as a whole. He was quite clear that the realistic story as developed by himself and his fellow Canadian

Ernest Thompson Seton represented "a culmination" and a return to origins. In "The Animal Story" he argues that the first manifestations of the form were to be found in primitive man's realistic accounts of successful hunts. While interesting in terms of Roberts' own turn to realism, this view is questionable in the light of the animism, transformations, and supernatural influences that we find in a great many of the animal and etiological tales of aboriginal peoples. There is a greater degree of continuity than Roberts suggests between primitive animal tales (with their manitous and magic) and classical mythic tales (with their centaurs and unicorns). Roberts' account of the presentation of animals in classical and Christian literature is largely one of the growing alienation between man and animals. As human reason is elevated to a supreme position, so animals sink in the scale of esteem, and in literature a mode of abstraction comes to prevail. As Roberts suggests, the animals of classical fable and myth become more and more the vehicles for human qualities; in Aesop's work, Raynard the Fox and Isegrim the Wolf (the fabled embodiments of craftiness and cruelty) become "alien to the truths of wild nature" (*KW*, 20). Christianity, he goes on, only exacerbated the situation: "While militant, fighting for its life against the forces of paganism, its effort was to set man at odds with the natural world...the inarticulate kindred reaped small comfort from the Dispensation of Love." Roberts acknowledges the softening influence of the gentle friars and hermits, Francis of Assisi, Anthony of Padua and Colomb of the Bees, but his argument requires him to avoid dwelling on the animal stories associated with these and other great Christian saints. His emphasis, rather, is consistent with the way in which medieval writers in their bestiaries and allegorical writing ignored animals in themselves, so as to use animal images to signify moral qualities and human passions.

In concentrating on animals in themselves as the subjects of his stories and rejecting some aspects of the classical tradition, Roberts was both one of the last romantics, and one of the first writers to be radically influenced by Darwin. His birth followed the 1859 publication of *On the Origin of Species by Natural Selection* within little more than a month, and his work was profoundly conditioned by Charles Darwin's theory of evolution, and particularly by the great man's desire to bridge the rift between man and animals, to assuage the alienation. Where many of Darwin's readers were disgusted to discover their kinship with hairy beasts, walking on all fours and sporting fluffy tails, Roberts rejoiced in this newly discovered kinship.[11] This faith in the kinship of man with the creatures of the wild is the rock on which the project of his animal stories rests, though the associated Darwinian ideas of the struggle for survival and the effects of natural selection in evolving princely creatures are important supporting notions.

In the last thirty or forty years of the nineteenth century, the Darwinian sense of man's kinship with the animals combined with the Victorian delight in tear-squeezing melodrama (so evident in passages of Dickens and Hardy) to give rise to a vogue for sentimental animal stories by such writers as Ouida and Alfred Ollivant. The best known of these tales is Anna Sewell's *Black Beauty* (1877) with its wrenching account of a high-spirited mare's sufferings at the hands of a cruel cabby. In Canada, Sewell's fervent admirer Marshall Saunders won a large public with her melodramatic and moralizing story of a homely dog, *Beautiful Joe* (1894). The American Dudley Warner with his finely told *A Hunting of the Deer* shifts the focus to a wild animal, but the preoccupation remains with an animal's sufferings, and the tone is of the tear-inducing variety. Rudyard Kipling more than anyone else was responsible for energizing the animal story, and so paving the way for Roberts and Seton with the immense success of his *Jungle Books* (1894/5)—though the stories contained in these are in no sense realistic. Kipling's hero, the wild boy Mowgli, is no genuine wolf child, and the speaking animals echo Indian folk wisdom more than they do genuine animal compulsions. What Kipling did do was to create a taste for well-told exuberant tales, filled with the struggle and suspense of animal life. The English-speaking public's taste had been whetted for stories of the wild, and the stage was set for the appearance of the genuine animal story, as shaped by two gifted Canadians—Ernest Thompson Seton and Charles G.D. Roberts.

Roberts included three animal stories in *Earth's Enigmas* (1896), but it was not until the publication of Seton's *Wild Animals I Have Known* (1898) that the vogue became really established. The international success of *Kindred of the Wild* (1902) confirmed the popularity of a new kind of story, which for years to come commanded widespread interest and admiration. Roberts characterized it as "a psychological romance constructed on a framework of natural science" (*KW*, 24). Basing the imaginative picture on the empirical observations of naturalists, Roberts and Seton strove to give an accurate representation of an animal's attempts to answer the imperatives of its nature in the quest for food, the nurture and protection of the young, the escape from predators, the winning of a mate, or the preservation of its freedom from man. At the same time, as romancers (and Seton was much more the romancer than Roberts) they aimed to suggest "the motive beneath the action" and to capture "the varying elusive personalities of the animals" (*KW*, 24). Moved by the Darwinian faith in the kinship of man and animals, their purpose, as far as possible, was to create an animal's eye view of experience, which they regarded as different in kind but not in quality to that of human beings.

Seton took considerable liberties in depicting the animal heroes in his stories. The fact that he was briefly provincial naturalist for Manitoba has misled some critics into suggesting that in his tales he was the more empirical and scientific of the two writers. A perusal of his stories gives the lie to this, and shows that a modest adherence to the minutiae of nature was not his forte. As a born raconteur, he excelled in heightening the facts of natural history, in boldly divining individuality and burgeoning mental capacities in his animal heroes, and evolving highly dramatic plots. Like the man himself, Seton's stories are larger than life, large in their power to awaken our fascination about the hidden psyches of animals, and large in their tragic sense of animal magnificence as it is confronted by the near certainty of violent death. Whatever the doubts the scientist may advance, Seton's delightful account of the extraordinary capacity of the veteran crow "Silverspot" to meaningfully use a wide variety of calls, of his strange propensity to collect treasures, and of his uncanny control of the fledglings raises endlessly intriguing questions.[12] And there is a dark classical simplicity in his depiction of the epic hunt by the remorseless trapper Scotty MacDougall of the Kootenay ram Krag, "majestic as a bull, graceful as a deer, with horns that rolled around his head like thunder-clouds about a peak."[13]

Where Seton is an expansive first-person presence in his stories, explaining how a fox cub learns from a vixen, or slanting a grouse story towards the conservationist, or pointing up the pathos in the persecution of a killer wolf, Roberts' hallmark is restraint. He keeps out of his stories, and is careful not to outdo the "modesty of nature." Unlike Seton, Roberts plots his stories very lightly. He will typically introduce his animal protagonist by setting a scene which offers a series of casual impressions of animals going about their own business. It is as if Blue Fox, in "The Master of Supply," registers the caribou browsing, the bold indifference of the Trumpeter Swans, the "clamouring" ducks, the twittering of the juncos and snow buntings, and the lemming mice squeaking and scurrying along their runways (*infra*, p. 9). Roberts lets his reader share Blue Fox's vigilance, and the latter's quick recognition of an airborne shadow—"slow moving deliberate wings"—and he delays, as the fox might, before identifying the bird as dangerous (the predatory Arctic Hawk-Owl). We find the same casualness punctuated by surprise in many of the stories, notably in "The Keeper of the Water Gate" and "The Homeless One."

Part of the reader's faith in the truth of Roberts' representations of the wild creatures can be ascribed to the forms in which he focuses his stories.[14] The simplest of these is "the anecdote of observation" (*KW*, p. 21), which he describes as a story which treats "of a single incident" that lies "within the scope of a single observation"

(*Watchers of the Trails*, p. viii). Of the stories included in this selection, "The Wolf of the Pool" offers the clearest example of this form. The effect of such stories is to make us see with the astonished eyes of the exploring observer facets of wilderness life which we have scarcely imagined before. In "The Little Wolf" we are taken into the submarine depths of a pond, and invited to pay microscopic attention to "a fantastic looking creature," the back of whose head is almost covered "by two dully staring globes of eyes" (*infra*, p. 101). These are partially veiled by "a shield-like mask," which hinges back in a most sinister fashion when edible creatures appear in view. The story in such 'anecdotes' exists for the observations, and their capacity to quicken the reader's imaginative recognition of the strange otherness of living beings. These stories depend for their effect on the intensity and brevity of the observations.[15]

Closely connected to 'the anecdote' is a form much favoured by Roberts which he calls "the piece of animal biography" (*WT*, p. viii). This, as he goes on, "follows the wild creature through wide intervals of time and space." Though the writer must necessarily build it up "from observations detached and scattered," he can by artfully linking discrete episodes make his story "not less true to nature than the transcript of an isolated fact." "The Keepers of the Nest," "The Master of Supply," and "The Keeper of the Water Gate" are most clearly instances of "the piece of animal biography." In each case, the story follows a creature or creatures though episodes that are widely scattered in time, but each is unified by a couple of main motifs or images. The great whistling swans who are "The Keepers of the Nest" triumph again and again through their mastery of the elements of air and water; while in "The Master of Supply" it is Blue Fox's gregarious siting of his lair and his provident digging of cold storage caches that etch themselves in the reader's imagination. With "The Keeper of the Water Gate," the muskrat's cunningly angled submarine tunnel to his nest figures again and again as an indicator of his preferred strategy for survival. These partial animal biographies, like Roberts' 'anecdotes,' tend not so much to highlight the narrative sequence, as to set the reader to musing on the extraordinary as it manifests itself in the ordinary lives of the wild creatures.

The 'piece' of animal biography ought, I think, to be distinguished from the rounded animal biography or complete chronicle (*infra*, p. 81). Where the more fragmentary 'piece' lays emphasis on some distinctive facet of an animal's life, the fuller 'biography' makes it possible for us to gain an impression of the emergent individuality of its animal hero, as the reader may confirm by looking closely at "The Homeless One," "The King of the Mamozekel," and "Queen Bomba of the Honey-Pots." Each of these stories offers a cumulative account of an animal's experience in such a way that we almost inevitably see the animal modifying his or her survival strategy in the light of remembered experience. In "The Homeless One" there is one episode where the big buck is marshalled down 'rabbit' runways by a huge goshawk behaving in a very peculiar manner (*infra*, p. 41). On this occasion, the snowshoe hare just manages to evade the hawk's mate hovering over the outlet; but when he later encounters a fox with comparable intent, he makes a much prompter escape. Similarly, in "The King" the old bull moose at the last discovers the fortitude to overcome his fear of ambushing bears which has plagued him all his life. To use Roberts' words, "In the wilderness world...history has a way of repeating itself" (*infra*, p. 97); but a major theme of his stories is that animals do not always repeat themselves. His animal biographies force us to recognize the possibility that animals are capable of applying intelligence to memory, and as a result modifying their instinctive behaviour patterns. Fred Cogswell has good reason for calling these stories "existential," for in the 'biographies' we see their animal protagonists remaking themselves at particular critical moments in their lives.[16]

In his "Introduction" to *Kindred of the Wild* (one of his first collections), Roberts mentions "the adventure story" as being the framing form for some of the pieces included. While there are some drawbacks to shaping animal happenings in terms of this form, there are significant advantages as well. The form is considerably less episodic and haphazard than the biographical and anecdotal forms that Roberts tended to prefer, and so might be thought of as less appropriate to reflecting the chance patterns of animal life. However, when Roberts offers an account of one animal hunting another, or trying to escape man, or protecting its young from predators, the episode frequently contains within itself the constituent elements of the adventure story. These include unity of action, a strong element of suspense, and a bold and simple rendering of the protagonist; and while these may be simple, they are adapted by Roberts with thoroughly satisfying effects in "Mothers of the North," "Lord of the Air," and "By the Winter Tide."

In the last mentioned of these, every detail of the story contributes to our sense of the inexorability of the fate awaiting the little muskrat, but we continue to hope throughout that he will be delivered from his adventure, and somehow escape the glaring eyes of the great white owl perched above him.[17] Roberts' depiction of setting helps to create the story's mood of suspense. The panorama is laid out in a series of precariously ephemeral planes: the moonscape, the precarious blue-white radiance of the marshes, the mile-on-mile of the Tantramar mud flats, and beyond them all the line of the swift Fundy tide. With the inexorable approach of the flood, a sinister shape "floats over the dyke top" (*infra*, p. 29). Roberts' language here lures us into seeing the great white owl with his "flaming eyes" as being almost as inescapable as the tide.

The main convention of the adventure story makes us cling to the hope that the little creature will miraculously escape. And Roberts' employment of a further convention of the adventure story makes this matter to us, for he presents the muskrat's inner reaction to the emergency in the simplest, and yet the most sympathetic, terms. Simple characterization is a standard convention in the adventure story, but it happens to be more appropriate to the rendering of animals than of human beings. Roberts shows us action and reaction in the muskrat primarily through images. The little creature's hope of submarine escape arises when "the first frothy rivulets" trickle through the ice cakes to touch his feet, and this hope is given force by his longing for "the narrow safe hole, the long, ascending burrow, and the soft warm-lined chamber that was his nest" (*infra*, p. 31). The very simplicity of the images which embody the longing make Roberts' rendering credible. Without them we would not be able to identify as strongly as we do with the warm little speck of consciousness in the centre of the cold-blue radiance of the story's cruel landscape. Any excess of sentiment in us is checked by Roberts' laying stress on the fact that the would-be predator, the great white owl, is driven by a compelling necessity, "the face of his hunger."

W.H. Magee in a very useful article has argued that Roberts' unique contribution to the animal story was to capture the non-human aspect of a creature's experience.[18] On a more questionable line, he has gone on to suggest not only that Roberts is at his best when his theme is an animal's quest for prey or provender, but also that he seldom writes really well "with any want for his heroes but food." This is surely to fail to do justice to Roberts' handling of some of the other great compulsions of an animal's nature. In "The Lord of the Air" he treats the great bird's untameable instinct for freedom with absolute conviction. The picture he gives of the eagle's "watchtower," a lightning struck pine, which is hummed about by the untrammelled winds, and which gives unmatchable vistas of valley brims stretching endlessly to the horizon, conveys a superb impression of the eagle's utterly unfettered freedom. And when we see the bird at "the supreme altitude" of his immense spiral, we share for an instant the feeling of superiority to every creature and circumstance in creation. The story depends for its final effect on irony. In the slight heightening of the language, the very occasional introduction of a phrase associated with pomp ("he sailed away majestically"; "the stone...was a provision of destiny for his convenience"), Roberts reveals the habit-bound complacency which will betray the eagle to the designs of the trapper. Then when we see the terrible constriction placed on the freedom of the bird—he is chained by a rusty dog-chain to a perch in a rude shack—we become aware of the far greater complacency in the bird's jailers. The dimension of their ignorance is the bird's hunger for freedom, the extent of his gaze from chained entrapment to distant mountaintop. In the dénouement the men's ignorance turns out to be comic when the eagle works free, and leaves them like Laurel and Hardy grasping a broken chair and a useless silver chain, while the great bird mounts to his native element, and the men seem nothing more than grotesque dwarves.

The narrative point of view which Roberts adopts in his stories is admirably suited to conveying the inexorable nature of the evolutionary struggle. It can best be described as "the intimate omniscient," for while the principal attention is directed to the external setting and action, the picture will often come to centre momentarily on the animal in itself—through emotionally charged descriptive details, and a presentation of the creature's simple thoughts. Furthermore Roberts will quite frequently employ the equivalent of a split scene focus, divided between protagonist and antagonist to enhance our understanding of the dynamics of the conflict. In "Mothers of the North" Roberts gives us a parallel picture of the two mothers—the emaciated polar bear making scarcely enough milk to keep her cub alive, and the walrus anxiously coaxing her wounded calf to nurse. We are made to see the source of the walrus' protective feeling in the description of "the truculence" of her calf's sprouting tusks which is "belied by the mildness of its baby eyes." We see the same material solicitude reflected in the description of the bear whose eyes "film" when her cub whimpers at the too thin stream of milk. For a time the story's focus centres on one of the mothers, and we follow the actions and reactions of the polar bear mother, who has caught the scent of the walruses, knows that they are at their ease, recognizes them as formidable adversaries, yet is driven by hunger to hunt them. At the crisis, however, we again have a double picture, when we see the bear as she must appear to the walrus, and the walrus as she must appear to the bear. Roberts' narrative technique is designed to enable him to offer the most balanced and objective account possible of the inevitable conflict at the heart of nature.

It is only in the stories where human beings figure significantly that Roberts adopts the limited third person narrative perspective which allows him to offer a fairly full picture of the inner life of the protagonists as well as to depict the external action in which they participate. In "Vagrants of the Barren" we follow the story by following the movements of its hero, Pete Noel, but at the same time come to know a great deal about his thoughts and feelings. Even here, we are not confined to seeing the story from the standpoint of a single figure, because, as we will see, Roberts offers his characteristic double perspective at the moment of the story's concluding crisis.

When attending to the external appearance and actions of Pete Noel, Roberts uses metaphoric and descriptive language which underline the veteran woodsman's animal affinities. This is a story very much in key with the purely 'animal' stories. When burnt out of his shack, Noel "in the deprivation of his tree roof" has been taken back "appreciably nearer to the elemental brute (*infra*, p. 148). We see him devouring the charred remnant of a side of bacon "with as much ceremony as a hungry wolf," and later after a hard day's trek, he 'claws' himself a deep sleeping hole (*infra*, p. 149). His one hope is to find an animal and kill it for the nourishment which will give him the strength to endure; and his opportunity arises when a herd of caribou appear on the ridge above his sleeping hole. Roberts now draws attention again and again to the parallels between Noel and a hunting beast. To prevent the caribou from scenting his man "taint," he must painstakingly get upwind of them, which he does "by slipping furtively from rampike to rampike, now creeping, now worming his way like a snake" (*infra*, p. 152). When the caribou subsequently take alarm, Noel doggedly trails them, his eyes "automatically" downwards, and when he loses the trail in a sudden storm, he plunges into it with a grim animal courage. Finally, in the last extremity of hunger and exhaustion, he literally falls on the caribou; he now reacts with the fury of a beast at bay, his unsheathed knife being the human equivalent of the sharp antlers with which the floundering caribou prods at him (*infra*, p. 157). The external perspective offered by Roberts thus compels us to see Noel as a hunting creature, almost indistinguishable in attributes to many of the animal denizens of his stories.

The inner aspect of the third person narrative perspective, which allows us to discover a good deal about the thoughts and feelings running through Noel's mind, significantly modifies this picture. What Roberts emphasizes here in his protagonist is the reflective habit of mind of an equable philosophic temperament. Even as his lonely home is being consumed by the flames, the woodsman, far from giving way to understandable spasms of anguish and dismay, is taking stock of his means of survival and figuring on turning the catastrophic flames to advantage. Noel's defiant reflective powers, which both here and subsequently hold his impulses in check, are presented in different terms than those of the animals. In Roberts' work, the wild creatures are shown as having memories which work through relatively simple image patterns, but these memories only comparatively rarely impel them to modify instinctive behaviour, and then only in fairly predictable ways. By contrast, Noel's reflective powers are forcibly counterpointed to his impulses, and permit a very strong awareness of the human self. This is most apparent when in his sleeping trench under the icy stars, he weighs the full strength of his silent adversary (Nature in her cruel and predatory phase). At this point he becomes self consciously aware of "the indomitable man-spirit" within him (*infra*, p. 150).

What Roberts means by this expression becomes clear at critical moments during Noel's struggle for survival. When he works his way up on the caribou, only to discover that they have moved off some distance, his impulses tempt him to rush off in pursuit. But a voice within him which blends resolution, restraint and calculation tells him that the exercise of intelligent patience is his best hope, even if it is a forlorn one. Later when all seems lost, and the storm has swallowed the animals' trail and all signs of refuge, he finds his way in terms of the direction of the wind, and its relation to what he remembers of the lay of the land. In the overwhelming confusion of the storm, he knows that the caribou will "forget both their cunning and the knowledge that they are being hunted," but for himself he does not forget these things.

To this point, the heart of the story lies in Noel's subjective experience, as this reaches us through the intimate aspect of the third person technique. As the story moves to its conclusion, however, Roberts offers us his characteristic double perspective. The homeless woodsman is tempted to make good his loss by preying on the stormbound herd, but the moment his hand touches his first victim's flank, he is powerless to act. The flow of sympathy from beast to man and from man to beast breaks the hard shell of Noel's self-absorption. At the point where Roberts writes "when his hand strayed down the muzzle, the animal gave a terrified snort at the dreaded man smell so violently invading his nostrils," we recognize that both the author and his protagonist have the imaginative capacity to live within the hide of the caribou, if only for an instant (*infra*, p. 157). A single sentence here serves to provide a surprisingly strong counterpoint to the human tone and perspective of much of the story.

The human perspective of the protagonist is more radically undercut in "The Ledge on Bald Face," which can best be described as an ironic parable. It should serve to remind the reader of how ardently Roberts desired to achieve "a purely objective" presentation in his best work. Here the veteran woodsman, Joe Peddler, in his attempt to cross a high and perilous ledge, presumes that he can "take full measure of these splendid breadths of sunlit, wind-washed space" (*infra*, p. 161). Throughout his long climb across the brow of the mountain, which conceals layer on layer of geologic time, he persists in nursing the conviction that his right to life is almost as superior to those of the animals he meets, as he is to "the interminable leagues of cedar swamp" far below (*infra*, p. 159). As he perseveres in striding into the glare of the sun, we are brought to see the utter delusion in his pride in his eagle perspective. The eagles circling about the heights know what he does not: that the 'Law' requires that creatures cross the ledge with the sun behind them and not in front of them, so that they will avoid "unnecessary—and necessarily deadly...struggle" (*infra*, p. 160).

Roberts' achievement in this story is to make it a closely observed and credible story of a knowledgeable woodsman's exploration of a new trail through the high country; and at the same time to incorporate into it his recognition of the qualities of his protagonist which make him an unlikely exemplar of the inner forces that set man against the possibilities and necessities of nature. For, though the story may be the unfolding of an enthralling adventure for its human protagonist, it is also a record of understated but sustained terror for the wild creatures who are following nature's primitive imperative by crossing the ledge with the sun behind them. Joe Peddler is able to overcome them with his bold confidence, and sends one bear scurrying, followed by his mocking laughter (a potent means of human domination as we see in the "Mrs. Gammit" story). He is able to dominate a second bear by the steady authority of his voice, and to compel him to retrace his footsteps. If we are to take the story as parable, the picture of Peddler driving the bear forward suggests the way man in general is herding the animals the wrong way down a perilous and deadly path.

The overall effect of Roberts' animal stories is to remind us of what Joe Peddler knows and has forgotten, and to impress on our imaginations what we see Pete Noel experiencing so comprehensively. For these stories serve to restore "confidence in the reality of the universal and original impulses" and to reemphasize "the distinction between the essentials and the accessories of life."[19]

Notes

[1] Terry Whalen's view, "Charles G.D. Roberts," *Canadian Writers and their Works: Fiction Series*, Vol 1, ed. by Robert Lecker et al. (Toronto: ECW Press, 1989), 174.

[2] The seven are: E.H. Bennett, ed., *Forest Folk* (Toronto: Ryerson, 1949); *Thirteen Bears* (Toronto: Ryerson, 1947); *Seven Bears* (Richmond Hill: Scholastic, 1977); Alec Lucas, ed., *The Last Barrier and Other Stories* (Toronto: McClelland & Stewart, 1958); Joseph Gold, ed., *King of Beasts and Other Stories* (Toronto: Ryerson, 1967); *Eyes of the Wilderness*, Copyright Joan Roberts, illustrated by Brian Carter (Toronto: McGraw-Hill Ryerson, 1980); and John Coldwell Adams' edition of the three last unpublished stories *The Lure of the Wild* (Ottawa: Borealis, 1980).

[3] From "The Iceberg," reprinted in W.J. Keith, ed., *Selected Poetry and Critical Prose: Sir Charles G.D. Roberts* (Toronto: University of Toronto Press), 207.

[4] Fred Cogswell, "Charles G.D. Roberts (1860-1943)," in *Canadian Writers and their Works: Poetry Series*, Vol 2, ed. by Robert Lecker et al. (Toronto: ECW Press, 1983), 209.

[5] "Poet: Irving Layton Observed," Canadian National Film Board Documentary.

[6] "The Excursion: Preface," 11. 66, 68.

[7] Quoted from Roberts' poem "The Marvellous Work," 1.22.

[8] "Lines Composed a Few Miles above Tintern Abbey," 11. 75, 122-3.

[9] Wordsworth, "The Mutability Sonnet," quoted in J. Gold, "The Precious Speck of Life," *Canadian Literature*, No. 26 (Aut 1965), 22-32.

[10] Letter to *Century Magazine*, 26 Oct. 1908.

[11] For a colourful characterization of Darwinian theories, see J. Travers Lewis, *Agnosticism* (Kingston, 1883) and *Second Lecture on Agnosticism* (Ottawa, 1884). These were Bishop Lewis' contributions

to a pamphlet campaign that he undertook against W.D. LeSueur who was championing Darwinian ideas.

[12] "Silverspot, the Story of a Crow," reprinted in *Selected Stories of Ernest Thompson Seton*, ed. by Patricia Morley (Ottawa: University of Ottawa Press, 1977), 19-32.

[13] "Krag, the Kootenay Ram," *ibid.*, 129-66.

[14] W.J. Keith has set the terms for the discussion of the types of Roberts' animal stories, though the account given here differs in some respects from his. See W.J. Keith, "Stories of Wild Life," *Charles G.D. Roberts* (Toronto: Copp Clark, 1969).

[15] "The Little Wolf of the Pool" had a companion piece "The Little Wolf of the Air." Roberts combined the two and rewrote the story which he called "In a Summer Pool." This has recently been published in *The Lure of the Wild: the last three animal stories by Sir Charles G.D. Roberts*, ed. by John Coldwell Adams (Ottawa: Borealis Press, 1980).

[16] Cogswell, 219.

[17] For a story about an Arctic Owl driven south by hunger, see "The Odyssey of the Great White Owl," in *The Lure of the Wild*, 11-21.

[18] W.H. Magee, "The Animal Story: A Challenge in Technique," *Dalhousie Review* XLIV (1961), 161 ff.

[19] Roberts' words as a young man in his twenties, "Introduction" to *Poems of Wild Life* (1888), reprinted in W.J. Keith, ed., *Selected Poetry and Critical Prose: Sir Charles G.D. Roberts* (Toronto: University of Toronto Press, 1974), 266.

Martin Ware
Sir Wilfred Grenfell College
Memorial University of
Newfoundland

Mothers of the North

It was in the first full, ardent rush of the Arctic spring.

Thrilling to the heat of the long, long days of unobstructed sun, beneath the southward-facing walls of the glaciers, the thin soil, clothing the eternal ice, burst into green and flowering life. In the sunward valleys brooks awoke, with a sudden filming of grass along their borders, a sudden passionate unfolding of star-like blooms, white, yellow, and blue. As if summoned from sleep by the impetuous blossoms, eager to be fertilized, came the small northern butterflies in swarms, with little wasp-like flies and beetles innumerable. Along the inaccessible ledges of the cliffs the auks and gulls, in crowded ranks, screamed and quarrelled over their untidy nests, or filled the air with wings as they flocked out over the gray-green, tranquil sea. The world of the north was trying to forget for a little the implacable savagery, the deathly cold and dark, of its winter's torment.

The great, unwieldy, grunting walruses felt it, too, and responded to it—this ardor of the lonely Arctic spring, astray in the wastes. On the ledges of a rocky islet, just off shore, the members of a little herd were sunning themselves. There were two old bulls and four cows with their sprawling lumps of calves. All were in a good humor with each other, lying with heads or foreflippers flung amicably across each other's grotesque bodies, and grunting, groaning, grumbling in various tones of content as the pungent sunlight tickled their coarse hides. All seemed without a care beneath the sky, except one of the old bulls. He, being on watch, held his great tusked and bewhiskered head high above his wallowing fellows, and kept eyes, ears, and nose alert for the approach of any peril. One of the unshapely, helpless-looking calves, with its mother, lay in a hollow of the rock, perhaps twenty feet back from the water's edge—a snug spot, sheltered from all winds of north and east. The rest of the herd were grouped so close to the water's edge that from time to time a lazy, leaden-green swell would come lipping up and splash them. The cubs had a tendency to flounder away out of reach of these chill douches; but their mothers were very resolute about keeping them close to the water.

Presently the little group was enlarged by one. Another old bull, who had been foraging at the sea-bottom, grubbing up clams, star-fish, and oysters with his tusks, and crushing them in the massive mill of his grinders, suddenly shot his ferocious-looking head above the surface. For all his gross bulk, in the water he moved with almost the speed and grace of a seal. In a second he was at the rock's edge. Hooking his immense tusks over it, he drew himself up by the force of his mighty neck, flung forward a broad flipper, dragged himself out of the water, and flopped down among his fellows with an explosive grunt of satisfaction.

They were not, it must be confessed, a very attractive company, these uncouth sea-cattle. The adults were from ten to eleven feet in length, round and swollen-looking as hogsheads, quite lacking the adornment of tails, and in color of a dirty yellow-brown. Sparse bristles, scattered over their hides in rusty patches, gave them a disreputable, moth-eaten look. Their short but powerful flippers were ludicrously splayed. They had the upper half of the head small, flat-skulled, and earless; while the lower half, or muzzle, was enormously developed to support the massive, downward-growing tusks, twelve to fifteen inches in length. This grotesque enlargement of the lower jaw was further emphasized by the bristling growth of long stiff whiskers which decorated it, giving the wearer an air of blustering irascibility. As for the calves, their podgy little forms had the same over-blown look as those of their parents, but their clean young hides were not so wrinkled, nor were they anywhere disfigured by lumps and scars. They were without tusks, of course, but the huge development of their muzzles, in preparation for the sprouting of the tusks, gave them a truculent air that was ludicrously belied by the mildness of their baby eyes. They rolled and snuggled against the mountainous flanks of their mothers, who watched them with vigilant devotion. The calf which lay farthest inland, apart from the rest, was in some pain, and whimpering. That morning it had got a nasty prod in the shoulder from the horn of a passing narwhal, and the anxious mother was trying to comfort it, gathering it clumsily but tenderly against her side and coaxing it to nurse. The rest of the herd, for the moment, was utterly content with life; but the troubled mother was too much engrossed with her little one's complaints to notice how caressing was the spring sun.

Meanwhile, not far away, was another mother who, in spite of the spring, was equally ill-content. Down to the shore of the mainland, behind the island, came prowling a lean white bear with a cub close at her heels. The narrow bay between island and mainland was full of huge ice-cakes swung in by an eddy of the tides. Many of these wave-eaten and muddied floes were piled up on the shore along the tide-mark, and as their worn edges softened under the downpour of the sun, they crumbled and fell with small glassy crashes. Hither and thither among them stole the fierce-eyed mother, hoping to find some dead fish or other edible drift of the sea. She had had bad hunting of late—the shoals of the salmon had been inexplicably delaying their appearance on the coast—and she was feeling the pangs of famine. To be sure, she was filling her stomach, after a fashion, with the young shoots of rushes and other green stuff, but this was not the diet which Nature had framed her for. And in her lack of right nourishment she was pouring her very life itself into her breasts, in the effort to feed her little one. He, too, was suffering, so scanty was the supply of mother's milk. Even now, as the great bear stopped to nose a mass of seaweed, the cub crowded under her flank and began to nurse, whimpering with disappointment at the too thin stream he drew. Her fierce eyes filmed, and she turned her head far round in order to lick him tenderly.

The stranded ice-floes yielded nothing that a bear could eat, and she was ranging on down the shore, disconsolately, when all at once a waft of air drew in from seaward. It came direct from the island, and it brought the scent of walrus. She lifted her long, black-edged muzzle and sniffed sharply, then stood as rigid as one of the ice-cakes, and searchingly scrutinized the island. The cub, either imitating his mother or obeying some understood signal, stood moveless also. One of the earliest lessons learned by the youngsters of the wild is to keep still.

There was not a walrus in sight, but the bear's nostrils could not deceive her. She knew the huge sea-beasts were there, on the other side of the island, and she knew they would be very much at ease on such a day as this, basking in the sun. Walruses were not the quarry she would have chosen. The great bulls, courageous and hot-tempered, the powerful cows, dauntless as herself in defence of their young—she knew them for antagonists to be avoided whenever possible. But just now she had no choice. Her cub was not getting food enough. To her there was nothing else in the world so important as that small, troublesome, droll-eyed, hungry cub.

Keeping herself now well out of sight behind the ice-floes, with the cub close at her heels, she stole down to the edge of the retreating tide. The bay was too crowded with slowly-moving floes to be quite as safe for the cub as she would have had it, but she could not leave him behind. She kept him close at her side as she swam. He was a good swimmer, diving fearlessly when she dived, his little black nose cutting the gray-green water bravely and swiftly. In everything he imitated her stealth, her speed, her vigilance, for he knew there was big game in this hunting.

The island was a ridge of some elevation, shelving down by ledges to the sea. The white bear knew better than to climb the ridge and try to steal down upon the walruses. She was well aware that they would be keenly on the watch against any approach from the landward side. From that direction came all they feared. When she arrived at the island, she swam along, close under shelter of the shore, till she reached the extremity. Then, behind the shelter of a stranded floe, she drew herself out, at the same time flattening herself to the rock till she seemed a part of it. Every movement the cub copied assiduously. But when she rose upon her haunches, and laid her narrow head in a cleft of the ice-floe to peer over, he kept himself in the background and watched her with his head cocked anxiously to one side.

The walruses were in full view, not fifty yards away. For all the pangs of her hunger, the mother bear never stirred, but remained for long minutes watching them, studying the approaches, while the scent of them came on the light breeze to her nostrils. She saw that the herd itself was inaccessible, being well guarded and close to the water. If she should try to rush them, they would escape at the first alarm; or if she should succeed in catching one of the cubs in the water, she would be overwhelmed in a moment—caught by those mighty tusks, dragged to the bottom, drowned and crushed shapeless. But with gleaming eyes she noted the cow and calf lying further up the slope. Here was her chance—a dangerous one enough, but still a chance. She dropped down at last to all fours, crouched flat, and began worming her way upward among the rocks, making a covert of the smallest hummock or projection. The cub still followed her.

It was miraculous how small the great white beast managed to make herself as she slowly crept up upon her quarry. Her movements were as noiseless as a cat's. They had need to be, indeed, for the hearing of the walrus is keen. There was not a sound upon the air but the heavy breathings and gruntings of the herd, and the occasional light tinkle and crash of crumbling ice.

At a distance of not more than twenty paces from the prey, the old bear stopped and gave a quick backward glance at her cub. Instantly the latter stopped also, and crouched warily behind a rock. Then his mother crept on alone. She knew that he was quite agile enough to avoid the floundering rush of any walrus, but with him she would take no risks.

Suddenly, as if some premonition of peril had smitten her, the mother walrus lifted her head and stared about her anxiously. There was no danger in sight, but she had grown uneasy. She lowered her head against her calf's plump flank, and started to push him down the slope toward the rest of the herd.

Not a dozen feet away, an enormous form, white and terrible, arose as if by magic out of the bare rocks. A bellow of warning came from the vigilant old bull down below. But in the same instant that white mass fell upon the cringing calf, and smashed its neck before it knew what was happening.

With a roar the mother walrus reared herself and launched her huge bulk straight forward upon the enemy. She was swift in her attack—amazingly so—but the white bear was swifter. With astonishing strength and deftness, even in the moment of delivering that fatal blow, she had pushed the body of her prey aside, several feet up the slope. At the same time, bending her long back like a bow, she succeeded in evading the full force of the mother's assault, which otherwise would have pinned her down and crushed her. She caught, however, upon one haunch, a glancing blow from those descending tusks, which came down like pile-drivers; and a long red mark leaped into view upon her white fur. The next moment she had dragged her prey beyond reach of the frantic mother's next plunging charge.

The rocky slope was now in an uproar. The other cows had instantly rolled their startled young into the sea, and were tumbling in after them with terrific splashing. The three bulls, grunting furiously, were floundering in great loose plunges up the slope, eager to get into the fray. The bereaved mother was gasping and snorting with her prodigious efforts, as she hurled herself in huge sprawling lunges after the slayer of her young. So agile was she proving herself, indeed, that the bear had enough to do in keeping out of her reach, while half lifting, half dragging the prize up the incline.

At last the body of the calf caught in a crevice, and the bear had to pause to wrench it free. It was for a moment only, but that moment came very near being her last. She felt, rather than saw, the impending mass of the cow as it reared itself above her. Like a spring suddenly loosed, she bounded aside, and those two straight tusks came down, just where she had stood, with the force of a ton of bone and muscle behind them.

Wheeling in a flash to follow up her assault, the desperate cow reared again. But this time she was caught at a disadvantage. Her far more intelligent adversary had slipped around behind her, and now, as she reared, struck her a tremendous buffet on the side of the neck. Caught off her balance, the cow rolled down the slope, turning clean over before she could recover her footing. The three bulls, in the midst of their floundering charge up the hill, checked themselves for a moment to see how she had fared. And in that moment the bear succeeded in dragging her prize up a steep where the walruses could not hope to follow. A few yards more, and she had gained a spacious ledge some twenty feet above the raging walruses. A second or two later, in answer to her summons, the cub joined her there, scrambling nimbly over the rocks at a safe distance from the foe.

Realizing now that the marauder had quite escaped their vengeance, the three bulls at length turned away, and went floundering and snorting back to the sea. The mother, however, inconsolable in her rage and grief, kept rearing herself against the face of the rock, clawing at it impotently with her great flippers, and striking it with their tusks till it seemed as they must give way beneath the blows. Again and again she fell back, only to renew her futile and pathetic efforts the moment she could recover her breath. And from time to time the old bear, nursing the cub, would glance down upon her with placid unconcern. At last, coming in some sort to her senses, the unhappy cow turned away and crawled heavily, with a slow jerky motion, down the slope. Slowly, and with a mighty splash, she launched herself into the sea, and swam off to join the rest of the herd a mile out from shore.

A Master of Supply

Unlike his reserved and supercilious red cousin of kindlier latitudes, Blue Fox was no lover of solitude; and seeing that the only solitude he knew was the immeasurable desolation of the Arctic barrens, this was not strange. The loneliness of these unending and unbroken plains, rolled out flat beneath the low-hung sky to a horizon of white haze, might have weighed down even so dauntless a spirit as his had he not taken care to fortify himself against it. This he did, very sagaciously, by cultivating the companionship of his kind. His snug burrow beneath the stunted bush-growth of the plains was surrounded by the burrows of perhaps a score of his race.

During the brief but brilliant Arctic summer, which flared across the lonely wastes with a fervour which strove to compensate for the weary duration of its absence, the life of Blue Fox was not arduous. But during the long, sunless winters, with their wild snows, their yelling gales, their interminable night, and their sudden descents of still, intense frost, so bitter that it seemed as if the incalculable cold of outer space were invading this undefended outpost of the world, then Blue Fox and his fellows would have had a sorry time of it but for two considerations. They had their cheer of association in the snug burrows deep beneath the covering of the snows; and they had their food supplies, laid by with wise forethought in the season when food was abundant.

Therefore, when the old bear, grown too restless and savage to hibernate, had often to roam the darkness hungry, and when the wolf-pack was forced to range the frozen leagues for hardly meat enough to keep their gaunt flanks from falling in, the provident foxes had little to fear from either cold or famine.

The burrow of Blue Fox was dug in a patch of dry, sandy soil that formed a sort of island half a dozen acres broad in the vast surrounding sea of the swampy tundra. The island was not high enough or defined enough to be called a knoll. To the eye it was nothing more than an almost imperceptible bulge in the enormous monotony of the levels. But its elevation was enough to secure it good drainage and a growth of more varied herb and bush than that of the moss-covered tundra, with here and there a little open space of turf and real grass which afforded its tenants room to bask deliciously in the glow of the precipitate summer.

Hot and melting as the Arctic summer might be, it could never reach with its ardent fingers the foundations of eternal frost which underlay all that land at a depth of a very few feet. So Blue Fox dug his burrow not too deep, but rather on a gentle slant, and formed his chamber at a depth of not much more than two feet below the roots of the bushes. Abundantly lined with fine, dry grasses, which he and his family kept scrupulously clean, it was always warm and dry and sweet.

It was an afternoon in the first of the summer, one of those long, unclouded, glowing, warm afternoons of the Arctic, when the young shoots of herb and bush seem to lengthen visibly under the eye of the watcher, and the flower-buds open impetuously as if in haste for the caresses of the eager moths and flies. For the moment the vast expanses of the barren were not lonely. The nesting juncos and snow-buntings twittered cheerfully among the busy growths. The mating ducks clamoured harshly along the bright coils of the sluggish stream which wound its way through the marshes. On an islet in the middle of a reedy mere, some half mile to the east, a pair of great white trumpeter swans had their nest, scornful of concealment. A mile or more off to the west a herd of caribou browsed the young green shoots of the tundra growth, moving slowly northward. The windless air was faintly musical with the hum of insects and with the occasional squeaks and scurryings of unseen lemming mice in their secret roadways under the dense green sphagnum. Blue Fox sat up, not far from the entrance to his tunnel, blinking lazily in the glow and watching the play of his fuzzy cubs and their slim, young, blue-grey mother in and out their doorway. Scattered here and there over their naked little domain he saw the families of his kindred, similarly care-free and content with life.

But care-free as he was, Blue Fox never forgot that the price of freedom from care was eternal vigilance. Between his eyes and the pallid horizon he detected a wide-winged bird swinging low over the marshes. He knew at once what it was that with slow-moving, deliberate wings came up, nevertheless, so swiftly. It was no goose, or brant, or fish-loving merganser, or inland wandering saddleback gull that flew in such a fashion. He gave a shrill yelp of warning, answered at once from all over the colony; and at once the playing cubs whisked into their burrows or drew close to their mothers, and sat up to stare with bright, suspicious eyes at the strong-winged flier.

Blue Fox himself, like most of his full-grown fellows, never stirred. But his eyes never swerved for a second from the approach of that ominous, winnowing shape. It was a great Arctic hawk-owl, white mottled with chocolate; and it seemed to be hunting in a leisurely fashion, as if well fed and seeking excitement rather than a meal. It came straight on toward the colony of the foxes, flying lower and lower, till Blue Fox began to gather his steel-like muscles to be ready for a spring at its throat if it should come within reach. It passed straight over his head, its terrible hooked beak half open, its wide, implacable eyes, jewel bright and hard as glass, glaring downward with still menace. But, with all its courage, it did not dare attack any one of the calmly watchful foxes. It made a sweeping half circuit of the colony, and then sailed on toward the mere of the white swans. Just at the edge of the mere it dropped suddenly into a patch of reeds, to flap up again, a second later, with a limp form trailing from its talons—the form of a luckless mother-duck surprised in brooding her eggs. A great hubbub of startled and screaming water-fowl pursued the marauder; but the swans from their islet, as the foxes from their colony, looked on with silent indifference.

Blue Fox, basking in the sun, was by and by seized with a restlessness, a sense of some duty left undone. He was not hungry, for the wastes were just now so alive with nesting birds and swarming lemmings, and their fat little cousins, the lemming mice, that his hunting was a swift and easy matter. He did not even have to help his mate, occupied though she was, in a leisurely way, with the care of her cubs. But across his mind came an insistent memory of the long and bitter Arctic night, when the world would seem to snap under the deadly intensity of the cold, and there would be no birds but a few ptarmigan in the snow, and the fat lemmings would be safe beneath the frozen roofs of their tunnels, and his cleverest hunting would hardly serve him to keep the keen edge off his hunger. In the first sweet indolence of spring he had put far from him the remembrance of the famine season. But now it was borne in upon him that he must make provision against it. Shaking off his nonchalance, he got up, stretched himself elaborately, and trotted down briskly into the tundra.

He picked his way daintily over the wide beds of moist sphagnum, making no more sound as he went than if his feet had been of thistledown. At some distance from the skirts of the colony the moss was full of scurrying and squeaking noises. Presently he crouched and crept forward like a cat. The next instant he pounced with an indescribable speed and lightness, his head and forepaws disappearing into the moss. He had penetrated into one of the screened runways of the little people of the sphagnum. The next moment he lifted his head with a fat lemming dangling from either side of his fine jaws. He laid down the prize and inspected it with satisfaction—a round-bodied creature some six inches long, of a grey colour mottled with rusty red, with a mere apology for a tail, and with the toes of its fore-paws exaggeratedly developed, for use, perhaps, in constructing its mossy tunnels. For a few seconds Blue Fox pawed his prey playfully, as one of his cubs would have done. Then, bethinking himself of the serious business which he had in hand, he picked it up and trotted off to a dry spot which he knew of, just on the fringe of the island.

Now, of one thing Blue Fox was well aware, it having been borne in upon him by experience—*viz.*, that a kill not soon eaten would speedily spoil in this weather. But he knew something else, which he could only have arrived at by the strictly rational process of putting two and two together—he understood the efficacy of cold storage.

Burrowing down through the light soil, he dug himself a little cellar, the floor of which was the stratum of perpetual frost. Here, in this preservative temperature, he deposited the body of the fat lemming, and covered the place from prying eyes with herbage and bush drawn lightly over it. Hunting easily and when the mood was upon him, he brought three more lemmings to the storehouse that same day. On the next day and the next an Arctic tempest swept over the plain, an icy rain drove level in whipping sheets, the low sky was crowded with hurrying ranks of torn black vapour, and the wise foxes kept to their holes. Then the sun came back to the waste places, and Blue Fox returned to his hunting.

Without in any way pushing himself, without stinting his own repasts or curtailing his hours of indolence or of play, Blue Fox attended to his problem of supply so efficiently that in the course of a couple of weeks he had perhaps two score plump carcasses, lemmings and mice, laid out in this cold storage cellar of his. Then he filled it in right to the top with grass-roots, turf, and other dry stuff that would not freeze into armour-plate, covered it over with light soil and bushes, and left it to await the hour of need.

In the course of the summer, Blue Fox, like all his fellows, established a number of these lemming *caches*, till by the time when the southward bird-flight proclaimed the summer at an end, the question of supply was one to give him no further anxiety. When the days were shrunken to an hour or two of sunlight, and the tundra was frozen to stone, and the winds drove the fine snow before them in blinding drifts, then Blue Fox dismissed his stores from his mind and devoted himself merrily to the hunting of his daily rations. The Arctic hares were still abundant, and not yet overwild from ceaseless harrying; and though the chase of these long-legged and nimble leapers was no facile affair, it was by no means too arduous for the tastes of an enterprising and active forager like Blue Fox.

In the meantime the household of Blue Fox, like all the other households in the little colony, had been substantially reduced in numbers. All the cubs, by this time grown nearly to full stature, if not to full wisdom, had migrated. There was neither room nor supply for them now in the home burrows, and they had not yet arrived at the sense of responsibility and forethought that would lead them to dig burrows for themselves. Gently enough, perhaps, but with a firmness which left no room for argument, the youngsters had all been turned out of doors. There seemed but one thing for them to do—to follow the southward migration of the game; and lightly they had done it. They had a hard winter before them, but with good hunting, and fair luck in dodging the traps and other perils that were bound to dog their inexperienced feet, they would return next spring, ripe with wisdom and experience, dig burrows of their own, and settle down to the responsibilities of Arctic family life.

To Blue Fox, sleeping warm in his dry burrow when he would, and secure in the knowledge of his deep-stored supplies, the gathering menace of the cold brought no terrors. By the time the sun had disappeared altogether, and the often brilliant but always terrible and mysterious Arctic night had settled firmly upon the barrens, game had grown so scarce and shy that even so shrewd a hunter as Blue Fox might often range a whole day without the luck to capture a ptarmigan or a hare. The hare, of course, like the ptarmigan, was at this season snowy-white; and Blue Fox would have had small fortune, indeed, in the chase had he himself remained in summer livery. With the setting in of the snow, he had quickly changed his coat to a like colour; and therefore, with his wariness, his unerring nose, and his marvellous lightness of tread, he was sometimes able to surprise the swift hare asleep. In this fashion, too, he would often capture a ptarmigan, pouncing upon it just as the startled bird was spreading its wings for flight. When he failed in either venture—which was often enough the case—he felt himself in no way cast down. He had the excitement of the chase, the satisfaction of stretching his strong, lithe muscles in the race across the hard snow. And then, when the storm clouds were down close upon the levels, and all the world was black, and the great winds from the Pole, bitterer than death, raved southward with their sheeted ghosts of fine drift—then Blue Fox, with his furry mate beside him, lay blinking contentedly in the deep of his burrow, with food and to spare close at hand.

But happy as he was in the main, Blue Fox was not without his cares. Two enemies he had, so strong and cunning that the menace of them was never very far from his consciousness. The wolf, his master in strength, though not in craft, was always ready to hunt him with a bitter combination of hunger and of hate. And the wolverine, cunning beyond all the other kindreds of the wild, and of a sullen ferocity which few would dare to cross, was for ever on the search for the stored supplies of the foxes.

The wolverine, solitary and morose, slow of movement, and defiant even toward the Polar storm, prowled in all weathers. One day chance led him upon one of Blue Fox's storage cellars. The snow had been recently pawed away, and the wolverine, quick to take the hint, began instantly to dig. It was astonishingly easy work. His short, powerful fore-paws made the dry turf and light earth fly, and speedily he came to the store of frozen lemmings. But before he had quite glutted his great appetite, he was interrupted.

Though the storm was raging over the outer world, to Blue Fox in his burrow had come a monition of evil. He had whisked out to inspect his stores. He found the wolverine head downward in his choicest cellar.

Hot as was his rage, it did not burn up his discretion. This was a peril to be dealt with drastically. He knew that, if the robber was merely driven off, he would return and haunt the purlieus of the colony, and end by finding and rifling every storehouse in the neighbourhood.

Blue Fox stole back and roused the occupants of the nearest burrows. In two minutes a dozen angry foxes were out and creeping through the storm. In vengeful silence they fell upon the thief as he feasted carelessly; and in spite of the savage fight he put up, they tore him literally to pieces.

The danger of the wolves was more terrible and more daunting. All through the first half of the winter there had been no sign of a wolf in the neighbourhood, the trail of the wandering caribou having lured them far to the eastward. Then it chanced, when Blue Fox was chasing a hare over the snow, beneath the green, rose, and violet dancing flames of the aurora, that a thin, quavering howl came to his ears. He stopped short. He lost all interest in the hare. Glancing over his shoulder, he saw a greyish patch moving swiftly under the shifting radiance. It was on his trail, that patch of death. He lengthened himself out, belly to earth, and sped for the burrows. And the dancing lights, shifting from colour to colour as they clustered and hurtled across the arch of sky, seemed to stoop in cold laughter over his lonely and desperate flight.

Blue Fox could run fast, but his best speed was slow in comparison with that of his gaunt and long-limbed foes. He knew that, had the race before him been a long one, it could have but one result. A glance over his shoulder, as he ran, showed him that the grey shapes were overhauling him; and, knowing that the distance to his burrow was not long, he felt that he had a chance. A sporting chance, however small, was enough for his courageous spirit, and he raced on with good heart at a pace which soon stretched his lungs near to bursting. But he spared breath for a sharp yelp of warning, which carried far in the stillness and signalled to his fellows the peril that approached.

As the wolves came up, the fugitive could hear the strong, relentless padding of their feet, and then, half a minute later, the measured hiss of their breathing, the occasional hard click of their fangs. But he did not look back. His ears gave him all the information he required, and he could not afford to risk the loss of the slenderest fraction of a second. As he reached the nearest burrow—it was not his own—it seemed as if the dreadful sounds were already overwhelming him. He dived into the burrow, and jaws of steel clashed at his tail as he vanished.

With a chorus of snarls, the disappointed pack brought up abruptly, checking themselves back upon their haunches. The leaders fell to digging at the burrow, while others scattered off to try the same experiment at the other burrows of the colony. But Blue Fox, breathless and triumphant, only showed his teeth derisively. He knew that no wolf-claws could make any impression on the hard-frozen earth surrounding the inner portals of the colony. The wolves discovered by chance one of the supply cellars, and quarrelled for a moment over the dozen or so of tit-bits which it contained. And then, realizing that it was no use hanging about in the expectation that any fox would come out to be eaten, the wise old pack-leader swung the pack into ranks and swept them off to hunt other quarry. When the thudding rhythm of their footsteps died into silence, the foxes all came out and sat under the dancing lights, and stared after the terrible receding shapes with a calm and supercilious scorn.

The Keepers of the Nest

Up from the south, and from the blue, palm-fringed lagoons, the giant white flock came beating, on wings that drove them through the heights of air at something like a mile and a half a minute. Over the rank, bright, mysterious solitudes and gold-green reek of the Everglades the shining wedge of their flight cleft the air unswervingly. In the mighty, throbbing rhythm of that flight, each vast white wing flashed momently like snow against the intense blue, struck by the level rays of a sun not yet an hour above the horizon.

In that high-voyaging flight went fifteen swans, those huge white, clarion-voiced birds so inaptly known as the "whistling swans." They flew in strict array with usually four in the shorter limb of the wedge, and eleven in the longer one, the wisest and most dominant of the flock, the undisputed leader, flying at the apex. The first far summons of the northern spring had come to him suddenly, in the blue and gold of the Floridian lagoons, and though he knew that spring was still deep wrapped in ice, howled over by the savage Arctic winds, he had lingered but a day or two before following the call. For a day or two the flock had been greatly excited, swimming this way and that, preening their feathers nervously, and making the yellow shores re-echo with their harshly sonorous cries. It was not an easy matter to tear themselves away from those milk-warm, teeming, green-azure tides; but at length, in the cool of the dawn, a flock of wild geese had gone musically *honking* overhead, bound for Hudson Bay. This was just the spur that he was needing. As if he had merely been waiting for these, his forerunners, to lead the way, he sprang into the air, with a long trumpeting call and a mighty beating of wings. The flock rose after him, in a snowy, tempestuous confusion of wings and cries. With much jealous wrangling the wedge formed itself as it rose, pounding upwards on a long slant, till at last having gained a cloudy height, it swept northward on the trail of the geese.

Not far under five feet in length, and with an enormous wing area, these "whistling swans" were the stateliest birds that the North American continent could boast. The whiteness of their plumage, radiantly flawless, save for a spot of yellow on each side of the face, was set off in a formal fashion by jet-black legs and bill. Their full-arched skulls betrayed a high degree of intelligence, and their wild eyes held a sort of aloof defiance.

Swerving rapidly inland, as if to avoid the Atlantic coast, the swans swept toward the Mississippi Valley. From time to time, with tremendous splashings and a noise as of a band of horns and bugles, they would come down from their heights to rest and feed, seeking always, for their halt, the loneliest of lakes or marshy pools. The weight of their great frames, and the fierce energy expended in the terrific speed of their flight, forced them to feed well and often.

From the altitude at which they journeyed the swans looked down on all the other migrant hosts, with the exception, perhaps, of the geese, who flew at about the same level. Above them, in the intense blue, they saw only a majestically wheeling eagle now and then, or the black, motionless wings of a soaring vulture, or some high-hawking falcon waiting to swoop upon her prey. But of none of these had the swans any fear. The harmless black vultures would not molest a kitten. And neither the eagle nor the swift gerfalcon, or goshawk, most bloodthirsty of his race, would lightly risk a buffet that might hurl him reeling to the earth. The swans, indeed, gave small thought to any possible enemies in their aërial path.

Yet, but for their confidence in their own power and courage, even the giant white swans might have had misgivings as the goshawk came gliding, a beautiful and sinister form, above the line of their flight. Flying as they were at a rate of not much less than a hundred miles an hour, the measured beat of their wings was a visible manifestation of splendid and adequate effort. But the goshawk swiftly overtook them, almost without seeming to hasten the slow sweep of his long, scythe-like pinions. Directly above the leader his wings came to a stop, and he glided motionless, with the wind of his speed hissing in the stiff-set feathers, and his flat, cruel head reaching downward as if he were about to strike. The longer limb of the wedge shortened a little, as certain of the younger birds at the rear nervously drew in closer to their fellows. But the leader and the other older birds paid no attention to the menace, beyond turning upwards, as they flew, a steady and watchful gaze. A few moments later, and apparently without an effort, the splendid marauder sailed on ahead. Two minutes more, and he had overtaken the journeying geese. Pouncing upon the hindermost, he gripped its outstretched neck with his clutching talons and fairly tore out its throat. But it was too heavy a bird for him to bear up, so, after a moment or two of tremendous flapping, he let it drop. It fell, sprawlingly, turning over several times in the air before it landed with a crash in the top of a dense old cedar. The great hawk, with half-folded wings, dropped after it straight as a stone and caught it again securely in his talons just as it touched the branches. With heavy flappings he guided it to a perch where he could devour it in comfort; and the swans, as they beat their way above the scene, stared down upon it with eyes of grave indifference.

Soon passing beyond the zones of cane-field, pine barren, and cypress swamp, they crossed the harsh and forbidding ridges of the Tennessee Mountains, running the gauntlet of the rifles of the wild mountaineers. In this perilous passage they lost three of their flock; but their leader swept them on without allowing the array to become demoralized. For a few seconds only was there some confusion, as a strong bird near the head of the wedge, having got his death wound, struggled blindly to keep on. A moment more, however, and he went plunging downward; and the line closed up.

And now the skies they traversed were no longer of so palpitating a blue, but more often of a sullen grey or lowering with black and wind-rent clouds. Gusts of icy rain burst over them, and those wanton storms which strive to buffet back the vanguards of the diffident northern spring. The rivers that now rolled swirling beneath them were cold and swollen floods, heavy with silt. The broad plains that stretched to the horizon and beyond began to be mottled uncouthly with patches of grey and shrinking snow. Soon the brown disappeared, and all was snow, white and interminable, broken only by the blue-black watercourses rolling along their burden of logs and ice, or by dark green, ragged belts of spruce forest. Such scattered cities as passed beneath them they hardly heeded, unless it chanced to be at night, and the city one of importance. Then the wide-flung glare always drew them, and there would be, on the part of the younger birds, a tendency to descend and investigate; but the leader always checked this inexorably, and swung the flock sometimes to a higher level.

Voyaging thus day by day toward ever more and more inhospitable lands and skies, they came at last to those shelterless and incredibly bleak expanses of the Barren Grounds which stretch along the north-west shores of Hudson Bay. In a blinding smother of snow they arrived at a small lake, a few miles inland from the sea, which had been the leader's objective ever since leaving the sun-drenched Floridian lagoons. But he had too far outflown the advance of the sluggish spring, and the little lake was not yet open. After circling above it with loud, disappointed cries, they flew off down the course of the shallow, turbulent stream which came boiling from under the ice, and alighted amid the muddy and wave-eaten floes which fringed the shores of the bay.

For nearly three weeks the flock held together and kept to the tide-waters. Their refuge was a narrow and shallow bay, its beaches piled with ice-cakes which gave them some shelter from the tearing winds. Here food was abundant, so they were well enough off, though restless and anxious to get about their nesting.

As the wind was off shore, under the lee of the ridged ice-cakes the water was comparatively still. And it was here they slept, rocking softly on the backwash. Here, for the most part, they were safe from all enemies. But one night, as they slept, shadowy, pale shapes on the dimly-shadowed water, there came another pallid shape, moving noiselessly as smoke, down to the water's edge, and paused among the huddled ice-cakes. Motionless it eyed the sleeping swans. Then, warily withdrawing, it entered the water some fifty yards away, swam out perhaps another fifty yards, and approached the sleepers from the direction of the open sea, the direction from which they least apprehended attack. Swimming so deep in the water that only a sharp, black muzzle appeared above the surface, the prowling shape came suddenly and without warning above the swans. Rearing half its length above the surface, it seized one off the sleepers by the neck and killed it with a single savage shake.

Wide awake on the instant, the flock beat up into the air with wild buglings of consternation, as the great white bear went splashing shoreward with his prize. The flock flew out to sea, mounting to a great height, and circled for nearly an hour in the glimmering twilight before they could recover their composure. Then they came dropping back in silence, ever eye alert, and settled once more upon the water a couple of hundred yards from their old sleeping-place. For perhaps another half-hour they floated with heads all erect, searching every ice-cake, every little lapping wave-crest. And thereafter, so long as the flock remained together, when they slept it was always with a sleepless sentinel on guard.

It was nearly a week later when there came a change—a change so sudden that all the forces of the cold were routed in a night. The spring, so long held back, came with a soft, delicious rush. No more shrieking of winds and roar of waves along the outer ledges, but, instead, bland airs that breathed of soaking moss, and wide, still waters gleaming under a desolate but tranquil sky. Through long, unclouded days the sun poured down lavishly, the snow fled like a lifting mist, and the ice, collapsing with silvery crash and tinkle, fell back into the floods that gave it birth. A wave of green, high, thin, ineffably tender, went washing in a day all across the illimitable wastes of the muskeg. Another day, and the green was starred with flowers.

The flock had scattered at once, flying off in pairs to their secluded nesting-places. The leader and his mate had no great way to go, for their place was already chosen. For several years they had held a tiny islet in the near-by lake, whose shores were a morass which gave them protection from most enemies. Their nest, of course, was invariably swept out of existence by the winter hurricanes, but they had no objection to the task of nest-building.

The islet was no more than a handful of moss and willow scrub caught in a jumble of uptilted rock, and it rose but a foot or so above the lake level. The two swans, working together—the splendid male as diligent in the task as his mate—collected dead sticks and brushwood from all around the shores of the lake, dragging it out with their powerful bills from where the storms had driven it into the tangle of the muskeg. They wove its foundations solidly, and reared it to a height of something over two feet, that its precious contents might be safe from any floods.

Almost before the nest was fairly finished, the female began to lay, the ample cup of the nest becoming lined with down as she went on laying. The eggs were big, obscurely-tinted affairs, a good twelve inches in the greater circumference, and with a dull, suède-like surface. She laid the full complement of her kind, which is six, and then began to sit.

In this long and arduous labour the male took no part. But this was not from any lack of sympathy on his part. He was ceaselessly on guard, and devoted in his attentions to his utterly preoccupied mate; and never did he allow his foraging expeditions to lead him any distance from the nest. When his mate came off to feed, he stayed close beside the nest, watching over the eggs. And if any inquisitive saddleback or herring gull flew over, peering down greedily at the coveted spheres in the nest, he would lift his wings threateningly and warn them off with a furious and strident hissing.

For a week or two, however, this assiduous guardianship put no great tax on anything but his patience. There was no serious danger in sight. A pair of the great white and grey Arctic hawk-owls, almost as big as eagles and far more savage, were nesting off on the muskeg, perhaps half a mile away. But these fierce marauders were not interested, for the present, in the nest of the swans. They had not the gulls' taste for eggs, and only the direst hunger could have driven them to try conclusions with the mighty wings and bills of the keepers of the nest on the islet. When the young cygnets should come to be hatched out, then might they begin to take an interest in the swans' nest; but for the present they never came near enough even to elicit a warning from the vigilant guardian.

Beside the hawk-owls, out there on the muskeg were stoats and ermine, a few mink, plenty of the little blue Arctic foxes, and a few of the larger and far more dangerous red species. But none of these could get to the nest except by swimming, and the swans knew that not one of these prowlers, unless, perhaps, a very daring red fox, would care to approach the islet as long as either one of its keepers was by. There were no wolves to fear, for they not only hated the half-floating edges of the lake, but they had followed the trail of the wandering caribou to some far-distant ranges. To be sure, there was the great grey lynx, seen picking his way stealthily, from time to time, about the drier portions of the muskeg, and sometimes stopping to glare hungrily across the water at the stately white guardian of the nest. But the swans knew that at this time of year—the season of good hunting—even the lynx was not ravenous enough to wet his well-kept fur by swimming out to the islet.

But one day there came a gliding over the muskeg, pausing and lurking behind the low bushes, a beautiful, dark-brown, sinister-looking stranger. He was long and low in the body, sinuous as a snake, and with a cruel, pointed head. He made his way down to the edge of the water, and stood looking steadily across at the brooding mother on her nest.

The watchful sentinel had never before seen a fisher, but he knew at once that this was an enemy, and a dangerous one. Spreading his vast wings, lowering and extending his long neck on a level with the ground, and hissing like an escape-pipe, he stalked around till he had put himself between his mate and those deadly eyes. At the edge of the water he stood poised, a splendid, gleaming, snowy figure; and for several seconds the two so strangely-matched antagonists surveyed each other across some twenty yards of clear water.

The fisher was not just then particularly hungry, but he was, as usual, in the mood for killing. His pause was not because of any hesitation, but simply because he had never seen a swan before, and, like the cunning tactician that he was, he took count of his opponent's points before attacking. Presently he slipped noiselessly into the water and came swimming at great speed toward the islet.

Ordinarily, perhaps, the swan would have chosen to await the attack on his own threshold. But some swift insight warned him now to join battle in that element where he was most at home. He launched himself smoothly as oil, and his powerful webs drove him gliding over the surface, apparently without effort, at a pace far beyond that of the fisher. But he did not sail direct to meet the foe. Rather it looked to the foe as if he were going to shun the encounter. He swept off on a curve, as if doubtful what do to in such an emergency.

The fisher was almost abreast of him, when he swerved like lightning, and, fairly lifting himself from the water, hurled himself straight at the swimmer's head. The swimmer dived; but, taken by surprise as he was, he was not quick enough to escape a bewildering blow over the right eye from the bird's powerful bill. Blinded for the moment on that side, he was at the same time filled with a very madness of rage. That any mere thing in feathers should dare to withstand him was unbelievable. He rose to the surface again instantly, shooting half his length out of water, and snapping viciously with his long white fangs. But he rose into an incomprehensible turmoil of enormous, battering wings, and lashed foam, and unheard-of hissings, and blinding, rigid white feathers; and it was nothing but a few feathers that his deadly jaws succeeded in grasping. Baffled and choking, he fell back with his mouthful of feathers; and as he dived once more, with a view to coming up again at some more convenient and satisfactory point of attack—at, perhaps, a foot below the surface—the back of his neck was clutched by a pair of steel-like mandibles. The swan had darted his long, snaky neck under water, as if to fish for lily roots; and now, having secured a good grip, he was shaking his enemy as a terrier would shake an old shoe. His neck and bill were excellently fitted to this employment, for lily roots are tough and require a lot of energetic persuasion.

On land, of course, those tactics would have proved promptly fatal to the bird. The fisher, with his lithe strength and swiftness, would have writhed about and fixed his teeth in his adversary's throat, and the fight would have been over. But here, in the water, he could get no leverage whereon to exert his strength. He could do nothing but kick and twist in futile fury. Moreover, not being accustomed to exerting himself under water, he involuntarily opened his mouth, and speedily felt himself choking. In fact, had the swan but understood the magnitude of his present advantage, he might now have drowned his assailant without further trouble, and rid the wilderness of one of its bloodiest scourges. But the indignant bird, having himself no objection to keeping his head under water several minutes at a time, little guessed that such an experience might be fatal to his enemy. He presently relaxed his terrible grip, and backing off lightly, waited to greet the foe's reappearance at the surface with a fresh buffeting of those great wing-elbows in which he put his faith.

Ordinarily speaking, the fisher is the last to cry quits or to lose heart under any punishment. But this kind of punishment was something so mysterious, so undreamed of, that it seemed for the moment to change his whole nature. It is more than probable that a good submersion would cool the battle lust even of a rhinoceros. It certainly cooled the fisher's. Though his lungs were bursting and his brain saw sparks, the moment he was freed from that grip on his neck, he had the presence of mind to remain yet a few seconds more under water, while he swam desperately toward his own shore. When at last he was forced to lift his head above the surface, he was within a few feet of the fringing bushes. But his adversary was there. He was met, as before, by a stupefying whirlwind of wings and blows and terrific sounds. Gulping a fresh lungful of the air he was agonizing for, he dived again, this time as deep as he could, escaping by a miracle a second darting clutch of his vanquisher's bill. Not till he was actually within the screening roots and stems did he come up again, and then it was to worm his way through them unseen till he was a good twenty paces or so from the water's edge. Then he slunk off without pausing to digest the situation—the most dispirited fisher that ever roamed the muskeg. The swan, catching a glimpse off his flight, filled the solitudes with the sonorous trumpetings of his triumph, and swam proudly back to the nest.

As the long five weeks of brooding, for the patient mother on her nest, drew near an end, there came to the Barren Grounds a time of unprecedented drought. The innumerable streams that drained the soaking muskeg ran shallow as they had never run before within the memory of the long-lived swans. Under the long, unshadowed warmth the lake shrank amazingly; and at last, to the vexation of the keepers of the nest, their islet ceased to be perfectly an islet. The group of tilted strata which formed it rose so far out of water that a thin-topped ledge was revealed, connecting them with the shore. It was no more than a series of widely-separated and precarious stepping-stones, awash in the smallest ripples, but it was enough to allow a sufficiently nimble wanderer to visit the islet dry-shod. The swans eyed it with glowing disquiet.

At last came the day when the patient brooder heard stirrings, and tappings, and thin little cries come from the six precious eggs beneath her breast. From time to time she would lower her head among them to listen enraptured, or to answer with soft sounds of encouragement in her throat. Her mate drew close to the nest, forgetting to eat, but never forgetting to keep a fiercely watchful eye upon the ledge connecting with the shore.

Soon one of the baby cygnets, having divided the shell into two halves by the ordered strokes of his sharp-tipped bill, thrust up the top portion as if it had been a lid, and sprawled forth all wet against its mother's hot and naked breast. The mother pushed one half of the shell within the other, that they might take up less room, and then, a little later, threw them out of the next, lest they should get fitted on over the end of another egg and smother the occupant.

Presently two more eggs hatched almost simultaneously. The ecstatic mother was now half standing in the nest to give the damp sprawlers room. It was at this time that the old grey lynx, prowling down nearer to the water's edge than was his wont, observed the stepping-stones and decided to come over. He had wanted those great white birds for a long time.

Now, the most powerful of swans, under usual circumstances and conditions, is no match for the lynx, but a helpless quarry merely for that fierce and powerful marauder. But often, in defence of their young, the wild creatures develop powers and heroisms undreamed of at other times. At such a period they become utterly reckless of odds; and such a temper may often accomplish the impossible. Moreover, it is one thing to hold a bridge, and another to fight in the open.

There was no uncertainty in the minds of the two swans as to the deadliness of this peril. They knew all about lynxes. The mother bird stood up among her eggs and young, and stepped delicately from the nest, hissing and beating her wings. Both birds knew better than to attack this foe by water or by land. With screams of hate they rose laboriously into the air.

The lynx had reached the second stepping-stone, a sharp and narrow one, and was balancing himself with the caution of a house cat afraid of wetting her feet, before taking the next leap. Just as he gathered himself to spring, the male swan struck him heavily on the side of the head, almost throwing him from his foothold. His fore-paws, indeed, and his whiskered muzzle went into the water, but his great hind claws, firm based for the spring, maintained their hold on the rock. Spitting harshly in his amazement, he clawed back to his position. But in the next instant he was so ill-advised and over-confident as to rise upon his hind legs, striking at his assailant in the hope of bringing him down. At the very moment when his balance was least secure, the female, utterly reckless, launched her whole buffeting weight against him. Hurling him irresistibly from the ledge, she fell with him and upon him, driving him deep into the water.

For one bewildering second he clawed at her, ripping off the strong white feathers, and inflicting cruel wounds on breast and thigh. But this was for a moment only. Daunted and choking, he loosed his grip in haste and pawed his way back to the surface. As he scrambled out upon the ledge, both birds were at him again instantly; but he had not an ounce of fight left in him. He was not at all hungry, and he did not like swans, and he wanted to get off to some quiet, sunny place and dry himself. Spitting loudly, head hunched down between his shoulders, ears flat, and stub of a tail pressed tight between his furry buttocks, he fled ignominiously through a pandemonium of wings and beaks and screams. When he was quite beyond their reach, the two swans stretched themselves to their full height, spread their wings as wide as possible, and trumpeted a raucous warning to all trespassers. Then they hurried back to the nest which they knew so well how to guard. The female, apparently unconscious of her wounds, resumed eagerly her brooding, with soft murmurs to the hatching young; while the male, as calm as if nothing out of the ordinary had happened, or was ever likely to happen, set himself to preening the ruffled snow of his plumage.

By the Winter Tide

Behind the long, slow-winding barrier of the dyke the marshes of Tantramar lay secure, mile on mile of blue-white radiance under the unclouded moon. Outside the dyke it was different. Mile on mile of tumbled mud-stained ice-cakes, strewn thickly over the Tantramar flats, waited motionless under the moon for the incoming tide. Twice in each day the far-wandering tide of Fundy would come in, to lift, and toss, and grind, and roll the ice-cakes, then return again to its deep channels; and with every tide certain of the floes would go forth to be lost in the open sea, while the rest would sink back to their tumbled stillness on the mud. Just now the flood was coming in. From all along the outer fringes of the flats came a hoarse, desolate roar; and in the steady light the edges of the ice-field began to turn and flash, the strange motion creeping gradually inland toward that impassive bulwark of the dyke. Had it been daylight, the chaotic ice-field would have shown small beauty, every wave-beaten floe being soiled and streaked with rust-coloured Tantramar mud. But under the transfiguring touch of the moon the unsightly levels changed to plains of infinite mystery—expanses of shattered, white granite, as it were, fretted and scrawled with blackness—reaches of loneliness older than time. So well is the mask of eternity assumed by the mutable moonlight and the ephemeral ice.

Nearer and nearer across the waste drew the movement that marked the incoming flood. Then from over the dyke-top floated a noiseless, winnowing, sinister shape which seemed the very embodiment of the desolation. The great white owl of the north, driven down from his Arctic hunting-grounds by hunger, came questing over the ragged levels. His long, soft-feathered wings moved lightly as a ghost, and almost touched the ice-cakes now and then as his round, yellow eyes, savagely hard and brilliant, searched the dark crevices for prey. With his black beak, his black talons protruding from the mass of snowy feathers which swathed his legs, and the dark bars on his plumage, one might have fancied him a being just breathed into menacing and furtive life by the sorcery of the scene.

Suddenly, with a motion almost as swift as light, the great owl swooped and struck. Swift as he was, however, this time he struck just too late. A spot of dark on the edge of an ice-cake vanished. It was a foraging muskrat who had seen the approaching doom in time and slipped into a deep and narrow crevice. Here, on the wet mud, he crouched trembling, while the baffled bird reached down for him with vainly clutching claws.

On either side of the two ice-cakes which had given the muskrat refuge, was a space of open mud which he knew it would be death to cross. Each time those deadly black talons clutched at him, he flattened himself to the ground in panic; but there were several inches to spare between his throat and death. The owl glared down with fixed and flaming eyes, then gave up his useless efforts. But he showed no inclination to go away. He knew that the muskrat could not stay for ever down in that muddy crevice. So he perched himself bolt upright on the very edge, where he could keep secure watch upon his intended victim, while at the same time his wide, round eyes might detect any movement of life among the surrounding ice-cakes.

The great flood-tides of Fundy, when once they have brimmed the steep channels and begun to invade the vast reaches of the flats, lose little time. When the baffled owl, hungry and obstinate, perched himself on the edge of the ice-cake to wait for the muskrat to come out, the roar of the incoming water and the line of tossing, gleaming floes were half a mile away. In about four minutes the fringe of tumult was not three hundred yards distant—and at the same time the vanguards of the flood, thin, frothy rivulets of chill water, were trickling in through the crevice where the little prisoner crouched. As the water touched his feet, the muskrat took heart anew, anticipating a way of escape. As it deepened he stood upright,—and instantly the white destruction cruelly watching struck again. This time the muskrat felt those deadly talons graze the long, loose fur of his back; and again he cowered down, inviting the flood to cover him. As much at home under water as on dry land, he counted on easy escape when the tide came in.

It happens, however, that the little kindreds of the wild are usually more wise in the general than in the particular. The furry prisoner at the bottom of the crevice knew about such regular phenomena as the tides. He knew, too, that presently there would be water enough for him to dive and swim beneath it, where his dreadful adversary could neither reach him nor detect him. What he did not take into account was the way the ice-cakes would grind and batter each other as soon as the tide was deep enough to float them. Now, submerged till his furry back and spiky tail were just even with the surface, his little, dark eyes glanced up with mingled defiance and appeal at the savage, yellow glare of the wide orbs staring down upon him. If only the water would come, he would be safe. For a moment his eyes turned longingly toward the dyke, and he thought of the narrow, safe hole, the long, ascending burrow, and the warm, soft-lined chamber which was his nest, far up in the heart of the dyke, high above the reach of the highest tides and hidden from all enemies. But here in the hostile water, with a cruel death hanging just above him, his valorous little heart ached with homesickness for that nest in the heart of the dyke; and though the water had no chill for his hardy blood, he shivered.

Meanwhile, the long line of clamour was rushing steadily inland. The roar suddenly crashed into thunder on the prisoner's ears and a rush of water swept him up. The white owl spread his wings and balanced himself on tiptoe, as the ice-cake on which he was perching lurched and rolled. Through all the clamour his ears, miraculously keen beyond those of other birds, caught an agonized squeak from below. The jostling ice had nipped the muskrat's hind quarters.

Though desperately hurt, so desperately that his strong hind legs were almost useless, the brave little animal was not swerved from his purpose. Straight from his prison, no longer now a refuge, he dived and swam for home through the loud uproar. But the muskrat's small forelegs are of little use in swimming, so much so that as a rule he carries them folded under his chin while in the water. Now, therefore, he was at a piteous disadvantage. His progress was slow, as in a nightmare,—such a nightmare as must often come to muskrats if their small, careless brains know how to dream. And in spite of his frantic efforts, he found that he could not hold himself down in the water. He kept rising toward the surface every other second.

Balancing had by this time grown too difficult for the great, white owl, and he had softly lifted himself on hovering wings. But not for an instant had he forgotten the object of his hunt. What were floods and cataclysms to him in the face of his hunger? Swiftly his shining eyes searched the foamy, swirling water. Then, some ten feet away, beside a pitching floe, a furry back appeared for an instant. In that instant he swooped. The back had vanished,—but unerringly his talons struck beneath the surface—struck and gripped their prey. The next moment the wide, white wings beat upward heavily, and the muskrat was lifted from the water.

As he rose into the air, though near blind with the anguish of that iron grip, the little victim writhed upward and bit furiously at his enemy's leg. His jaws got nothing but a bunch of fluffy feathers, which came away and floated down the moonlight air. Then the life sank out of his brain, and he hung limply; and the broad wings bore inland over the dyke-top—straight over the warm and hidden nest where he had longed to be.

The Little Homeless One

The icy rain of a belated Northern spring drove down steadily through the dark branches of the fir thicket, and the litter of young "snowshoe rabbits," shivering beneath the insufficient shelter, huddled themselves together, for warmth, into a reddish-brown ball of the same color as the dead fir needles which formed their bed. Their long-eared mother, after nursing them all through the harsh daylight and shielding them as best she could with her furry body, had slipped away to forage for her evening meal under cover of the gathering dusk, leaving her litter, perforce, to the chances of the wild.

Concealment being their only defense against their many prowling and hungry foes, the compact cluster of long-eared babies made no tiniest whimper of protest against their discomfort, lest the sound should betray them to some hunting fox or weasel. Had they kept still, as they should have done, they would have been invisible to the keenest passing eye; but just for the moment the cluster was convulsed by a silent struggle. One of the litter, chancing to have been left on the outer surface of the bunch, came to the conclusion that he would be more comfortable at the center, and set himself to force his way in. Being the biggest and strongest of the litter he presently succeeded, in spite of the resistance of his weaker brothers and sisters. And so, since he was the one least in need of warmth, he managed to get the most of it. For it is written in the Law of the Wilderness that to him that hath shall be given.

Fortunately for the defenseless litter no hungry prowler came by during the commotion, and the struggle was soon over. The ousted ones resigned themselves to the inevitable and settled themselves quietly on the cold exterior of the bunch. Some fifteen or twenty minutes later the mother returned, well stuffed with sprouting grasses and the aromatic leaf buds of the birch saplings. Through the gathering dark and the rain she came hopping in soundlessly on her broad furry pads. She slipped under the low-hanging branches of the thicket, curled herself about the shivering cluster of her little ones, and drew them close against her warm, wet body, where at once they fell to nursing greedily.

Soon the whole litter was sound asleep, so well warmed by their mother's abundant milk that the bitter rain lashing down upon them through the branches disturbed them not at all. The night was black and full of strange, subdued noises, the swish of sudden rain gusts, the occasional scraping of great branches against each other, and always, high overhead the sealike rush and muffled roar of the wind in the straining tops of the firs and hemlocks. While the little ones slept soundly, careless of the storm and unconscious of all danger, the mother's sleep was hardly sleep at all. While her eyes closed drowsily in the darkness, some portion of her senses was always on the alert, always standing sentry, ready to arouse her to instant and complete wakefulness. Her ears, attuned to catch the faintest doubtful sound, were never asleep, never quite at rest; her sensitive nostrils were always quiveringly attentive. If a twig snapped and was blown to earth her eyes opened wide at once, and both ears stood up in anxious interrogation. Once, through the hushed tumult, those vigilant ears caught a sound of light feet stealing past the edge of the thicket. Instantly they stiffened to a rigid stillness, as if frozen. But the menacing sound—so faint that few ears save hers could have detected it—passed on. The rigid ears relaxed; the round, bulging, anxious eyes of the furry mother closed again.

That night of rain and cold few of the hungry hunting beasts were on the prowl, and no further peril came near the shelterless family in the fir thicket. But had a fox or a weasel chanced upon them, the timorous mother would have been no protection to her young. With no defense against her swarming foes except her obscure coloring and her speed in flight, she would have had to choose between staying to die with the helpless litter or leaving them to their fate and escaping, if she could, to bear another litter in their place. And there is no doubt as to which course she would have chosen. She loved her young ones; but she loved life better. She had but one life; and she had had, and with luck could go on having, many young. She would have run away, careering with mighty bounds through the stormy darkness to hide at last, with pounding heart and panting lungs in some other thicket.

And the nurslings would have made a succulent meal for the lucky prowler.

Fortunately, however, for this little story, the timorous mother was not to be faced by any such harsh alternative. For in this particular litter of hers, as we have seen, there was one youngster so much stronger than his fellows as to have been singled out, apparently, for the special favour of the Unseen Powers of the Wilderness. To him fell more than his due share of the family warmth, the family nourishment, to the end that he should grow up a peculiarly fine, vigorous, and prepotent specimen of his race, and reproduce himself abundantly, to the advantage, not only of the whole tribe of the snowshoe rabbits, but of all the hunting beasts and birds of the wilderness, who chiefly depend upon that prolific and defenseless tribe for their prey. Hence it came about that, though death in many furred and feathered forms prowled about them and hovered over them by night and by day, this particular mother and her young escaped discovery. No dreadful, peering eyes chanced to penetrate their screen of drooping fir branches. And the mother, on her perilous foragings in the twilight or the rose-grey dawn, was never pounced upon or trailed. For that one sturdy youngling's sake, it would seem, the spirits of the wild had decreed it so.

Presently, the harsh season relented. The rain ceased except for an occasional warm, vitalizing shower; the wilderness was steeped in caressing sunshine; the leaf buds of the birch and poplar burst into a flood of tenderest green; and in every open glade the Painted Trillium unfolded its fairy blooms of white and carmine. Spring, in haste to make up for lost time, rushed forward glowing to meet the summer. The litter of young "snowshoes" had been, for a week or more, browsing upon the tender herbage on the skirts of the thicket, and depending daily less and less upon their mother's milk for their subsistence. Suddenly, on one of those rich days, warm yet tonic, when life runs sweetly in the veins of all the wilderness, the hitherto devoted mother looked coldly on her young and refused them her breasts. Her biggest and most favored son, unused to rebuffs, persisted obstinately. She fetched him a kick from her powerful hinder paws which sent him rolling over and over on the brown carpet of fir needles, whisked about impatiently, and went hopping off through the bushes to seek other interests and make ready to rear another family. The kicked one, recovering from his astonishment, scratched the needles from his ears with his hind paws, stared indignantly at his brothers and sisters as if he thought that they had done it, and hopped away, in the opposite direction to that which his unsympathetic mother had taken. He browsed upon the young grasses till his appetite was satisfied, then took cover beneath a thick low juniper bush and settled himself to sleep, his independent spirit refusing to be daunted by the unaccustomed loneliness. The rest of the litter, less venturesome, peered forth timorously from the edge of their shelter, nibbled the herbage that was within easy reach, and finally huddled down together, for comfort, on the old nest. That same night, while they slept in a furry bunch, a weasel came that way and took it into his triangular head to explore the thicket. He was not hungry, but after the manner of his bloodthirsty tribe he loved killing for its own sake—which most of the other hunting folk of the wilderness do not. He savagely dispatched the while litter, drank the blood of a couple, devoured the brains of another, tossed the mangled carcases wantonly about, and left them to the next prowler that might come by. A few minutes later a big "fisher" arrived, maliciously pursuing the weasel's trail, and did not disdain the easy repast that had been left for him.

During the sunlit, spring-scented weeks that followed, while the young snowshoe rabbit was growing swiftly to maturity, the favor of the Fates continued to shield him. If a prowling fox chanced to peer, sniffing hungrily, beneath the bush which formed his bivouac (for he knew no home, no specially preferred abiding place), it always happened that some caprice, perhaps some dim premonition of peril, would arouse him from his half slumber and send him off noiselessly through the shadows a few moments before the arrival of the foe, which would be left to smell angrily at the still warm couch. If, as he hopped buoyantly across some moonlit glade, the terrible horned owl, that scourge of the wilderness night, dropped down on him on soundless wings, it always happened that some great branch would magically interpose itself, just in time, and the clutching talons would be diverted from their aim. Such experiences—and they were many—served only to sharpen his vigilance and drive home upon his narrow brain the lesson, more vital to a snowshoe rabbit than all others put together, that destruction lay in wait for him every hour.

Thus well schooled by that rough but most efficient teacher, the wilderness, and well nourished by the abundance of the growing season, young Snowshoe came swiftly to his full stature. Though universally called a rabbit, and, more definitely, a "snowshoe" rabbit by reason of his great, spreading, furry feet, he was in reality a true hare, larger than the rabbits, much longer and more powerful in the hind legs, incomparably swifter in flight, but quite incapable of making himself a home by burrowing in the earth. He was of the tribe of the homeless ones, who knew no shelters but the overhanging branches of bush or thicket, no snug lairs in which to hide from storm or cold, no nests save such dead leafage as they might find to crouch upon. In color he was of a rusty reddish brown above and pure white underneath, and he had the long, alert ears, narrow skull, and protruding, guileless eyes of all the hare family.

And now the Unseen Powers, taking stock of their favorite, perceived that he was bigger, stronger, fleeter, and more alert in all his senses, than any other buck snowshoe in the whole wide basin of the Ottanoonsis Stream. Thereupon they decided to leave him to his own resources. And straightway life grew even more eventful for him than it had been hitherto.

It was high summer in the Ottanoonsis Valley. The air, hot but wholesome, and sweet with faint, wild smells of moss and balsam fir and juniper, breathed softly through the dense, dark patches of evergreens, and rustled lightly among the birches and poplars which clothed the tumbled rocky ridges. The river, shrunken in its channel, here brawled musically over its shallow rapids, there widened out into still reaches where the great black moose would wade belly-deep as they fed upon the roots of the water lilies. Here and there a fract of dark cedar swamps gave shelter to the bears. The Valley, an epitome of the wilderness, was the congenial home of foxes, lynxes, fishers, minks, weasels, skunks, and porcupines; and every single one of these, the blameless vegetarian porcupine excepted, was a tireless and implacable hunter of the snowshoe rabbits. Moreover, in the deeper recesses of the fir and hemlock woods several pairs of the murderous giant-horned owls had their retreats; and in the high ravines of the hills that rimmed the valley were the nests of the white-headed eagles and of the great, blue goshawks, those swiftest and most relentless of all the marauders of the air, who also looked upon the long-eared tribe as their most natural prey and easiest quarry. It would seem that, in the game of life as played in the Ottanoonsis Valley, the dice were heavily loaded against the Homeless One.

It was a sultry, drowsy afternoon, and the Homeless One, crouched beneath a thick juniper bush, was more nearly asleep than was at all usual with him. Indeed, it was the safest time of the day, when most of the hunting beasts were apt to be curled up in their lairs, when the giant owl slumbered in the depths of the hemlock glooms, when few enemies were abroad except the soaring eagles and the long-winged, tireless goshawks. But it is the exceptions rather than the rules which make the life of the wilderness exciting. Just as young Snowshoe, who had browsed comfortably, was in his deepest drowse, his quivering nostrils, which never slept, signalled to his brain—"DEATH!" In that same lightning fraction of a second all his powers were wide awake, and, resting as he did in the position of a coiled spring, he shot into the air through the thin fringes of his shelter just as the slender, yellow shape of a hungry weasel alighted on the spot where he had been lying. His great furry hind paws, as they left the ground, just brushed the weasel's pointed nose.

The weasel's narrow mouth opened in a snarl of savage disappointment. Never before, in all his sanguinary experience of snowshoe rabbits, had he missed what seemed to him so sure and easy a kill. But it was not in the weasel nature to be discouraged, as one of the cat tribe might have been, by the failure of his first spring. Though his intended victim was already many feet away, lengthening out in great bounds which propelled him through the bushes at an amazing pace, the weasel darted after him confidently, trusting to his endurance and tenacity of purpose to win in the end against his quarry's greater speed. In a few seconds the fugitive was lost to sight among the leafage, but the relentless pursuer followed the trail by scent for several hundred yards. Then, because he knew it was the habit of the snowshoe tribe to circle back so as to regain the familiar feeding grounds and coverts, this craftiest of hunters left the trail and cut a chord to the circle, expecting to intercept his quarry's flight. Had he been dealing with an ordinary, average snowshoe, things would have fallen out something after this fashion. He would have shown himself suddenly right in the fugitive's path and jumped at him with a terrifying snarl. The fugitive, panic-stricken to find himself thus confronted by the foe whom he had thought left far behind, would have cowered down trembling in his tracks and yielded up his life with a scream of anguish.

But in this case the weasel found his calculations all astray. This quarry's flight was so unexpectedly swift that the pursuer reached the point of interception too late to lie in ambush. He arrived just as young Snowshoe came by with a wild rush. He sprang, of course, but from too great a distance for his spring to be effective. Snowshoe, catching sight of him just in time, was not panic-stricken, but, without swerving from his course, went clean over him in one tremendous bound, and at the same time, as luck would have it, fetched him a convulsive kick on the side of the head with one powerful hind paw as he passed. The weasel went sprawling, with a startled squeak. And the fugitive, tearing on, had vanished before he could recover himself. Refusing to be discouraged, however, and blazing with fury at his discomfiture, he settled himself down again doggedly to the pursuit. He had now a more just appreciation of his quarry's pace and powers; so he drew a longer chord to the circle, determined that this time he would get well ahead and make certain of his prey.

But unfortunately for his enemy's designs, the Homeless One was no slave to the traditions of his tribe. He was now thoroughly frightened. He changed his mind about running in a circle. He lost all desire to get back to his familiar haunts. Untiring and swift he kept straight on; and the weasel, after waiting in vain for many minutes at the point where, by all the rules of rabbit hunting, the prey should have been intercepted and pulled down, gave up the chase in disgust and fell furiously to hunting wood mice. But his brain retained a vindictive memory of the great snowshoe who had so outwitted him.

The Homeless One, meanwhile, had reached a part of the valley which wore a novel air to him. This section had been chopped over by the lumbermen some seven or eight years before, and cleared of nearly all of the heavy timber. There were few trees of any size; and most of the ground was covered with dense thickets of birch, poplar, Indian pear, wild cherry, and mountain ash, with here and there a patch of young balsam firs, darkly but richly green and giving forth an aromatic perfume in the heat. All the thickets were traversed by the runways of the snowshoe rabbits—narrow, well-trodden trails frequented by all the tribe.

The Homeless One, by this time, had got over his fright. Having a conveniently short memory, he had forgotten why he was frightened. And also, which was altogether unusual, he had forgotten the haunts of his past life, a mile or so away. A sleek young doe met him in the runway, and waved long ears of admiration at his comely stature and length of limb. He stopped to touch noses and exchange compliments with her. Coyly she hopped away, leading him into a cool, green-shadowed covert of sumach scrub.

The Homeless One was well content with his new feeding grounds. The strange does all received him with frank approval. He found the bucks, to be sure, by no means so friendly; but this was of small concern to him. If any of them tried to drive him away he bowled them over with a careless rush, or treated them to a scornful kick, of such vigor as to bring them promptly to their manners. Being a philosophic folk they accepted his society forthwith and forgot that he was a stranger and an interloper.

As was the custom of the snowshoe tribe, the Homeless One was in the habit of passing most of the hours of full daylight crouched in a half doze in some dim covert. When hungry, or in the mood for diversion, he would slip forth, after assuring himself that there was no danger in the air, and either go leaping along the runways in playful pursuit of his acquaintances or fall to browsing upon the wild grasses and tender herbage.

One afternoon as he was hopping lazily after a pair of does who were merely pretending, by way of sport, to evade him, he was amazed and startled by the sight of a big goshawk shuffling at an awkward gait along the runway behind him. The runway was narrow, and densely overarched by low branches, so it was impossible that the great hawk could have seen him from the upper air. Obviously, the enterprising bird had entered the runway at its outlet on a little glade some forty or fifty yards back; and here he was now foolishly undertaking to hunt the fleet snowshoes on their own domain.

The first impulse of the Homeless One, naturally, was flight. He knew that terrible long-winged hawk, swiftest and most valiant of all the marauders of the air. With one bound he cleared the two does and raced on for a score of yards. Then curiosity overcame his fear. He stopped short and turned to stare at his pursuer; and the brightened does, blundering against him as they fled past, nearly knocked him over.

Paying no attention to the does he sat up on his hind quarters, ears erect and eyes bulging, and watched the hawk's approach with mingled wonder and contempt. The beautiful, fierce-eyed bird was not at home upon the level earth. His deadly talons were not made for walking, but for perching and for slaying. His realm was the free spaces of the air, and here in the runway he could not spread his wings. His progress was so slow, laborious, and clumsy that, but for the glare of his level, piercing eyes he would have seemed grotesque. The Homeless One, deeply puzzled, kept hopping away along the runway as the clumsy bird approached, preserving a safe distance of ten or a dozen yards, and ready to make an instantaneous dart into the underbrush on either side if the enemy should show the slightest sign of rising into the air. The two does, meanwhile, reassured by their companion's boldness, had ventured back to peer at the strange intruder from farther up the runway.

Apparently undiscouraged by his failure to overtake the mocking fugitives, the great hawk shuffled steadily on, the three rabbits giving way rather contemptuously and at their leisure before him. This went on for a distance of perhaps a hundred yards, till the runway came to an end in a patch of grassy open. As the foremost of the two does hopped forth into the sunlight there came a rush of wings overhead and a bright form, sweeping from just above the green birchtops, struck her down. Her scream of terror was strangled in her throat as the talons of a second hawk, larger and more powerful than the first, clutched her life out in an instant. The other does and the Homeless One, horrified out of their complacence, shot off in opposite directions through the densest of the underbrush. And the victor, standing erect and trim with one foot upon her still quivering prey, stared about her with hard, bright eyes like jewels, waiting for her mate, who had so cleverly driven the runway for her, to emerge from the shadows and join her in the feast.

After this adventure the Homeless One, who was gifted beyond his fellows with the power of learning from experience, was always a little suspicious of the tribal runways. He used them, for his convenience and for his amusement, as much as ever, but he had gained a dim notion of the advantages which they offered to his enemies. One evening, on the violet edge of dusk, when he was gambolling with another buck and several frisky does, a red fox came racing down the runway without making any attempt to disguise his approach. Swift as he was the swifter snowshoes easily outstripped him as they fled from his terrifying attack. Toward the other end of the runway they darted pell-mell, to be met by another fox, who, leaping among them and slashing from side to side with his long white fangs, brought down two of the panic-stricken fugitives before they could scatter across the open, while the original pursuer was able to seize a third in the momentary confusion. But the Homeless One was not there. At the first appearance of the red-furred enemy he had darted aside from the runway and slipped off like a ghost through the gloom of the underbrush. He was not badly frightened, so he only ran a dozen yards or so. Then he stopped and complacently fell to browsing, quite careless as to the fate of his companions. A snowshoe rabbit has enough to think of in guarding his own skin, and it had never occurred to him to try and warn his fellows of the trap they were running into.

It was through such experiences, such hairbreadth adventures and escapes, that the Homeless One, always in hourly peril of his life but not without distractions and joys of his own to make that life sweet to him, saw the hot, bright summer pass into the crisp, exhilarating autumn, with its glories of scarlet on the maple leaves, dull crimson on the sumachs, aërial gold on the birches and poplars, and vivid, waxy vermilion on the heavy fruit clusters of the mountain ash trees overhanging the amber eddies of the Ottanoonsis Stream. The patches of barren, clothed only with a bushy scrub not more than a foot and a half in height, were tinged to a rich cobalt by the crowded masses of the blueberries. These luscious berries gave the snowshoes a pleasant variation to their diet, and the matted scrub was traversed abundantly by their runways. The black bears of the Ottanoonsis, also, would come to these blue berry patches and squat upon their plump haunches to feast greedily on the juicy harvest. The Homeless One, rejoicing in his swiftness of foot, regarded these huge, black, cunning-eyed beasts with scorn, because they were so slow and lumbering in their movements. One day he saw a bear apparently asleep, its rusty-black snout all purple-streaked with the juices of the berries it had been devouring. Yes, it was clear the bear was sleeping soundly, well stuffed with food and well content with the warm sun. The Homeless One had never before enjoyed such a chance to examine a bear at close quarters. It almost looked to him as if that bear was dead. A shrewd blue jay in a neighboring bush shrieked a note of warning. It was ignored. The Homeless One hopped closer and closer, investigating the monster with eyes and nose alike intensely interested. All at once, a huge, black paw, armed with mighty claws, swept down upon him with the speed of a trained boxer's fist. But the Homeless One was no such fool as the blue jay had taken him to be. When that murderous paw descended he was no longer just there but some seven or eight feet away and waving his long ears innocently. The bear, trying to look unconcerned, fell to munching blueberries again; and the Homeless One hopped off with his curiosity quite satisfied.

It was not until November came, with its biting sleet showers, its snows that fell, rested a few days, and vanished, its spells of sharp frost and sudden, bone-reaching cold, that the Homeless One began really to suffer the penalties of his inherited incapacity to make or find himself a home. The comfortable leafage had fallen from all the trees and bushes except the evergreens, the firs and pines, hemlocks and cedars. It was dreary work to crouch beneath a dripping bush while the icy winds scourged the high valley of the Ottanoonsis. Nevertheless, he kept heart to play with his furry companions; and life grew more eventful day by day as his enemies grew more and more hungry and persistent in their hunting. It was about this time, when the snow began to linger upon the ground in glaring patches, that his coat began to change in color in order to make him less conspicuous. He was moulting his rusty-colored summer fur, and the new fur, as it came in, was pure white. By the time the snow had come to stay for the winter his clean, new, snowy coat was in readiness to match it, so that when he crouched motionless, his ears laid back and his nose between his paws, the keenest and hungriest of eyes would usually fail to distinguish him.

One windless, biting afternoon about sunset, when the shadows were stretching long and blue across the snow, the Homeless One was just stirring from his chilly couch to go and feed when from behind his sheltering bush a lean weasel darted upon him. Thanks to his amazing alertness—and his luck—he shot aside in time. But just in time. It was the narrowest shave he had ever had; and he left a tantalizing mouthful of fur in the weasel's jaws.

As it happened, this was the same big weasel, swift and cunning, whom he had balked so ignominiously in the early part of the summer; and by some freak of chance the incident—and possibly some peculiarity in the scent of this huge snowshoe—now revived in the weasel's memory, and he took up the pursuit with a special fury. The snow lay thin and hard, so that the Homeless One was deprived of the advantage which his wide, furry feet would have given him had the snow been soft and deep. To make matters worse he was feeling slack and tired that day, and so fell short of his accustomed speed. As was his rule when pursued, he neither followed the runways nor fled in a circle, but raced straight off through the thickets, dodging erratically and traversing whatever obstacles he thought most likely to embarrass his pursuer. But to his horror he found that pursuer still close upon his heels. The shock of this discovery almost brought upon him that fatal panic which so often overtakes a hunted rabbit and makes him yield himself suddenly as an easy prey. But the Homeless One was of sterner stuff, and that moment's panic only stung him to fiercer effort.

Nevertheless, for the weasel's endurance was greater than his, the Homeless One's career would have come to an end in this last desperate adventure, but for the fact that the Unseen Powers once more woke up and took a whimsical hand in the affair. Just as he was darting, stretched out to his limit, beneath the shelter of a snowy bush, a great owl swooped and made a clutch at him. But the owl had miscalculated the speed which the Homeless One was displaying. She missed him; and she was just in time to seize his pursuer instead. Infuriated at this disappointment—for she would have greatly preferred tender rabbit to tough weasel—her talons closed like steel jaws upon the weasel's neck and loins. Rising noiselessly into the air she swept away into the shadows with her writhing victim. And the Homeless One, presently realizing that he was no longer pursued, hid himself in the deepest thicket he could find, with his heart nearly bursting between his ribs.

When winter had finally closed down upon the Ottanoonsis Valley, with snow four and five feet deep on the levels and a cold that made the trees snap like gunshots in the stillness, the Homeless One, though with no lair to hide in, was in reality less uncomfortable than he had been in the variable weather. The cold, though so intense, was of a sparkling dryness; and every snow-covered bush was ready to afford him a secluded shelter. For him and his tribe—more fortunate in this hard season than their enemies—food was fairly abundant, for the depth of the snow enabled them to reach the tender twigs of the birches and willows and poplars. Moreover, alone among the kindreds of the wild, these weak, defenseless, homeless tribes of the snowshoes managed to find heart for gaiety and play amid the white desolation. When the full moon flooded the wastes with her sinister, icy-blue light, the snowshoes would hop forth from their coverts and gather in the open glades. There they would amuse themselves for hours with a strange game, leaping over each other, and chasing each other till their tracks made curious patterns on the snow almost as if they were performing some wild quadrille. But during these gaieties they were never unmindful of their caution. They could not afford to be, in that world of prowling death. At every entrance to the glade there would be stationed a sentinel, erect upon his hind quarters, long ears waving warily, every sense at utmost tension, ready to give the alarm by a loud pounding with his hind feet at the faintest sign of peril.

It was during one such moonlit revel that the Homeless One stood sentry at the post of chief danger, where a dense growth of hemlocks overhung the edge of the glade. He had been some time on duty, and was just about to give up his post to one of the revelers, who was even then hopping over to relieve him, when he caught sound of a stealthy movement close behind the screen of branches. He gave three frantic thumps with his powerful hind feet, and the revelers vanished as if wiped out by a giant breath. In the next instant he leapt for his life, desperately.

But he was too late—by just the moment it had taken him to give the warning signal. Even as he sprang a shape of shadowy grey, like a huge cat with pale moon-eyes and tufted ears, launching itself through the branches, fell upon him and bore him down; and long fangs reached his throat. With a snarl of triumph the famished lynx tore at the warm prey between his paws, and a dark stain spread upon the trampled snow. The Homeless One, as truly as many a hero of history and song, had died for the safety of his tribe.

The Lord of the Air

The chill glitter of the northern summer sunrise was washing down over the rounded top of old Sugar Loaf. The sombre and solitary peak, bald save for a ragged veil of blueberry and juniper scrub, seemed to topple over the deep enshadowed valley at its foot. The valley was brimmed with crawling vapours, and around its rim emerged spectrally the jagged crests of the fir wood. On either side of the shrouded valley, to east and west, stretched a chain of similar basins, but more ample, and less deeply wrapped in mist. From these, where the vapours had begun to lift, came radiances of unruffled water.

Where the peak leaned to the valley, the trunk of a giant pine jutted forth slantingly from a roothold a little below the summit. Its top had long ago been shattered by lightning and hurled away into the depths; but from a point some ten or twelve feet below the fracture, one gaunt limb still waved green with persistent, indomitable life. This bleached stub thrust out over the vast basin, hummed about by the untrammelled winds, was the watch-tower of the great bald eagle who ruled supreme over all the aerial vicinage of the Squatooks.

When the earliest of the morning light fell palely on the crest of Sugar Loaf, the great eagle came to his watch-tower, leaving the nest on the other side of the peak, where the two nestlings had begun to stir hungrily at the first premonition of dawn. Launching majestically from the edge of the nest, he had swooped down into the cold shadow, then, rising into the light by a splendid spiral, with muffled resonance of wing-stroke, he had taken a survey of the empty, glimmering world. It was still quite too dark for hunting, down there on earth, hungry though the nestlings were. He soared, and soared, till presently he saw his wide-winged mate, too, leave the nest, and beat swiftly off toward the Tuladi Lakes, her own special hunting-grounds. Then he dropped quietly to his blanched pine-top on the leaning side of the summit.

Erect and moveless he sat in the growing light, his snowy, flat-crowned head thrust a little forward, consciously lord of the air. His powerful beak, long and scythe-edged, curved over sharply at the end in a rending hook. His eyes, clear, direct, unacquainted with fear, had a certain hardness in their vitreous brilliancy, perhaps by reason of the sharp contrast between the bright gold iris and the unfathomable pupil, and the straight line of the low overhanging brow gave them a savage intensity of penetration. His neck and tail were of the same snowy whiteness as his snake-like head, while the rest of his body was a deep, shadowy brown, close kin to black.

Suddenly, far, far down, winging swiftly in a straight line through the topmost fold of the mist drift, he saw a duck flying from one lake to another. The errand of the duck was probably an unwonted one, of some special urgency, or he would not have flown so high and taken the straight route over the forest; for at this season the duck of inland waters is apt to fly low and follow the water-course. However that may be, he had forgotten the piercing eyes that kept watch from the peak of old Sugar Loaf.

The eagle lifted and spread the sombre amplitude of his wings, and glided from his perch in a long curve, till he balanced above the unconscious voyager. Then down went his head; his wings shut close, his feathers hardened till he was like a wedge of steel, and down he shot with breathless, appalling speed. But the duck was travelling fast, and the great eagle saw that the mere speed of dropping like a thunderbolt was insufficient for his purpose. Two or three quick, short, fierce thrusts of his pinions, and the speed of his descent was more than doubled. The duck heard an awful hissing in the air above him. But before he could swerve to look up he was struck, whirled away, blotted out of life.

Carried downward with his quarry by the rush of his descent, the eagle spread his pinions and rose sharply just before he reached the nearest tree-tops. High he mounted on still wings with that tremendous impulse. Then, as the impulse failed, his wings began to flap strongly, and he flew off with business-like directness toward the eyrie on the other slope of Sugar Loaf. The head and legs of the duck hung limply from the clutch of his talons.

The nest was a seemingly haphazard collection of sticks, like a hay-cart load of rubbish, deposited on a ledge of the mountainside. In reality, every stick in the structure had been selected with care, and so adeptly fitted that the nest stood unshaken beneath the wildest storms that swept old Sugar Loaf. The ground below the ledge was strewn with the faggots and branches which the careful builders had rejected. The nest had the appearance of being merely laid upon the ledge, but in reality its foundations were firmly locked into a ragged crevice which cleft the ledge at that point.

As the eagle drew near with his prey, he saw his mate winging heavily from the Tuladis, a large fish hanging from her talons. They met at the nest's edge, and two heavy-bodied, soot-coloured, half-fledged nestlings, with wings half spread in eagerness, thrust up hungry, gaping beaks to greet them. The fish, as being the choicer morsel, was first torn to fragments and fed to these greedy beaks; and the duck followed in a few moments, the young ones gulping their meal with grotesque contortions and ecstatic liftings of their wings. Being already much more than half the size of their parents, and growing almost visibly, and expending vast vitality in the production of their first feathers, their appetites were prodigious. Not until these appetites seemed to be, for the moment, stayed, and the eaglets sank back contentedly upon the nest, did the old birds fly off to forage for themselves, leaving a bloody garniture of bones and feathers upon the threshold of their home.

The king—who, though smaller than his mate, was her lord by virtue of superior initiative and more assured, equable daring—returned at once to his watch-tower on the lake side of the summit. It had become his habit to initiate every enterprise from that starting-point. Perching motionless for a few minutes, he surveyed the whole wide landscape of the Squatook Lakes, with the great waters of Lake Temiscouata gleaming to the north-west, and the peak of Bald Mountain, old Sugar Loaf's rival, lifting a defiant front from the shores of Nictau Lake, far to the south.

The last wisp of vapour had vanished, drunk up by the rising sun, and the eagle's eye had clear command of every district of his realm. It was upon the little lake far below him that his interest presently centred itself. There, at no great height above the unruffled waters, he saw a fish-hawk sailing, now tilted to one side or the other on moveless wing, now flapping hurriedly to another course, as if he were scrupulously quartering the whole lake surface.

The king recognized with satisfaction the diligence of this, the most serviceable, though most unwilling, of his subjects. In leisurely fashion he swung off from his perch, and presently was whirling in slow spirals directly over the centre of the lake. Up, up he mounted, till he was a mere speck in the blue, and seemingly oblivious of all that went on below; but, as he wheeled, there in his supreme altitude, his grim white head was stretched ever earthward, and his eyes lost no detail of the fish-hawk's diligence.

All at once, the fish-hawk was seen to poise on steady wing. Then his wings closed, and he shot downward like a javelin. The still waters of the lake were broken with a violent splash, and the fish-hawk's body for a moment almost disappeared. Then, with a struggle and a heavy flapping of wings, the daring fisher arose, grasping in his victorious claws a large "togue" or gray lake trout. He rose till he was well above the tree-tops of the near-by shore, and then headed for his nest in the cedar swamp.

This was the moment for which the eagle had been waiting, up in the blue. Again his vast wings folded themselves. Again his plumage hardened to a wedge of steel. Again he dropped like a plummet. But this time he had no slaughterous intent. He was merely descending out of the heavens to take tribute. Before he reached the hurrying fish-hawk he swerved upward, steadied himself, and flapped a menacing wing in the fish-hawk's face, heading it out again toward the centre of the lake.

Frightened, angry, and obstinate, the big hawk clutched his prize the closer, and made futile efforts to reach the tree-tops. But, fleet though he was, he was no match for the fleetness of his master. The great eagle was over him, under him, around him, all at once, yet never striking him. The king was simply indicating, quite unmistakably, his pleasure, which was that the fish should be delivered up.

Suddenly, however, seeing that the fish-hawk was obstinate, the eagle lost patience. It was time, he concluded, to end the folly. He had no wish to harm the fish-hawk,—a most useful creature, and none too abundant for his kingly needs. In fact, he was always careful not to exact too heavy a tribute from the industrious fisherman, lest the latter should grow discouraged and remove to freer waters. Of the spoils of his fishing the big hawk was always allowed to keep enough to satisfy the requirements of himself and his nestlings. But it was necessary that there should be no foolish misunderstanding on the subject.

The eagle swung away, wheeled sharply with an ominous, harsh rustling of stiffened feathers, and then came at the hawk with a yelp and a sudden tremendous rush. His beak was half open. His great talons were drawn forward and extended for a deadly stroke. His wings darkened broadly over the fugitive. His sound, his shadow,—they were doom itself, annihilation to the frightened hawk.

But that deadly stroke was not delivered. The threat was enough. Shrinking aside with a scream the fish-hawk opened his claws, and the trout fell, a gleaming bar of silver in the morning light. On the instant the eagle half closed his wings, tilted sideways, and swooped. He did not drop, as he had descended upon the voyaging duck, but with a peculiar shortened wing-stroke, he flew straight downward for perhaps a hundred feet. Then, with this tremendous impulse driving him, he shot down like lightning, caught the fish some twenty feet above the water, turned, and rose in a long, magnificent slant, with the tribute borne in his talons. He sailed away majestically to his watch-tower on old Sugar Loaf, to make his meal at leisure, while the ruffled hawk beat away rapidly down the river to try his luck in the lower lake.

Holding the fish firmly in the clutch of one great talon, the eagle tore it to pieces and swallowed it with savage haste. Then he straightened himself, twisted and stretched his neck once or twice, settled back into erect and tranquil dignity, and swept a kingly glance over all his domain, from the far head of Big Squatook, to the alder-crowded outlet of Fourth Lake. He saw unmoved the fish-hawk capture another prize, and fly off with it in triumph to his hidden nest in the swamp. He saw two more ducks winging their way from a sheltered cove to a wide, green reed-bed at the head of the thoroughfare. Being a right kingly monarch, he had no desire to trouble them. Untainted by the lust of killing, he killed only when the need was upon him.

Having preened himself with some care, polished his great beak on the dry wood of the stub, and stretched each wing, deliberately and slowly, the one after the other, with crisp rustling noises, till each strong-shanked plume tingled pleasantly in its socket and fitted with the utmost nicety to its overlapping fellows, he bethought him once more of the appetites of his nestlings. There were no more industrious fish-hawks in sight. Neither hare nor grouse was stirring in the brushy opens. No living creatures were visible save a pair of loons chasing each other off the point of Sugar Loaf Island, and an Indian in his canoe just paddling down to the outlet to spear suckers.

The eagle knew that the loons were no concern of his. They were never to be caught napping. They could dive quicker than he could swoop and strike. The Indian also he knew, and from long experience had learned to regard him as inoffensive. He had often watched, with feelings as near akin to jealousy as his arrogant heart could entertain, the spearing of suckers and whitefish. And now the sight determined him to go fishing on his own account. He remembered a point of shoals on Big Squatook where large fish were wont to lie basking in the sun, and where sick or disabled fish were frequently washed ashore. Here he might gather some spoil of the shallows, pending the time when he could again take tribute of the fish-hawk. Once more he launched himself from his watch-tower under the peak of Sugar Loaf, and sailed away over the serried green tops of the forest.

II

Now it chanced that the old Indian, who was the most cunning trapper in all the wilderness of Northern New Brunswick, though he seemed so intent upon his fishing, was in reality watching the great eagle. He had anticipated and indeed prepared for the regal bird's expedition to those shoals of the Big Squatook; and now, as he marked the direction of his flight, he clucked grimly to himself with satisfaction, and deftly landed a large sucker in the canoe.

That very morning, before the first pallor of dawn had spread over Squatook, the Indian had scattered some fish, trout and suckers, on the shore adjoining the shoal water. The point he chose was where a dense growth of huckleberry and withe-wood ran out to within a few feet of the water's edge, and where the sand of the beach was dotted thickly with tufts of grass. The fish, partly hidden among these tufts of grass, were all distributed over a circular area of a diameter not greater than six or seven feet; and just at the centre of the baited circle the Indian had placed a stone about a foot high, such as any reasonable eagle would like to perch upon when making a hasty meal. He was crafty with all the cunning of the woods, was this old trapper, and he knew that a wise and experienced bird like the king of Sugar Loaf was not to be snared by any ordinary methods. But to snare him he was resolved, though it should take all the rest of the summer to accomplish it; for a rich American, visiting Edmundston on the Madawaska in the spring, had promised him fifty dollars for a fine specimen of the great white headed and white tailed eagle of the New Brunswick lakes, if delivered to Edmundston alive and unhurt.

When the eagle came to the point of shoals he noticed a slight change. That big stone was something new, and therefore to be suspected. He flew over it without stopping, and alighted on the top of a dead birch-tree near-by. A piercing scrutiny convinced him that the presence of the stone at a point where he was accustomed to hop awkwardly on the level sand, was in no way portentous, but rather a provision of destiny for his convenience. He sailed down and alighted upon the stone.

When he saw a dead sucker lying under a grass tuft he considered again. Had the fish lain at the water's edge he would have understood; but up among the grasses, that was a singular situation for a dead fish to get itself into. He now peered suspiciously into the neighbouring bushes, scanned every tuft or grass, and cast a sweeping survey up and down the shores. Everything was as it should be. He hopped down, captured the fish, and was about to fly away with it to his nestlings, when he caught sight of another, and yet another. Further search revealed two more. Plainly the wilderness, in one of those caprices which even his old wisdom had not yet learned to comprehend, was caring very lavishly for the king. He hastily tore and swallowed two of the fish, and then flew away with the biggest of the lot to the nest behind the top of old Sugar Loaf. That same day he came twice again to the point of shoals, till there was not another fish left among the grass tufts. But on the following day, when he came again, with hope rather than expectation in his heart, he found that the supply had been miraculously renewed. His labours thus were greatly lightened. He had more time to sit upon his wind-swept watch-tower under the peak, viewing widely his domain, and leaving the diligent fish-hawks to toil in peace. He fell at once into the custom of perching on the stone at every visit, and then devouring at least one fish before carrying a meal to the nest. His surprise and curiosity as to the source of the supply had died out on the second day. The wild creatures quickly learn to accept a simple obvious good, however extraordinary, as one of those beneficences which the unseen powers bestow without explanation.

By the time the eagle had come to this frame of mind, the old Indian was ready for the next move in his crafty game. He made a strong hoop of plaited withe-wood, about seven feet in diameter. To this he fastened an ample bag of strong salmon-netting, which he had brought with him from Edmundston for this purpose. To the hoop he fixed securely a stiff birch sapling for a handle, so that the affair when completed was a monster scoop-net, stout and durable in every part. On a moonlight night when he knew that the eagle was safely out of sight, on his eyrie around at the back of Sugar Loaf, the Indian stuck his gigantic scoop in the bow of his canoe, and paddled over to the point of shoals. He had never heard of anyone trying to catch an eagle in a net; but, on the other hand, he had never heard of anyone wanting an eagle alive, and being willing to emphasize his wants with fifty dollars. The case was plainly one that called for new ideas, and the Indian, who had freed himself from the conservatism of his race, was keenly interested in the plan which he had devised.

The handle of the great scoop-net was about eight feet in length. Its butt the trapper drove slantingly into the sand where the water was an inch or two deep, bracing it securely with stones. He fixed it at an angle so acute that the rim of the net lay almost flat at a height of about four feet above the stone whereon the eagle was wont to perch. Under the uppermost edge of the hoop the trapper fixed a firm prop, making the structure steady and secure. The drooping slack of the net he then caught up and held lightly in place on three or four willow twigs, so that it all lay flat within the rim. This accomplished to his satisfaction, he scattered fish upon the ground as usual, most of them close about the stone and within the area overshadowed by the net, but two or three well outside. Then he paddled noiselessly away across the moon-silvered mirror of the lake, and disappeared into the blackness about the outlet.

On the following morning, the king sat upon his watch-tower while the first light gilded the leaning summit of Sugar Loaf. His gaze swept the vast and shadowy basin of the landscape with its pointed tree-tops dimly emerging above the vapour-drift, and its blank, pallid spaces whereunder the lakes lay veiled in dream. His golden eye flamed fiercely under the straight and fierce white brow; nevertheless, when he saw, far down, two ducks winging their way across the lake, now for a second visible, now vanishing in the mist, he suffered them to go unstricken. The clear light gilded the white feathers of his head and tail, but sank and was absorbed in the cloudy gloom of his wings. For fully half an hour he sat in regal immobility. But when at last the waters of Big Squatook were revealed, stripped and gleaming, he dropped from his perch in a tremendous, leisurely curve, and flew over to the point of shoals.

As he drew near, he was puzzled and annoyed to see the queer structure that had been erected during the night above his rock. It was inexplicable. He at once checked his flight and began whirling in great circles, higher and higher, over the spot, trying in vain to make out what it was. He could see that the dead fish were there as usual. And at length he satisfied himself that no hidden peril lurked in the near-by huckleberry thicket. Then he descended to the nearest tree-top and spent a good half-hour in moveless watching of the net. He little guessed that a dusky figure, equally moveless and far more patient, was watching him in turn from a thicket across the lake.

At the end of this long scrutiny, the eagle decided that a closer investigation was desirable. He flew down and alighted on the level sand well away from the net. There he found a fish which he devoured. Then he found another; and this he carried away to the eyrie. He had not solved the mystery of the strange structure overhanging the rock, but he had proved that it was not actively inimical. It had not interfered with his morning meal, or attempted to hinder him from carrying off his customary spoils. When he returned an hour later to the point of shoals the net looked less strange to him. He even perched on the sloping handle, balancing himself with outspread wings till the swaying ceased. The thing was manifestly harmless. He hopped down, looked with keen interested eyes at the fish beside the rock, hopped in and clutched one out with beak and claw, hopped back again in a great hurry, and flew away with the prize to his watch-tower on Sugar Loaf. This caution he repeated at every visit throughout that day. But when he came again on the morrow, he had grown once more utterly confident. He went under the net without haste or apprehension, and perched unconcernedly on the stone in the midst of his banquet. And the stony face of the old Indian, in his thicket across the lake, flashed for one instant with a furtive grin. He grunted, melted back into the woods, and slipped away to resume his fishing at the outlet.

The next morning, about an hour before dawn, a ghostly birch canoe slipped up to the point of shoals, and came to land about a hundred yards from the net. The Indian stepped out, lifted it from the water, and hid it in the bushes. Then he proceeded to make some important changes in the arrangement of the net.

To the topmost rim of the hoop he tied a strong cord, brought the free end to the ground, led it under a willow root, and carried it some ten paces back into the thicket. Next he removed the supporting prop. Going back into the thicket, he pulled the cord. It ran freely under the willow root, and the net swayed down till it covered the rock, to rebound to its former position the moment he released the cord. Then he restored the prop to its place; but this time, instead of planting its butt firmly in the sand, he balanced it on a small flat stone, so that the least pull would instantaneously dislodge it. To the base of the prop he fixed another cord; and this also he ran under the willow root and carried back into the thicket. To the free end of this second cord he tied a scrap of red flannel, that there might be no mistake at a critical moment. The butt of the handle he loosened, so that if the prop were removed the net would almost fall of its own weight; and on the upper side of the butt, to give steadiness and speed of action, he leaned two heavy stones. Finally, he baited his trap with the usual dead fish, bunching them now under the centre of the net. Then, satisfying himself that all was in working order, he wormed his way into the heart of the thicket. A few leafy branches, cunningly disposed around and above his hiding-place, made his concealment perfect, while his keen black beads of eyes commanded a clear view of the stone beneath the net. The ends of the two cords were between his lean fingers. No waiting fox or hiding grouse could have lain more immovable, could have held his muscles in more patient perfect stillness, than did the wary old trapper through the chill hour of growing dawn.

At last there came a sound that thrilled even such stoic nerves as his. Mighty wings hissed in the air above his head. The next moment he saw the eagle alight upon the level sand beside the net. This time there was no hesitation. The great bird, for all his wisdom, had been lured into accepting the structure as a part of the established order of things. He hopped with undignified alacrity right under the net, clutched a large whitefish, and perched himself on the stone to enjoy his meal.

At that instant he felt, rather than saw, the shadow of a movement in the thicket. Or rather, perhaps, some inward, unaccredited guardian signalled to him of danger. His muscles gathered themselves for that instantaneous spring wherewith he was wont to hurl himself into the air. But even that electric speed of his was too slow for this demand. Ere he could spring, the great net came down about him with a vicious swish; and in a moment beating wings, tearing beak, and clutching talons were helplessly intertangled in the meshes. Before he could rip himself free, a blanket was thrown over him. He was ignominiously rolled into a bundle, picked up, and carried off under the old Indian's arm.

III

When the king was gone, it seemed as if a hush had fallen over the country of the Squatooks. When the old pine beneath the toppling peak of Sugar Loaf had stood vacant all the long golden hours of the morning, two crows flew up from the firwoods to investigate. They hopped up and down on the sacred seat, cawing impertinently and excitedly. Then in a sudden flurry of apprehension they darted away. News of the great eagle's mysterious absence spread quickly among the woodfolk—not by direct communication, indeed, except in the case of the crows, but subtly and silently, as if by some telepathic code intelligible alike to mink and wood-mouse, kingfisher and lucifee.

When the noon had gone by, and the shadow of Sugar Loaf began to creep over the edge of the nest, the old mother eagle grew uneasy at the prolonged absence of her mate. Never before since the nestlings broke the shell had he been so long away. Never before had she been compelled to realize how insatiable were the appetites of her young. She flew around to the pine-tree on the other side of the peak—and finding it vacant, something told her it had been long unoccupied. Then she flew hither and thither over all the lakes, a fierce loneliness growing in her heart. From the long grasses around the mouth of the thoroughfare between third and fourth lakes a heron arose, flapping wide bluish wings, and she dropped upon it savagely. However her wild heard ached, the nestlings must be fed. With the long limp neck and slender legs of the heron trailing from her talons, she flew away to the eyrie; and she came no more to the Squatooks.

The knowledge of all the woodfolk around the lakes had been flashed in upon her, and she knew some mysterious doom had fallen upon her mate. Thereafter, though the country of the Squatooks was closer at hand and equally well stocked with game, and though the responsibilities of her hunting had been doubled, she kept strictly to her old hunting-ground of the Tuladis. Everything on the north side of old Sugar Loaf had grown hateful to her; and unmolested within half a mile of the eyrie, the diligent fish-hawks plied their craft, screaming triumphantly over every creature. The male, indeed, growing audacious after the king had been a whole week absent, presumed so far as to adopt the old pine-tree under the peak for his perch, to the loud and disconcerting derision of the crows. They flocked blackly about with vituperative malice, driving him to forsake his seat of usurpation and soar indignantly to heights where they could not follow. But at last the game palled upon their whimsical fancies, and they left him in peace to his aping of the king.

Meanwhile, in the village of Edmundston, in the yard of a house that stood ever enfolded in the sleepless roar of the Falls of Madawaska, the king was eating out his sorrowful and tameless heart. Around one steely-scaled leg, just above the spread of the mighty claws, he wore the ragged ignominy of a bandage of soiled red flannel. This was to prevent the chafing of the clumsy and rusty dog-chain which secured him to his perch in an open shed that looked out upon the river. Across the river, across the cultivated valley with its roofs, and farther across the forest hills than any human eye could see, his eye could see a dim summit, as it were a faint blue cloud on the horizon, his own lost realm of Sugar Loaf. Hour after hour he would sit upon his rude perch, unstirring, unwinking, and gaze upon this faint blue cloud of his desire.

From his jailers he accepted scornfully his daily rations of fish, ignoring the food while anyone was by, but tearing it and gorging it savagely when left alone. As week after week dragged on, his hatred of his captors gathered force, but he showed no sign. Fear he was hardly conscious of; or, at least, he had never felt that panic fear which unnerves even kings, except during the one appalling moment when he felt the falling net encumber his wings, and the trapper's smothering blanket shut out the sun from his eyes. Now, when any one of his jailers approached and sought to win his confidence, he would shrink within himself and harden his feathers with wild inward aversion, but his eye of piercing gold would neither dim nor waver, and a clear perception of the limits of his chain would prevent any futile and ignoble struggle to escape. Had he shown more fear, more wildness, his jailers would have more hope of subduing him in some measure; but as it was, being back country men with some knowledge of the wilderness folk, they presently gave him up as tameless and left off troubling him with their attentions. They took good care of him, however, for they were to be well paid for their trouble when the rich American came for his prize.

At last he came; and when he saw the king he was glad. Trophies he had at home in abundance—the skins of lions which he had shot on the Zambesi, of tigers from Himalayan foothills, of grizzlies from Alaskan canyons, and noble heads of moose and caribou from these very highlands of Squatook, whereon the king had been wont to look from his dizzy gyres of flight above old Sugar Loaf. But the great white-headed eagle, who year after year had baffled his woodcraft and eluded his rifle, he had come to love so that he coveted him alive. Now, having been apprised of the capture of so fine and well-known a bird as the king of old Sugar Loaf, he had brought with him an anklet of thick, soft leather for the illustrious captive's leg, and a chain of wrought steel links, slender, delicate, and strong. On the morning after his arrival the new chain was to be fitted.

The great eagle was sitting erect upon his perch, gazing at the faint blue cloud which he alone could see, when two men came to the shed beside the river. One he knew. It was his chief jailer, the man who usually brought fish. The other was a stranger, who carried in his hand a long, glittering thing that jangled and stirred a vague apprehension in his heart. The jailer approached, and with a quick movement wrapped him in a coat, till beak and wings and talons alike were helpless. There was one instinctive, convulsive spasm within the wrapping, and the bundle was still, the great bird being too proud as well as too wise to waste force in a vain struggle.

"Seems pretty tame already," remarked the stranger, in a tone of satisfaction.

"Tame!" exclaimed the countryman. "Them's the kind as don't tame. I've give up trying to tame him. Ef you keep him, an' feed him, an' coax him for ten year, he'll be as wild as the day Gabe snared him up on Big Squatook."

"We'll see," said the stranger, who had confidence in his knowledge of the wild folk.

Seating himself on a broken-backed chair just outside the shadow of the shed, where the light was good, the countryman held the motionless bundle firmly across his knees, and proceeded cautiously to free the fettered leg. He held it in an inflexible grip, respecting those knife-edged claws. Having removed the rusty dog-chain and the ignominious red flannel bandage, he fitted dexterously the soft leather anklet, with its three tiny silver buckles, and its daintily engraved plate, bearing the king's name with the place and date of his capture. Then he reached out his hand for the new steel chain.

The eagle, meanwhile, had been slowly and imperceptibly working his head free; and now, behind the countryman's arm, he looked out from the imprisoning folds of the coat. Fierce, wild, but unaffrighted, his eye caught the glitter of the chain as the stranger held it out. That glitter moved him strangely. On a sudden impulse he opened his mighty beak, and tore savagely at the countryman's leg.

With a yell of pain and surprise the man attempted to jump away from this assault. But as the assailant was on his lap this was obviously impossible. The muscles of his leg stiffened out instinctively—and the broken-backed chair gave way under the strain. Arms and legs flew wildly in the air as he sprawled backward—and the coat fell apart—and the eagle found himself free. The stranger sprang forward to clutch his treasured captive, but received a blinding buffet from the great wings undestined to captivity. The next moment the king bounded upward. The air whistled under his tremendous wing-strokes. Up, up he mounted, leaving the men to gape after him, flushed and foolish. Then he headed his flight for that faint blue cloud beyond the hills.

That afternoon there was a difference in the country of the Squatooks. The nestlings in the eyrie—bigger and blacker and more clamorous they were now than when he went away—found more abundant satisfaction to their growing appetites. Their wide-winged mother, hunting away on Tuladi, hunted with more joyous heart. The fish-hawks on the Squatook waters came no more near the blasted pine; but they fished more diligently, and their hearts were big with indignation over the spoils which they had been forced to deliver up.

The crows far down in the fir-tops were garrulous about the king's return, and the news spread swiftly among the mallards, the muskrats, the hares, and the careful beavers. And the solitude about the toppling peak of old Sugar Loaf seemed to resume some lost sublimity, as the king resumed his throne among the winds.

The Keeper of the Water-Gate

Some distance below the ice, through the clear, dark water of the quiet-running stream, a dim form went swimming swiftly. It was a sturdy, broad-headed, thick-furred form, a little more than a foot in length, with a naked, flattened tail almost as long as the body. It held its small, handlike fore paws tucked up under its chin, and swam with quick strokes of its strong hind legs and eellike wrigglings of the muscular tail. It would have seemed like no more than a darker, swiftly-moving shadow in the dark water, save for a curious burden of air-bubbles which went with it. Its close under-fur, which the water could not penetrate, was thickly sprinkled with longer hairs, which the water seemed, as it were, to plaster down; and under these long hairs the air was caught in little silvery bubbles, which made the swimmer conspicuous even under two inches of clear ice and eighteen inches of running water.

As he went, the swimmer slanted downward and aimed for a round hole at the bottom of the bank. This hole was the water-gate of his winter citadel; and he, the keeper of it, was the biggest and pluckiest muskrat on the whole slow-winding length of Bitter Creek.

At this point Bitter Creek was about four feet deep and ten or twelve feet wide, with low, bushy shores subject to overflow at the slightest freshet. Winter, setting in suddenly with fierce frost, had caught it while its sluggish waters were still so high from the late autumn rains that the bushes and border grasses were all awash. Now the young ice, transparent and elastic, held them in firm fetters. The flat world of field and wood about Bitter Creek was frozen as hard as iron, and a biting gale, which carried a thin drift of dry, gritty snow, was lashing it pitilessly. The branches snapped and creaked under the cruel assault, and not a bird or beast was so hardy as to show its head abroad. But in the muskrat's world, there under the safe ice, all was as tranquil as a May morning. The long green and brown water-weeds swayed softly in the faint current, with here and there a silvery young chub or an olive-brown sucker feeding lazily among them. Under the projecting roots lurked water-snails, and small, black, scurrying beetles, and big-eyed, horn-jawed larvae which would change next spring to aerial forms of radiance. And not one of them, muskrat, chub, or larva, cared one whit for the scourge of winter on the bleak world above the ice.

The big muskrat swam straight to the mouth of the hole, and plunged half-way into it. Then he suddenly changed his mind. Backing out abruptly, he darted up to the surface close under the edge of the bank. Along the edge of the bank the ice-roof slanted upward, the water having fallen several inches since the ice had set. This left a covered air space, about two inches in height, all along the fringes of the grass roots; and here the muskrat paused, head and shoulders half out of water, to take breath. He was panting heavily, having come a long way under water without stopping to empty and refill his long-suffering little lungs. Two inches over his head, on the other side of the ice, the thin, hard snow went driving and swirling, and he could hear the alders straining under the bitter wind. His little, bead-bright eyes, set deep in his furry face, gleamed with satisfaction over his comfortable security.

Having fully eased his lungs, the muskrat dived again to the bottom, and began to gnaw with fierce energy at a snaky mass of the roots of the yellow material. Having cut off a section about as long as himself, and more than an inch in thickness, he tugged at it fiercely to loosen the fibres which held it to the bottom. But this particular piece was more firmly anchored than he had expected to find it, and presently, feeling as if his lungs would burst, he was obliged to ascend to the air-space under the ice for a new breath. There he puffed and panted for perhaps a minute. But he had no thought of relinquishing that piece of succulent, crisp, white-hearted lily-root. As soon as he had rested, he swam down again, and gripping it savagely tore it loose at the first pull. Holding the prize lengthwise that it might not obstruct his entrance, he plunged into the hole in the bank, the round, black water-gate to his winter house.

The house was a most comfortable and strictly utilitarian

structure. The entrance, dug with great and persistent toil from the very bottom of the bank, for the better discouragement of the muskrat's deadliest enemy, the mink, ran inward for nearly two feet, and then upward on a long slant some five or six feet through the natural soil. At this point the shore was dry land at the average level of the water; and over this exit, which was dry at the time of the building, the muskrat had raised his house.

The house was a seemingly careless, roughly rounded heap of grass-roots, long water-weeds, lily-roots and stems, and mud, with a few sticks woven into the foundation. The site was cunningly chosen, so that the roots and stems of a large alder gave it secure anchorage; and the whole structure, for all its apparent looseness, was so well compacted as to be secure against the sweep of the spring freshets. About six feet in diameter at the base, it rose about the same distance from the foundation, a rude, sedge-thatched dome, of which something more than three feet now showed itself above the ice.

To the unobservant eye the muskrat house in the alders might have looked like a mass of drift in which the rank water-grass had taken root. But within the clumsy pile, about a foot below the centre of the dome, was a shapely, small, warm chamber, lined with the softest grasses. From one side of this chamber the burrow slanted down to another and much larger chamber, the floor of which, at the present high level of the water, was partly flooded. From this chamber led downward two burrows—one, the main passage, by which the muskrat had entered, opening frankly, as we have seen, in the channel of the creek, and the other, longer and more devious, terminating in a narrow and cunningly concealed exit, behind a deeply submerged willow-root. This passage was little used, and was intended chiefly as a way of escape in case of an extreme emergency—such as, for example, the invasion of a particularly enterprising mink by way of the main water-gate. The muskrat is no match for the snake-swift, bloodthirsty mink, except in the one accomplishment of holding his breath under water. And a mink must be very ravenous, or quite mad with the blood-lust, to dare the deep water-gate and the long subaqueous passage to the muskrat's citadel, at seasons of average high water. In time of drought, however, when the entrance is nearly uncovered and the water goes but a little way up the dark tunnels, the mink will often glide in, slaughter the garrison, and occupy the well-built citadel.

The big muskrat, dragging his lily-root, mounted the narrow, black, water-filled passage till he reached the first chamber. Here he was met by his mate, just descending from the upper room. She promptly appropriated the piece of lily-root, which the big muskrat meekly gave up. He had fed full before coming, and now had no care except to clean his draggled fur and make his toilet before mounting to the little dry top chamber and curling himself up for a nap.

This toilet was as elaborate and painstaking as that of the cleanliest of cats or squirrels. He was so loose-jointed, so loose-skinned, so flexibly built in every way, that he could reach every part of his fur with his teeth and claws at once. He would seem to pull great folds of skin from his back around under his breast, where he could comb it the more thoroughly. It was no trouble at all for him to scratch his left ear with his right hind foot. He went about his task with such zeal that in a very few minutes his fur was as fluffy and exquisite as that of a boudoir kitten. Then he rubbed his face, eyes, and ears vigorously with both fore paws at once in a half-childish fashion, sitting up on his hind-quarters as he did so. This done, he flicked his tail sharply two or three times, touched his mate lightly with his nose, and scurried up to the little sleeping-chamber. Something less than a foot above his head the winter gale howled, ripped the snow-flurries, lashed the bushes, sent the snapped twigs hurtling through the bare branches, turned every naked sod to stone. But to the sleeping muskrat all the outside sound and fury came but as a murmur of June trees.

His mate, meanwhile, was gobbling the lily-root as if she had not eaten for a week. Sitting up like a squirrel, and clutching the end of the root with both little fore paws, she crushed the white esculent into her mouth and gnawed at it ravenously with the keen chisels of her teeth. The root was as long as herself, and its weight perhaps a sixth of her own. Yet when it was all eaten she wanted more. There were other pieces stored in the chamber; and indeed the whole house itself was in great part edible, being built largely of such roots and grasses as the muskrat loves to feed on. But such stores were for emergency use. She could forage for herself at present. Diving down the main passage she presently issued from the water-gate, and immediately rose to the clear-roofed air-space. Here she nibbled tentatively at some stems and withered leafage. These proving little to her taste, she suddenly remembered a clam-bed not far off, and instantly set out for it. She swam briskly downstream along the air-space, her eyes and nose just out of the water, the ice gleaming silvery above her head.

She had travelled in this position perhaps fifty yards when she saw, some twelve or fifteen feet ahead of her, a lithe, dark, slender figure with a sharp-nosed, triangular head, squeeze itself over a projecting root which almost touched the ice. The stranger was no larger than herself—but she knew it was not for her to try conclusions with even the smallest of minks. Catching a good lungful of air, she dived on the instant, down, down, to the very bed of the creek, and out to mid-channel.

The mink, eagerly desirous of a meal of muskrat meat, dived also, heading outward to interrupt the fugitive. He swam as well as the muskrat—perhaps faster, indeed, with a darting, eel-like, deadly swiftness. But the stream at this point had widened to a breadth of twelve or fifteen yards—and this was the little muskrat's salvation. The mink was afraid to follow her to such a distance from the air-space. He knew that by the time he overtook her, and fixed his teeth in her throat, he would be fairly winded; and then, with no breathing-hole at hand, he would die terribly, bumping up against the clear ice and staring madly through at the free air for which his lungs were agonizing. His fierce heart failed him, and he turned back to the air-space under the bank. But the sight of the muskrat had whetted his appetite, and when he came to the muskrat house in the alders, he swam down and thrust his head inside the water-gate. He even, indeed, went half-way in; but soon instinct, or experience, or remembered instruction, told him that the distance to the air-chamber was too great for him. He had no more fancy to be drowned in the muskrat's winding black tunnel, than under the clear daylight of the ice; so he turned away, and with red, angry eyes resumed his journey up-stream.

The little muskrat, seeing that her enemy was disheartened, went on cheerfully to the clam-bed. Here she clawed up from the oozy bottom and devoured almost enough clams to make a meal for a full-grown man. But she took longer over her meal than the man would, thereby saving herself from an otherwise imminent indigestion. Each bivalve, as she got it, she would carry up to the air-space among the stones, selecting a tussock of grass on which she could rest half out of the water. And every time, before devouring her prize, she would carefully, though somewhat impatiently, cleanse her face of the mud and dead leafage which seemed to be an inseparable concomitant of her digging. When she had eaten as many clams as she could stuff into her little body, she hastened back to join her mate in the safe nest over the water-gate.

In the upper world the winter was a severe one, but of all its bitterness the muskrats knew nothing, save by the growing thickness of the ice that sheltered them. As Bitter Creek shrank to normal, winter level, and the strong ice sank in mid-channel, the air-space along shore increased till they had a spacious, covered corridor in which to disport themselves. Food was all about them—an unlimited abundance of lily-roots and clams; and once in awhile their diet was varied by the capture of a half-torpid sucker or chub. There were no otters in Bitter Creek; and the mink, which had investigated their water-gate so hungrily, got caught in a trap at an open spring up-stream, where he was accustomed to fish for eels. So the muskrats had no dangerous enemies to mar their peace.

The spring thaws came suddenly, while the ice was yet strong, and the flood went wide over the low banks of Bitter Creek. But the little house among the alders withstood them sturdily. The water rose till it filled the lower chamber. Inch by inch it crept up the last passage, till it glistened dimly just an inch below the threshold. But it never actually touched that threshold; and the little grass-lined retreat stayed warm and dry. Then the ice went out, under the sun and showers of late April, and the waters shrank away as rapidly as they had risen; and the muskrats, wild with the intoxication of spring, rolled, played, and swam gaily hither and thither on the surface of the open creek. They made long excursions up and down-stream for the sheer delight of wandering, and found fresh interest in every clam-flat, lily cove, or sprouting bed of sweet-flag. Their appetites they had always with them; and though it was fun to chase each other, or to roll and wallow luxuriously on the cool surface of the water when the sun shone warm, there was nothing quite so worth while, day in and day out, as eating. Other muskrats now appeared, the wander-spirit seizing them all at once; and the males had many fierce fights, which left their naked tails scarred and bleeding. But the big muskrat, from the house in the alders, was denied the joy of battle, because none of his rivals were so hardy as to confront him.

About this pleasant season, in the upper chamber over the water-gate, was born a family of nine very small and very naked young muskrats. Their big father was amiably indifferent to them, and spent most of his time, when at home, in the lower chamber, which was now dry and clean enough for his luxurious tastes. Their small mother, however, was assiduous in her care; and in an exceedingly short time the youngsters, very sleek and dark in their first fur, were investigating the wonderful, great world beyond their water-gate. They had prodigious appetites, and they grew prodigiously. One, on their very first outing, got snapped up by a greedy black duck. The attention of the little mother was just then occupied, and, never having learned to count up to nine, she, apparently, never realized her loss; but she was destined to avenge it, a week or two later, by eating two new-hatched ducklings of that same black duck's brood. Another of the little muskrats encountered fate on the threshold of his existence, being snatched by the hungry jaws of a large pickerel, which darted upon him like lightning from under the covert of a lily-pad. But in this case, vengeance was instant and direct. The big muskrat chanced to be near by. He caught the pickerel, while the latter was preoccupied with his meal, bit clean through the back of his neck, and then and there devoured nearly half of him. In the engrossing task of cleaning his fur after this feast, and making his toilet, which he did with minute nicety on a stranded log by the shore, he promptly forgot the loss to his little family, the wrong which he had so satisfactorily and appropriately avenged. As for the remaining seven, they proceeded to grow up as rapidly as possible, and soon ceased to stand in any danger of pickerel or mallard.

Though fairly omnivorous in his tastes, the big muskrat, like all his tribe, was so content with his lilies, flag-root, and clams, that he was not generally regarded as a foe by the birds and other small people of the wilderness. He was too well fed to be a keen hunter.

Having learned (and taught his fellows) to avoid muskrat-traps, the big muskrat enjoyed his lazy summer life on Bitter Creek with a care-free spirit that is permitted to few, indeed, of the furtive kindred of the wild. There was no mink, as we have seen, to beware of; and as for hawks, he ignored them as none of the other small wild creatures—squirrels, hares, or even the fierce and fearless weasel—could afford to do. The hawks knew certain inconvenient capacities of his kind. When, therefore, that sudden alarm would ring clamorous over the still, brown woods, that shrill outcry of the crows, jays, and king-birds, which sends every weak thing trembling to cover, the big muskrat would sit up, untroubled, on his log, and go on munching his flat-root with as fine an unconcern as if he had been a bear or a bull moose.

But one day, one late, rose-amber afternoon, when the gnats were dancing over the glassy creek, he was startled out of this confidence. He was standing in shallow water, digging out an obstinate, but tempting root, when there arose a sudden great outcry from all the birds. It meant "A hawk!—A hawk!—A hawk!—A hawk!" He understood it perfectly; but he never lifted his head from his task. Next moment there was a mighty rush of wind in his ears; a thunderbolt seemed to strike him, frightful claws gripped him, piercing his pack, and he was swept into the air. But it was a young hawk, unversed in the way of the muskrat, which had seized him. What those steely claws really clutched was little more than a roll of loose skin. Hurt, but not daunted, the muskrat twisted his head up and back, and sank his long, punishing incisors in the enemy's thigh. He did not hang on, in bulldog fashion but cut, cut, cut, deep through the bird's hard feather armour, and into the cringing red strata of veins and muscles. With a scream of pain and fear, the bird dropped him, and he fell into the water. At first, he dived deep, fearing a second attack, and came up under a tangle of grasses, from which he could peer forth unseen. Then, perceiving that the hawk had vanished, he, by and by, came out of the grass, and paddled to his favourite log. He was bleeding profusely, and his toilet that evening was long and painful. But in a few days he was as well as ever, with an added confidence.

About this time, however, a small, inquisitive, and particularly bloodthirsty mink came down from the upper waters of the creek, where game had grown scarce under the ravages of her insatiable and implacable family. One of her special weaknesses was for muskrat-meat, and many a muskrat house she had invaded so successfully that the long, smothering, black, drowned galleries had no more terrors for her.

She came to the house in the alders. She noted its size, and realized that here, indeed, was good hunting. She swam down to the water-gate at the bottom of the channel, poked her nose in, and returned to the surface for a full supply of air. Then, with great speed, she dived again, and disappeared within the blackness of the water-gate.

It chanced that the big muskrat was just descending. From the inner darkness he saw the enemy clearly, before her savage, little, peering eyes could discover him. He knew all the deadliness of the peril. He could easily have escaped, turning back and fleeing by the other passage while the foe went on to her bloody work in the chambers. There was no time to warn the rest.

But flight was far from the big muskrat's mind in that crucial moment. Not panic, but a fierce hate blazed in his usually good-natured eyes. With a swift, strenuous kick of his powerful hind legs, he shot downward upon the enemy, and grappled with her in the narrow tunnel.

The mink had seen him just before he fell upon her, and quicker than thought itself had darted up her snake-like jaws to gain the fatal throat-hold. But long success had made her over-confident. No muskrat had ever, within her experience, even tried to fight her. This present impetuous attack she mistook for a frantic effort to crowd past her and escape. Half careless, therefore, she missed the fatal hold, and caught only a mouthful of yielding skin. Before she could try again—borne down and hampered as she was by the muskrat's weight—a set of long, tenacious teeth, crunching and cutting, met in the side of her face, just at the foot of the jaw.

This time the muskrat was wise enough to hold on. His deep grip held like a vise. The mink's teeth, those vindictive teeth that had killed and killed for the mere joy of killing, now gnashed impotently. In utter silence, there in the choking deep, the water in their eyes and ears and jaws, they writhed and strove, the mink's lithe body twisting around her foe like a snake. Then, with a convulsive shudder, her struggles ceased. Her lungs had refused to hold the strained breath any longer. They had opened—and the water had fill them. Her body trailed out limply; and the muskrat, still maintaining that inexorable grip, dragged her out through the water-gate which he had so well kept. Out in the brown, blurred light of the current he still held her down, jamming her head into a patch of bright sand, until the ache of his own lungs gave him warning. Then, carrying the body to the surface, he flung it scornfully over a root to await the revival of his appetite, and proceeded to calm his excitement by a long, elaborate toilet. Steely dark and cold the waters of Bitter Creek slipped by between their leafless, bushy banks. And inside the dome of the house in the alders the thick-furred muskrat colony slept luxuriously, little dreaming of the doom just averted from their door.

The King of the Mamozekel

I

When the king of the Mamozekel barrens was born, he was one of the most ungainly of all calves—a moose-calf.

In the heart of the tamarack swamp, some leagues south from Nictau Mountain, was a dry little knoll of hardwood and pine undiscovered by the hunters, out of the track of the hunting beasts. Neither lynx, bear, nor panther had tradition of it. There was little succulent undergrowth to tempt the moose and the caribou. But there the wild plum each summer fruited abundantly, and there a sturdy brotherhood of beeches each autumn lavished their treasure of three-cornered nuts; and therefore the knoll was populous with squirrels and grouse. Nature, in one of those whims of hers by which she delights to confound the studious naturalist, had chosen to keep this spot exempt from the law of blood and fear which ruled the rest of her domains. To be sure, the squirrels would now and then play havoc with a nest of grouse eggs, or, in the absence of their chisel-beaked parents, do murder on a nest of young goldenwings; but, barring the outbreaks of those bright-eyed incorrigible marauders—bad to their very toes, and attractive to their plumy tail-tips—the knoll in the tamarack swamp was a haven of peace amid the fierce but furtive warfare of the wilderness.

On this knoll, when the arbutus breath of the northern spring was scenting the winds of all the Tobique country, the king was born—a moose-calf more ungainly and of mightier girth and limb than any other moose-calf of the Mamozekel. Never had his mother seen such a one—and she a mother of lordly bulls. He was uncouth, to be sure, in any eyes but those of his kind—with his high humped fore-shoulders, his long, lugubrious, over-hanging snout, his big ears set low on his big head, his little eyes crowded back toward his ears, his long, big-knuckled legs, and the spindling, lank diminutiveness of his hindquarters. A grotesque figure, indeed, and lacking altogether in that pathetic, infantile winsomeness which makes even little pigs attractive. But anyone who knew about moose would have said, watching the huge baby struggle to his feet and stand with sturdy legs well braced, "There, if bears and bullets miss him till his antlers get full spread, is the king of the Mamozekel." Now, when his mother had licked him dry, his coat showed a dark, very sombre, cloudy, secretive brown, of a hue to be quite lost in the shadows of the fir and hemlock thickets, and to blend consummately with the colour of the tangled alder trunks along the clogged banks of the Mamozekel.

The young king's mother was perhaps the biggest and most morose cow on all the moose ranges of northern New Brunswick. She assuredly had no peer on the barrens of the upper Tobique country. She was also the craftiest. That was the reason why, though she was dimly known and had been blindly hunted all the way from Nictau Lake, over Mamozekel, and down to Blue Mountain on the main Tobique, she had never felt a bullet wound, and had come to be regarded by the backwoods hunters with something of a superstitious awe. It was of her craft, too, that she had found this knoll in the heart of the tamarack swamp, and had guarded the secret of it from the herds. Hither, at calving time, she would come by cunningly twisted trails. Here she would pass the perilous hours in safety, unharassed by the need of watching against her stealthy foes. And when once she had led her calf away from the retreat, she never returned to it, save alone, and in another year.

For three days the great cow stayed upon the knoll, feeding upon the overhanging branch tips of mountain-ash and poplar. This was good fodder, for buds and twigs were swollen with sap, and succulent. In those three days her sturdy young calf made such gains in strength and stature that he would have passed in the herd for a calf of two weeks' growth. In mid-afternoon of the third day she led the way down from the knoll and out across the quaking glooms of the tamarack swamp. And the squirrels in the budding branches chattered shrill derision about their going.

The way led through the deepest and most perilous part of the swamp; but the mother knew the safe trail in all its windings. She knew where the yielding surface of moss with black pools on either side was not afloat on fathomless ooze, but supported by solid earth or a framework of ancient tree roots. She shambled onward at a very rapid walk, which forced the gaunt calf at her heels to break now and then into the long-striding, tireless trot which is the heritage of his race.

For perhaps an hour they travelled. Then, in a little, partly open glade where the good sound earth rose up sweet from the morass, and the mountain-ash, the viburnum, and the moose-wood grew thinly, and the ground was starred with spring blooms—painted trillium and wake-robin, claytonia and yellow dog-tooth and wind-flower—they stopped. The calf, tired from his first journeying, nursed fiercely, twitching his absurd stub of a tail, butting at his mother's udder with such discomforting eagerness that she had to rebuke him by stepping aside and interrupting his meal. After several experiences of this kind, he took the hint and put curb upon his too robust impatience. The masterful spirit of a king is liable to inconvenience its owner if exercised prematurely.

By this time the pink light of sunset was beginning to stain the western curves of branch and stem and bud, changing the spring coolness of the place into a delicate riot of fairy colour and light intervolving form. Some shadows deepened, while others disappeared. Certain leaves and blossoms and pale limbs stood out with a clearness almost startling, suddenly emphasized by the level rays, while others faded from view. Though there was no wind, the changed light gave an effect of noiseless movement in the glade. And in the midst of this gathering enchantment the mother moose set herself to forage for her own meal.

Selecting a slim young birch-tree, whose top was thick with twigs and greening buds, she pushed against it with her massive chest till it bent nearly to the ground. Then straddling herself along it, she held it down securely between her legs, moved forward till the succulent top was within easy reach, and began to browse with leisurely jaws and selective reachings out of her long, discriminating upper lip. The calf stood close by, watching with interest, his legs sympathetically spread apart, his head swung low from his big shoulders, his great ears swaying slowly backward and forward, not together, but one at a time. When the mother had finished feeding, there were no buds, twigs or small branches left on the birch sapling; and the sunset colours had faded out of the glade. With dusk a chilly air breathed softly through the trees, and the mother led the way into a clump of thick balsam firs near the edge of the good ground. In the heart of the thicket she lay down for the night, facing away from the wind; and the calf, quick in perception as in growth, lay down close beside her in the same position. He did not know at the time the significance of the position, but he had a vague sense of its importance. He was afterward to learn that enemies were liable to approach his lair in the night, and that as long as he slept with his back to the wind, he could not be taken unawares. The wind might be trusted to bring to his marvellous nostrils timely notice of danger from the rear; while he could depend upon his eyes and his spacious, sensitive, unsleeping ears to warn him of anything ascending against the wind to attack him in front.

At the very first suggestion of morning the two light sleepers arose. In the dusk of the fir thicket the hungry calf made his meal. Then they came forth into the grayness of the spectral spring dawn, and the great cow proceeded as before to breast down a birch sapling for fodder. Before the sun was fairly up, they left the glade and resumed their journey across the swamp.

It was mid-morning of a sweet-aired, radiant day when they emerged from the swamp. Now, through a diversified country of thick forests and open levels, the mother moose swung forward on an undeviating trail, perceptible only to herself. Presently the land began to dip. Then a little river appeared, winding through innumerable alders, with here and there a pond-like expansion full of young lily-leaves; and the future king of the Mamozekel looked upon his kingdom. But he did not recognize it. He cared nothing for the little river of alders. He was tired, and very hungry, and the moment his mother halted he ran up and nursed vehemently.

II

Delicately filming with the first green, and spicy-fragrant, were the young birch-trees on the slopes about the Mamozekel water. From tree-top to tree-top, across the open spaces, the rain-birds called to each other with long falls of melody and sweetly insistent iteration. In their intervals of stillness, which came from time to time as if by some secret and preconcerted signal, the hush was beaded, as it were, with the tender and leisurely staccatos of the chickadees. The wild kindreds of the Tobique country were all happily busy with affairs of spring.

While the great cow was pasturing on birch-twigs, the calf rested, with long legs tucked under him, on the dry, softly carpeted earth beneath the branches of a hemlock. At this pleasant pasturage the mother moose was presently joined by her calf of the previous season, a sturdy bull-yearling, which ran up to her with a pathetic little bleat of delight, as if he had been very desolate and bewildered during the days of her strange absence. The mother received him with good-natured indifference, and went on pulling birch-tips. Then the yearling came over and eyed with curiosity the resting calf—the first moose-calf he had ever seen. The king, unperturbed and not troubling himself to rise, thrust forward his spacious ears, and reached out a long inquiring nose to investigate the newcomer. But the yearling was in doubt. He drew back, planted his forehoofs firmly, and lowered and shook his head, challenging the stranger to a butting bout. The old moose, which had kept wary eye upon the meeting, now came up and stood over her young, touching him once or twice lightly with her upper lip. Then, swinging her great head to one side, she glanced at the yearling, and made a soft sound in her throat. Whether this were warning or mere pertinent information, the yearling understood that his smaller kinsman was to be let alone, and not troubled with challenges. With easy philosophy, he accepted the situation, doubtless not concerned to understand it, and turned his thoughts to the ever fresh theme of forage.

Through the spring and summer the little family of three fed never far from the Mamozekel stream; and the king grew with astonishing speed. Of other moose families they saw little, for the mother, jealous and overbearing in her strength, would tolerate no other cows on her favourite range. Sometimes they saw a tall bull, with naked forehead, come down to drink or to pull lily-stems in the still pools at sunset. But the bull, feeling himself discrowned and unlordly in the absence of his antlers, paid no attention to either cows or calves. While waiting for autumn to restore to his forehead its superb palmated adornments, he was haughty and seclusive.

By the time summer was well established in the land, the moose-calf had begun to occupy himself diligently with the primer-lessons of life. Keeping much at his mother's head, he soon learned to pluck the tops of tall seeding grasses; though such low-growing tender herbage as cattle and horses love, he never learned to crop. His mother, like all his tribe, was too long in the legs and short in the neck to pasture close to the ground. He was early taught, however, what succulent pasturage of root and stem and leaf the pools of Mamozekel could supply; and early his sensitive upper lip acquired the wisdom to discriminate between the wholesome water-plants and such acrid, unfriendly growths as the water-parsnip and the spotted cowbane. Most pleasant the little family found it, in the hot, drowsy afternoons, to wade out into the leafy shallows and feed at leisure belly-deep in the cool, with no sound save their own comfortable splashings, or the shrill clatter of a kingfisher winging past up-stream. Their usual feeding hours were just before sunrise, a little before noon, and again in the late afternoon, till dark. The rest of the time they would lie hidden in the deepest thickets, safe, but ever watchful, their great ears taking in and interpreting all the myriad fluctuating noises of the wilderness.

The hours of foraging were also—for the young king, in particular, whose food was mostly provided by his mother—the hours of lesson and the hours of play. In the pride of his growing strength he quickly developed a tendency to butt at everything and test his prowess. His yearling brother was always ready to meet his desires in this fashion, and the two would push against each other with much grunting, till at last the elder, growing impatient, would thrust the king hard back upon his haunches, and turn aside indifferently to his browsing. Little by little it became more difficult for the yearling to close the bout in this easy way; but he never guessed that in no distant day the contests would end in a very different manner. He did not know that, for a calf of that same spring, his lightly tolerated playfellow was big and strong and audacious beyond all wont of the wide-antlered kindred.

The young king was always athrill with curiosity, full of interest in all the wilderness folk that chanced to come in his view. The shyest of the furtive creatures were careless about letting him see them, both his childishness and his race being guarantee of good will. Very soon, therefore, he became acquainted, in a distant, uncomprehending fashion, with the hare and the mink, the wood-mouse and the muskrat; while the mother mallard would float amid her brood within a yard or two of the spot where he was pulling at the water-lilies.

One day, however, he came suddenly upon a porcupine which was crossing a bit of open ground—came upon it so suddenly that the surly little beast was startled and rolled himself up into a round, bristling ball. This was a strange phenomenon indeed! He blew upon the ball, two or three hard noisy breaths from wide nostrils. Then he was so rash as to thrust at it, tentatively rather than roughly, with his inquisitive nose—for he was most anxious to know what it meant. There was a quiver in the ball; and he jumped back, shaking his head, with two of the sharp spines sticking in his sensitive upper lip.

In pain and fright, yet with growing anger, he ran to his mother where she was placidly cropping a willow-top. But she was not helpful. She knew nothing of the properties of porcupine quills. Seeing what was the matter, she set the example of rubbing her nose smartly against a stump. The king did likewise. Now, for burrs, this would have been all very well; but porcupine quills—the malignant little intruders throve under such treatment, and worked their way more deeply into the tender tissues. Smarting and furious, the young monarch rushed back with the purpose of stamping that treacherous ball of spines to fragments under his sharp hoofs. But the porcupine, meanwhile, had discreetly climbed a tree, whence it looked down with scornful red eyes, bristling its barbed armory, and daring the angry calf to come up and fight. For days thereafter the young king suffered from a nose so hot and swollen that it was hard for him to browse, and almost impossible for him to nurse. Then came relief, as the quills worked their way through, one dropping out, and the other getting chewed up with a lily-root. But the young moose never forgot his grudge against the porcupine family; and catching one, years after, in a poplar sapling, he bore the sapling down and trod his enemy to bits. In his wrath, however, he did not forget the powers and properties of the quills. He took good care that none should pierce the tender places of his feet.

Some weeks after his meeting with the porcupine, when his nose and his spirits together had quite recovered, he made a new acquaintance. The moose family had by this time worked much farther up the Mamozekel, into a region of broken ground, and steep up-thrusts of rock. One day, while investigating the world at a little distance from his mother and brother, he saw a large, curious-looking animal at the top of a rocky slope. It was a light brown-gray in colour, with a big, round face, high-tufted ears, round, light, cold, eyes, long whiskers brushed back from under its chin, very long, sharp teeth displayed in its snarlingly open jaws, and big round pads of feet. The lynx glared at the young king, scornfully unacquainted with his kingship. And the young king stared at the lynx with lively, unhostile interest. Then the lynx cast a wary glance all about, saw no sign of the mother moose (who was feeding on the other side of the rock), concluded that this was such an opportunity as he had long been looking for, and began creeping swiftly, stealthily, noiselessly down the slope of rocks.

Any other moose-calf, though of thrice the young king's months, would have run away. But no so he. The stranger seemed unfriendly. He would try a bout of butting with him. He stamped his feet, shook his lowered head, snorted, and advanced a stride or two. At the same time, he uttered a harsh, very abrupt, bleating cry of defiance, the infantile precursor of what his mighty, forest-daunting bellow was to be in later years. The lynx, though he well knew that this ungainly youngster could not withstand his onslaught for a moment, was nevertheless astonished by such a display of spirit; and he paused for a moment to consider it. Was it possible that unguessed resources lay behind this daring? He would see.

It was a critical moment. A very few words more would have sufficed for the conclusion of this chronicle but for the fact that the young king's bleat of challenge had reached other ears than those of the great lynx. The old moose, at her pasturing behind the rock, heard it too. Startled and anxious, she came with a rush to find out what it meant; and the yearling, full of curiosity, came at her heels. When she saw the lynx, the long hair on her neck stood up with fury, and with a roar she launched her huge, dark bulk against him. But for such an encounter the big cat had no stomach. He knew that he would be pounded into paste in half a minute. With a snarl, he sprang backward, as if his muscles had been steel springs suddenly loosed; and before his assailant was half-way up the slope, he was glaring down upon her from the safe height of a hemlock limb.

This, to the young king, seemed a personal victory. The mother's efforts to make him understand that lynxes were dangerous had small effect upon him; and the experience advanced him not at all in his hitherto unlearned lesson of fear.

Even he, however, for all his kingly heart, was destined to learn that lesson—was destined to have it so seared into his spirit that the remembrance should, from time to time, unnerve, humiliate, defeat him through half the years of his sovereignty.

It came about in this way, one blazing August afternoon.

The old moose and the yearling were at rest, comfortably chewing the cud in a spruce covert close to the water. But the king was in one of those restless fits which, all through his calfhood, kept driving him forward in quest of experience. The wind was almost still; but such as there was blew up stream. Up against it he wandered for a little way, and saw nothing but a wood chuck, which was a familiar sight to him. Then he turned and drifted carelessly down the wind. Having passed the spruce thicket, his nostrils received messages from his mother and brother in their quiet concealment. The scent was companion to him, and he wandered on. Presently it faded away from the faintly pulsing air. Still he went on.

Presently he passed a huge, half-decayed windfall, thickly draped in shrubbery and vines. No sooner had he passed than the wind brought him from this dense hiding-place a pungent, unfamiliar scent. There was something ominous in the smell, something at which his heart beat faster; but he was not afraid. He stopped at once, and moved back slowly toward the windfall, sniffing with curiosity, his ears alert, his eyes striving to pierce the mysteries of the thicket.

He moved close by the decaying trunk without solving the enigma. Then, as the wind puffed a thought more strongly, he passed by and lost the scent. At once he swung about to pursue the investigation; and at the same instant an intuitive apprehension of peril made him shudder, and shrink away from the windfall.

He turned not an instant too soon. What he saw was a huge, black, furry head and shoulders leaning over the windfall, a huge black paw, with knife-like claws, lifting for a blow that would break his back like a bulrush. He was already moving, already turning, and with his muscles gathered. That saved him. Quick as a flash of light he sprang, wildly. Just as quickly, indeed, came down the stroke of those terrific claws. But they fell short of their intended mark. As the young moose sprang into the air, the claws caught him slantingly on the haunch. They went deep, ripping hide and flesh almost to the bone— a long, hideous wound. Before the blow could be repeated, the calf was far out of reach, bleating with pain and terror. The bear, much disappointed, peered after him with little red, malicious eyes, and greedily licked the sweet blood from his claws.

The next instant the mother moose burst from her thicket, the long hair of her neck and shoulders stiffly erect with rage. She had understood well enough that agonized cry of the young king. She paused but a second, to give him a hasty lick of reassurance, then charged down upon the covert around the windfall. She knew that only a bear could have done that injury; and she knew, without any help from ears, eyes, or nose, that the windfall was just the place for a bear's lying-in-wait. With an intrepidity beyond the boldest dreams of any other moose-cow on the Mamozekel, she launched herself crashing into the covert.

But her avenging fury found no bear to meet it. The bear knew well this mighty moose-cow, having watched her from many a hiding-place, and shrewdly estimated her prowess. He had effaced himself, melting away through the underwood as noiselessly and swiftly as a weasel. Plenty of the strong bear scent the old moose found in the covert, and it stung her to frenzy. She stamped and tore down the vines, and sent the rotten wood of the windfall flying in fragments. Then she emerged, powdered with débris, and roared and glared about for the enemy. But the wily bear was already far away, well burdened with discretion.

III

In a few weeks the king's healthy flesh, assiduously licked by his mother, healed perfectly, leaving long, hairless scars upon his hide, which turned in course of time from livid to a leaden whitish hue. But while his flesh healed perfectly, his spirit was in a different case. Thenceforward, one great fear lurked in his heart, ready to leap forth at any instant—the fear of the bear. It was the only fear he knew, but it was a terrible one; and when, two months later, he again caught that pungent scent in passing a thicket, he ran madly for an hour before he recovered his wits and stole back, humiliated and exhausted, to his mother's pasture-grounds.

In the main, however, he was soon his old, bold, investigating self, his bulk and his sagacity growing vastly together. Ere the first frosts had crimsoned the maples and touched the birches to a shimmer of pale gold, he could almost hold his own by sheer strength against his yearling brother's weight, and sometimes, for a minute or two, worst him by feint and strategy. When he came, by chance, in the crisp, free-roving weather of the fall, upon other moose-calves of that year's birth, they seemed pygmies beside him, and gave way to him respectfully as to a yearling.

About this time he experienced certain qualms of loneliness, which bewildered him and took much of the interest out of life. His mother began to betray an unexpected indifference, and his childish heart missed her caresses. He was not driven away, but he was left to himself; while she would stride up and down the open, gravelly meadows by the water, sniffing the air, and at times uttering a short, harsh roar which made him eye her uneasily. One crisp night, when the round October moon wrought magic in the wilderness, he heard his mother's call answered by a terrific, roaring bellow, which made his heart leap. Then there was a crashing through the underbrush; and a tall bull strode forth into the light, his antlers spreading like oak branches from either side of his forehead. Prudence, or deference, or a mixture of the two, led the young king to lay aside his wonted inquisitiveness and withdraw into the thickets without attracting the notice of this splendid and formidable visitor. During the next few days he saw the big bull very frequently, and found himself calmly ignored. Prudence and deference continued their good offices, however, and he was careful not to trespass on the big stranger's tolerance during those wild, mad, magical autumn days.

One night, about the middle of October, the king saw from his thicket a scene which filled him with excitement and awe, swelled his veins almost to bursting, and made his brows ache as if the antlers were already pushing to birth beneath the skin. It all came about in this fashion. His mother, standing out in the moonlight by the water, had twice with outstretched muzzle uttered her call, when it was answered not only by her mate, the tall bull, approaching along the shore, but by another great voice from up the hillside. Instantly the tall bull was in a rage. He rushed up to the cow, touched her with his nose, and then, after a succession of roars which were answered promptly from the hillside, he moved over to the edge of the open and began thrashing the bushes with his antlers. A great crashing of underbrush arose some distance away, and drew near swiftly; and in a few minutes another bull burst forth violently into the open. He was young and impetuous, or he would have halted a moment before leaving cover and stealthily surveyed the situation. But not yet had years and overthrows taught him the ripe moose wisdom; and with a reckless heart he committed himself to the combat.

The newcomer had barely the chance to see where he was before the tall bull was upon him. He wheeled in time, however, and got his guard down; but was borne back upon his haunches by the terrific shock of the charge. In a moment or two he recovered the lost ground, for youth had given him strength, if not wisdom; and the tall bull, his eyes flame-red with wrath, found himself fairly matched by this shorter, stockier antagonist.

The night forthwith became tempestuous with gruntings, bellowings, the hard clashing of antlers, the stamping of swift and heavy feet. The thin turf was torn up. The earthy gravel was sent flying from the furious hoofs. From his covert the young king strained eager eyes upon the fight, his sympathies all with the tall bull whom he had regarded reverently from the first moment he saw him. But as for the cow, she moved up from the waterside and looked on with a fine impartiality. What concerned her was chiefly that none but the bravest and strongest should be her mate—a question which only fighting could determine. Her favour would go with victory.

As it appeared, the rivals were fairly matched in vigour and valour. But among moose, as among men, brains count in the end. When the tall bull saw that, in a matter of sheer brawn, the sturdy stranger might hold him, he grew disgusted at the idea of settling such a vital question by mere butting and shoving. The red rage faded in his eyes, and a colder light took its place. On a sudden, when his foe had given a mighty thrust, he yielded, slipped his horns from the lock, and jumped nimbly aside. The stranger lunged forward, almost stumbling to his knees.

This was the tall bull's opportunity. In a whirlwind of fury he thrust upon the enemy's flank, goring him and bearing him down. The latter, being short and quick-moving, recovered his feet in a second, and wheeled to present his guard. But the tall bull was quick to maintain the advantage. He, too, had shifted ground; and now he caught his antagonist in the rear. There was no resisting such an attack. With hind legs weakly doubling under him, with the weight of doom descending upon his defenceless rump, the rash stranger was thrust forward, bellowing madly, and striving in vain to brace himself. His humiliation was complete. With staring eyes and distended nostrils, he was hustled across the meadow and over the edge of the bank. With a huge splash, and carrying with him a shower of turf and gravel, he fell into the stream. Once in the water and his courage well cooled, he did not wait for a glance at his snorting and stamping conqueror on the bank above, but waded desperately across, dripping, bleeding, crushed in spirit—and vanished into the woods. In the thicket, the king's heart swelled as if the victory had been his own.

By and by, when the last of the leaves had fluttered down with crisp whisperings from the birch and ash, maple and poplar, and the first enduring snows were beginning to change the face of the world, the tall bull seemed to lay aside his haughtiness. He grew carelessly good-natured toward the young king and the yearling, and frankly took command of the little herd. As the snow deepened, he led the way northward toward the Nictau Lake, and chose winter quarters on the wooded southward slopes of Bald Mountain, where there were hemlock groves for shelter and an abundance of young hardwood growth for browsing.

This leisurely migration was in the main uneventful, and left but one sharp impression on the young king's memory. On a wintry morning, when the sunrise was reaching long pink-saffron fingers across the thin snow, a puff of wind brought with it from a tangle of stumps and rocks a breath of that pungent scent so hateful to a moose's nostrils. The whole heard stopped; and the young king, his knees quaking under him and his eyes staring with panic, crowded close against his mother's flank. The tall bull stamped and bellowed his defiance to the enemy—but the enemy, being discreet, made no reply whatever. It is probable, indeed, that he was preparing his winter quarters, and getting too drowsy to hear or heed the angry challenge; but if he did hear it no doubt he noiselessly withdrew himself till the dangerous travellers had gone by. In a few minutes the herd resumed its march—the king keeping close to his mother's side, instead of in his proper place in the line.

The big-antlered bull now chose his site for the "yard," with "verge and room enough" for all contingencies. The "yard" was an ample acreage of innumerable winding paths, trodden ever deeper as the snow accumulated. These paths led to every spot of browse, every nook of shelter, at the same time twisting and crossing in a maze of intricacies. Thick piled the snows about the little herd, and the northern gales roared over the hemlocks, and the frost sealed the white world down into silence. But it was such a winter as the moose kin loved. No wolves or hunters came to trouble them, and the months passed pleasantly. When the days were lengthening and the hearts of all the wild folk beginning to dream of the yet unsignalled spring, the young king was astonished to see the great antlers of his leader fall off. Seeing that their owner left them lying unregarded on the snow, he went up and sniffed at them wonderingly, and pondered the incident long and vainly in his heart.

When the snows shrank away, departing with a sound of many waters, and spring returned to the Tobique country, the herd broke up. First the dis-antlered bull drifted off on his own affairs. Then the two-year-old went, with no word of reason or excuse. Though a well-grown young bull, he was now little larger or heavier than the king; and the king was now a yearling, with the stature and presence of a two-year-old. In a playful butting contest, excited by the joy of life which April put into their veins, he worsted his elder brother; and this, perhaps, though taken in good part, hastened the latter's going.

A few days later the old cow grew restless. She and the king turned their steps backward toward the Mamozekel, feeding as they went. Soon they found themselves in their old haunts, which the king remembered very well. Then one day, while the king slept without suspicion of evil, the old cow slipped away stealthily, and sought her secret refuge in the heart of the cedar swamp. When the king awoke, he found himself alone in the thicket.

All that day he was most unhappy. For some hours he could not eat, but strayed hither and thither, questing and wondering. Then, when hunger drove him to browse on the tender birch-twigs, he would stop every minute or two to call in his big, gruff, pathetic bleat, and look around eagerly for an answer. No answer came from the deserting mother, by this time far away in the swamp.

But there were ears in the wilderness that heard and heeded the call of the desolate yearling. A pair of hunting lynxes paused at the sound, licked their chops, and crept forward with a green light in their wide, round eyes.

Their approach was noiseless as thought—but the king, on a sudden, felt a monition of their coming. Whirling sharply about, he saw them lurking in the underbrush. He recognized the breed. This was the same kind of creature which he had been ready to challenge in his first calfhood. No doubt, it would have been more prudent for him to withdraw; but he was in no mood for concession. His sore heart made him ill-tempered. His lonely bleat became a bellow of wrath. He stamped the earth, shook his head as if thrashing the underbrush with imaginary antlers, and then charged madly upon the astonished cats. This was no ordinary moose-calf, they promptly decided; and in a second they were speeding away with great bounds, gray shadows down the gray vistas of the wood. The king glared after them for a moment, and then went back to his feeding, greatly comforted.

It was four days before his mother came back, bringing a lank calf at her heels. He was glad to see her, and contentedly renewed the companionship; but in those four days he had learned full self-reliance, and his attitude was no longer that of the yearling calf. It had become that of the equal. As for the lank little newcomer, he viewed it with careless complaisance, and no more dreamed of playing with it than if it had been a frog or a chipmunk.

The summer passed with little more event for the king than his swift increase in stature. One lesson then learned, however, though but vaguely comprehended at the time, was to prove of incalculable value in after years. He learned to shun man—not with fear, indeed, for he never learned to fear anything except bears—but with aversion and a certain half-disdainful prudence. It was as if he came to recognize in man the presence of powers which he was not anxious to put to trial lest he should be forced to doubt his own supremacy.

It was but a slight incident that gave him the beginning of this valuable wisdom. As he lay ruminating one day beside his mother and the gaunt calf, in a spruce covert near the water, a strange scent was wafted in to his nostrils. It carried with it a subtle warning. His mother touched him with her nose, conveying a silent yet eloquent monition, and got upon her feet with no more sound than if she had been compact of thistledown. From their thicket shelter the three stared forth, moveless and unwinking, ears forward, nostrils wide. Then a canoe with two men came into view, paddling lazily, and turning to land. To the king, they looked not dangerous; but every detail of them—their shape, motion, colour, and above all, their ominous scent—stamped itself in his memory. Then, to his great surprise, his mother silently signalled the gravest and most instant menace, and forthwith faded back through the thicket with inconceivably stealthy motion. The king and the calf followed with like care—the king, though perplexed, having faith in his mother's wise woodcraft. Not until they had put good miles between themselves and the strange-smelling newcomers did the old moose come to a halt; and from all this precaution the king realized that the mysterious strangers were something to be avoided by moose.

That summer the king saw nothing more of the man-creatures —and he crossed the scent of no more bears. His great heart, therefore, found no check to its growing arrogance and courage. When the month of the falling leaves and the whirring partridge-coveys again came round, he felt a new pugnacity swelling in his veins, and found himself uttering challenges, he knew not why, with his yet half infantile bellow. When, at length, his mother began to pace the open meadow by the Mamozekel, and startle the moonlit silences with her mating call, he was filled with strange anger. But this was nothing to his rage when the calls were answered by a wide-antlered bull. This time the king refused to slink obsequiously to cover. He waited in the open; and he eyed the new wooer in a fashion so truculent that at length he attracted notice.

For his dignity, if not for his experience, this was most unfortunate. The antlered stranger noted his size, his attitude of insolence, and promptly charged upon him. He met the charge, in his insane audacity, but was instantly borne down. As he staggered to his feet he realized his folly, and turned to withdraw—not in terror, but in acknowledgment of superior strength. Such a dignified retreat, however, was not to be allowed him. The big bull fell upon him again, prodding him cruelly. He was hustled ignominiously across the meadow and into the bushes. Thence he fled, bleating with impotent wrath and shame.

In his humiliation he fled far down along the river, through alder swamps which he had never traversed, by pools in which he had never pulled the lilies. Onward he pressed, intent on placing irrevocably behind him the scene of his chagrin.

At length he came out upon the fair river basin where the Mamozekel, the Serpentine, and the Nictau, tameless streams, unite to form the main Tobique. Here he heard the call of a young cow—a voice thinner and higher than his mother's deep-chested notes. With an impulse which he did not understand, he pushed forward to answer the summons, no longer furtive, but noisily trampling the brush. Just then, however, a pungent smell stung his nostrils. There, not ten paces distant, was a massive black shape standing out in the moonlight. Panic laid grip upon his heart, chilling every vein. He wheeled, splashed across the shallow waters of the Nictau, and fled away northward on tireless feet.

That winter the king yarded alone, like a morose old bull, far from his domain of the Mamozekel. In the spring he came back, but restricted his range to the neighbourhood of the Forks. And he saw his mother no more.

That summer he grew his first antlers. As antlers, indeed, they were no great thing; but they started out bravely, a massive cylindrical bar thrusting forth laterally, unlike the pointing horns of deer and caribou, from either side of his forehead. For all this sturdy start, their spiking and palmation did not amount to much; but he was inordinately proud of them, rubbing off the velvet with care when it began to itch, and polishing assiduously at the hardened horn. By the time the October moon had come round again to the Tobique country, he counted these first antlers a weapon for any encounter; and, indeed, with his bulk and craft behind them, they were formidable.

It was not long before they were put to the test. One night, as he stood roaring and thrashing the bushes on the bluff overlooking the Forks, he heard the call of a young cow a little way down the shore. Gladly he answered. Gladly he sped to the tryst. Strange ecstasies, the madness of the night spell, and the white light's sorcery made his heart beat and his veins run sweet fire. But suddenly all this changed; for another roar, a taunting challenge, answered him; and another bull broke from covert on the other side of the sandy level where stood the young cow coquettishly eyeing both wooers.

The new arrival was much older than the king, and nobly antlered; but in matter of inches the young king was already his peer. In craft, arrogance, and self-confident courage the king had an advantage that outweighed the deficiency in antlers. The fury of his charge spelled victory from the first; and though the battle was prolonged, the issue was decided at the outset, as the interested young cow soon perceived. In about a half-hour it was all over. The wise white moon of the wilderness looked down understandingly upon the furrowed sandspit, the pleased young cow, and the king making diffident progress with his first wooing. Some distance down the river-bank, she caught glimpses of the other bull, whose antlers had not saved him, fleeing in shame, with bleeding flanks and neck, through the light-patched shadows of the forest.

IV

During the next four years the king learned to grow such antlers as had never before been seen in all the Tobique country. So tall, impetuous, and masterful he grew, that the boldest bulls, recognizing the vast reverberations of his challenge, would smother their wrath and slip noiselessly away from his neighbourhood. Rumours of his size and his great antlers in some way got abroad among the settlements; but so crafty was he in shunning man—whom he did not really fear, and whom he was wont to study intently from safe coverts—that there was never a hunter who could boast of having got a shot at him.

Once, and once only, did he come into actual, face-to-face conflict with the strange man-creature. It was one autumn evening, at the first of the season. By the edge of a little lake, he heard the call of a cow. Having already found a mate, he was somewhat inattentive, and did not answer; but something strange in the call made him suspicious, and he stole forward, under cover, to make an observation. The call was repeated, seeming to come from a little, rushy island, a stone's throw from shore. This time there came an answer—not from the king, but from an eager bull rushing up from the outlet of the lake. The king listened, with some lazy interest, to the crashing and slashing of the impetuous approach, thinking that if the visitor were big enough to be worth while he would presently go out and thrash him. When the visitor did appear, however, bursting from the underbrush and striding boldly down to the water's edge, a strange thing happened. From the rushy island came a spurt of flame, a sharp detonating report. The bull jumped and wheeled in his tracks. Another report, and he dropped without a kick. As he lay in the pale light, close to the water, a canoe shot out from the rushy island and landed some distance from the body. Two men sprang out. They pulled up the canoe, leaving their rifles in it, and ran up to skin the prize.

The king in his hiding-place understood. This was what men could do—make a strange, menacing sound, and kill moose with it. He boiled with rage at this exhibition of their power, and suddenly took up the quarrel of the slain bull. But by no means did he lay aside his craft. Noiselessly he moved, a vast and furtive shadow, down through the thickets to a point where the underbrush nearly touched the water. This brought him within a few yards of the canoe, wherein the hunters had left their rifles. Here he paused a few moments, pondering. But as he pondered, redder and redder grew his eyes; and suddenly, with a mad roar, he burst from cover and charged.

Had the two men not been expert woodsmen, one or the other would have been caught and smashed to pulp. But their senses were on the watch. Cut off as they were from the canoe and from their weapons, their only hope was a tree. Before the king was fairly out into view, they had understood the whole situation, sprung to their feet, and sped off like hares. Just within the nearest fringe of bushes grew a low-hanging beech-tree; and into this they swung themselves, just as the king came raging beneath. As it was, one of them was nearly caught when he imagined himself quite safe. The king reared his mightly bulk against the trunk and with his keen-spiked antlers reached upward fiercely after the fugitives, the nearest of whom was saved only by a friendly branch which intervened.

For nearly an hour the king stamped and stormed beneath the branches, while the trapped hunters alternately cursed his temper and wondered at his stature. Then, with a swift change of purpose, he wheeled and charged on the canoe. In two minutes the graceful craft was reduced to raw material—while the hunters in the tree-top, sputtering furiously, vowed vengeance. All the kit, the tins, the blankets, the boxes, were battered shapeless, and the rifles thumped well down into the wet sand. In the midst of the cataclysm, one of the rifles somehow went off. The noise and the flash astonished the king, but only added to his rage and made him more thorough in his work of destruction. When there was nothing left that seemed worth trampling upon, he returned to the tree—on which he had kept eye all the time—and there nursed his wrath all night. At the first of dawn, however, he came to the conclusion that the shivering things in the tree were not worth waiting for. He swung off, and sought his favourite pasturage, a mile or two away; and the men, after making sure of his departure, climbed down. They nervously cut some steaks from the bull which they had killed, and hurried away, crestfallen, on the long tramp back to the settlements.

This incident, however, did not have the effect which it might have been expected to have. It did not make the king despise men. On the contrary, he now knew them to be dangerous, and he also knew that their chief power lay in the long dark tubes which spit fire and made fierce sounds. It was enough for him that he had once worsted them. Ever afterward he gave them wide berth. And the tradition of him would have come at last to be doubted in the settlements, but for the vast, shed antlers occasionally found lying on the diminished snows of March.

But all the time, while the king waxed huge and wise, and overthrew his enemies, and begot great offspring that, for many years after he was dead, were to make the Mamozekel famous, there was one grave incompleteness in his sovereignty. His old panic fear of bears still shamed and harassed him. The whiff of a harmless half-grown cub, engrossed in stuffing its greedy red mouth with blueberries, was enough to turn his blood to water and send him off to other feeding-grounds. He chose his ranges, indeed, first of all for their freedom from the dreaded taint, and only second for the excellence of their pasturage. This one unreasoning fear was the drop of gall which went far toward embittering all the days of his singularly favoured life. It was as if the wood-gods, after endowing him so far beyond his fellows, had repented of their lavishness, and capriciously poisoned their gifts.

One autumn night, just at the beginning of the calling season, this weakness of his betrayed the king to the deepest humiliation which had ever befallen him. He was then nearly seven years old; and because his voice was known to every bull in the Tobique country, there was never answer made when his great challenge went stridently resounding over the moonlit wastes. But on this particular night, when he had roared perhaps for his own amusement, or for the edification of his mate who browsed near by, rather than with any expectation of response, to his astonishment there came an answering defiance from the other side of the open. A big, wandering bull, who had strayed up from the Grand River region, had never heard of the king, and was more than ready to put his valour to test. The king rushed to meet him. Now it chanced that between the approaching giants was an old ash-tree growing out of a thicket. In this thicket a bear had been grubbing for roots. When he heard the king's first roar, he started to steal away from the perilous proximity; but the second bull's answer, from the direction in which he had hoped to retreat, stopped him. In much perturbation he climbed the ash-tree to a safe distance, and curled himself into a black, furry ball, in a fork of the branches.

The night was still, and no scents wafting to sensitive nostrils. With short roars, and much thrashing of the underbrush, the two bulls drew near. When the king was just about abreast of the bear's hiding-place, his arrogance broke into fury, and he charged upon the audacious stranger. Just as he did so, and just as his foe sprang to meet him, a wilful night-wind puffed lightly through the branches. It was a very small, irresponsible wind; but it carried sharply to the king's nostrils the strong, fresh taint of bear.

The smell was so strong, it seemed to the king as if the bear must be fairly on his haunches. It was like an icy cataract flung upon him. He shrank, trembled—and the old wounds twinged and cringed. The next moment, to the triumphant amazement of his antagonist, he had wheeled aside to avoid the charge, and was off through the underbrush in ignominious flight. The newcomer, who, for all his stout-heartedness, had viewed with concern the giant bulk of his foe, stopped short in his tracks and stared in bewilderment. So easy a victory as this was beyond his dreams—even beyond his desires. However, a bull moose can be a philosopher on occasion, and this one was not going to quarrel with good luck. In high elation he strode on up the meadow, and set himself, not unsuccessfully, to wooing the deserted and disgusted cow.

His triumph, however, was short-lived. About moon-rise of the following night the king came back. He was no longer thinking of bears, and his heart was full of wrath. His vast challenge came down from the near-by hills, making the night resound with its short, explosive thunders. His approach was accompanied by the thrashing of giant antlers on the trees, and by a crashing as if the undergrowths were being trodden by a locomotive. There was grim omen in the sounds; and the cow, waving her great ears back and forward thoughtfully, eyed the Grand River bull with shrewd interest. The stranger showed himself game, no whit daunted by threatenings and thunder. He answered with brave roarings, and manifested every resolution to maintain his conquest. But sturdy and valorous though he was, all his prowess went for little when the king fell upon him, thrice terrible from the memory of his humiliation. There was no such thing as withstanding that awful charge. Before it the usurper was borne back, borne down, overwhelmed, as if he had been no more than a yearling calf. He had no chance to recover. He was trampled and ripped and thrust onward, a helpless sprawl of unstrung legs and outstretched, piteous neck. It was luck alone—or some unwonted kindness of the wood-spirits—that saved his life from being trodden and beaten out in that hour of terror. It was close to the river-bank that he had made his stand; and presently, to his great good fortune, he was thrust over the brink. He fell into the water with a huge splash. When he struggled to his feet, and moved off, staggering, down the shallow edges of the stream, the king looked over and disdained to follow up the vengeance.

Fully as he had vindicated himself, the king was never secure against such a humiliation so long as he rested thrall to his one fear. The threat of the bear hung over him, a mystery of terror which he could not bring himself to face. But at last, and in the season of his weakness, when he had shed his antlers, there came a day when he was forced to face it. Then his kingliness was put to the supreme trial.

He was now at the age of nine years, in the splendour of his prime. He stood over seven feet high at the shoulders, and weighed perhaps thirteen hundred pounds. His last antlers, those which he had shed two months before, had shown a gigantic spread of nearly six feet.

It was late April. Much honeycombed snow and ice still lingered in the deeper hollows. After a high fashion of his own, seldom followed among the moose of the Tobique region, the king had rejoined his mate when she emerged from her spring retreat with a calf at her flank. He was too lordly in spirit to feel cast down or discrowned when his head was shorn of its great ornament; and he never felt the spring moroseness which drives most bull moose into seclusion. He always liked to keep his little herd together, was tolerant to the yearlings, and even refrained from driving off the two-year-olds until their own aggressiveness made it necessary.

On this particular April day, the king was bestriding a tall poplar sapling, which he had borne down that he might browse upon its tender, sap-swollen tips. By the water's edge the cow and the yearling were foraging on the young willow shoots. The calf, a big-framed, enterprising youngster two weeks old, almost as fine a specimen of young moosehood as the king had been at his age, was poking about curiously to gather knowledge of the wilderness world. He approached a big gray-white boulder, whose base was shrouded in spruce scrub, and sniffed apprehensively at a curious, pungent taint that came stealing out upon the air.

He knew by intuition that there was peril in that strange scent; but his interest overweighed his caution, and he drew close to the spruce scrub. Close, and yet closer; and his movement was so unusual that it attracted the attention of the king, who stopped browsing to watch him intently. A vague, only half-realized memory of that far-off day when he himself, a lank calf of the season, went sniffing curiously at a thicket, stirred in his brain; and the stiff hair along his neck and shoulder began to bristle. He released the poplar sapling, and turned all his attention to the behaviour of the calf.

The calf was very close to the green edges of the spruce scrub, when he caught sight of a great dark form within, which had revealed itself by a faint movement. More curious than ever, but now distinctly alarmed, he shrank back, turning at the same time, as if to investigate from another and more open side of the scrub.

The next instant a black bulk lunged forth with incredible swiftness from the green, and a great paw swung itself with a circular, sweeping motion, upon the retreating calf. In the wilderness world, as in the world of men, history has a trick of repeating itself; and this time, as on that day nine years before, the bear was just too late. The blow did not reach its object till most of its force was spent. It drew blood, and knocked the calf sprawling, but did no serious damage. With a bleat of pain and terror, the little animal jumped to its feet and ran away.

The bear would have easily caught him before he could recover himself; but another and very different voice had answered the bleat of the calf. At the king's roar of fury the bear changed his plans and slunk back into hiding. In a moment the king came thundering up to the edge of the spruces. There, planting his fore-feet suddenly till they ploughed the ground, he stopped himself with a mighty effort. The smell of the bear had smitten him in the face.

The moment was a crucial one. The pause was full of fate. Turning his head in indecision, he caught a cry of pain from the calf as it ran to its mother; and he saw the blood streaming down its flank. Then the kingliness of his heart arose victorious. With a roar, he breasted trampling into the spruce scrub, heedless at last of the dreaded scent.

The bear, meanwhile, had been seeking escape. He had just emerged on the other side of the spruces, and was slipping off to find a secure tree. As the king thundered down upon him, he wheeled with a savage growl, half squatted back, and struck out sturdily with that redoubtable paw. But at the same instant the king's edged hoofs came down upon him with the impact of a battering ram. They smashed in his ribs. They tore open his side. They hurled him over so that his belly was exposed. He was at a hopeless disadvantage. He had not an instant for recovery. Those avenging hoofs, with the power of a pile-driver behind them, smote like lightning. The bear struck savagely, twice, thrice; and his claws tore their way through hide and muscle till the king's blood gushed scarlet over his prostrate foe's dark fur. Then, the growls and the claw-strokes ceased; and the furry shape lay still, outstretched, unresisting.

For a moment or two the king drew off and eyed the carcass. Then the remembrance of all his past terror and shame surged hotly through him. He pounced again upon the body, and pounded it, and trampled it, and ground it down, till the hideous mass bore no longer a resemblance to any thing that ever carried the breath of life. It was not his enemy only, not only the assailant of the helpless calf, that he was thus completely blotting from existence, but it was fear itself that he was wiping out.

At last, grown suddenly tired of rage, and somewhat faint from the red draining of his veins, the king turned away and sought his frightened herd. They gathered about him, trembling with excitement —the light-coated cow, the dark yearling, the lank, terrified calf. They stretched thin noses toward him, questioning, wondering, troubled at his hot, steaming wounds. But the king held his head high, heeding neither the wounds nor the herd. He cast one long, proud look up the valley of the Mamozekel, his immediate, peculiar domain. Then he looked southward over the lonely Serpentine, northward across the dark-wooded Nictau, and westward down the flood of the full, united stream. He felt himself supreme now beyond challenge over all the wild lands of Tobique.

For a long time the group stood so, breathing at last quietly, still with that stillness which the furtive kindreds know. There was no sound save the soft, ear-filling roar of the three rivers, swollen with freshet, rushing gladly to their confluence. The sound was as a background to the cool, damp silence of the April wilderness. Some belated snow in a shaded hollow close at hand shrank and settled, with a hushed, evasive whisper. Then the earliest white-throat, from the top of a fir-tree, fluted across the pregnant spring solitudes the six clear notes of his musical and melancholy call.

The Little Wolf of the Pool

The bottom of the pool (it was too small to be called a pond) was muddy, with here and there a thicket of rushes or arrow-weed stems. Down upon the windless surface streamed the noon sun warmly. Under its light the bottom was flecked with shadows of many patterns,—circular, heart-shaped, spear-shaped, netted, and barred. There were other shadows that were no more than ghosts of shadows, cast by faint, diaphanous films of scum which scarcely achieved to blur the clear downpour of radiance, but were nevertheless perceived and appreciated by many of the delicate larval creatures which made a large part of the life of the pool.

For all its surface tranquillity and its shining summer peace, the pool was thronged with life. Beneath the surface, among the weeds and stalks, the gleams and shadows, there was little of tranquillity or peace. Almost all the many-formed and strange-shaped inhabitants of the pool were hunting or being hunted, preying or being preyed upon—from the goggle-eyed, green-throated bullfrog under the willow root, down to the swarming animalculae which it required a microscope to see. Small crawling things everywhere dotted the mud or tried to hide under the sticks and stones. Curled fresh-water snails moved up and down the stems of the lilies. Shining little black water-bugs scurried swiftly in all directions. In sheltered places near the surface, under the leaves, wriggled the slim gray larvae of the mosquitoes. And hither and thither, in flickering shoals, darted myriads of baby minnows, from half an inch to an inch and a half in length.

In a patch of vivid sunshine, about six inches from a tangle of arrow-weed stems, a black tadpole lay basking. Light to him meant not only growth, but life. Whenever, with the slow wheeling of the sun, the shadow of a lily leaf moved over him, he wriggled impatiently aside, and settled down again on the brightest part of the mud. Most of the time he seemed to be asleep; but in reality he was keeping that incessant sharp lookout which, for the pool-dwellers, was the price of survival.

Swimming slowly up toward the other side of the arrow-weed stems, came a fantastic-looking creature, something more than an inch and a half in length. It had a long, tapering, ringed and armoured body, ending in a spine; a thick, armoured thorax, with six legs attached; and a large head, the back of which was almost covered by two big, dully staring globes of eyes. The whole front of its head—part of the eyes, and all the face—was covered by a smooth, cleft, shieldlike mask, reaching well down under the breast, and giving the creature an expression both mysterious and terrible. On its back, folded close and obviously useless were rigidly encased attempts at wings.

The little monster swam slowly by the motion of its long and strong legs, thrusting out two short, hornlike antennae over the top of its mask. It seemed to be eying a snail-shell on a stem above, and waiting for the snail's soft body to emerge from the citadel; when on a sudden, through the stems, it caught sight of the basking tadpole. Instantly it became motionless, and sank, like a waterlogged twig, to the level of the mud. It crept around, effacing itself against the brown and greenish roots, till it was just opposite the quarry. Then it sprang, propelling itself not only by its legs, but by the violent ejection of a little stream of water from the powerful breathing-valves near its tail.

The tadpole, as we have seen, was not asleep. With a convulsive wriggle of its tail it darted away in a panic. It was itself no mean swimmer, but it could not escape the darting terror that pursued. When the masked form was almost within reach of its victim, the mask dropped down and shot straight out, working on a sort of elbow-shaped lever, and at the same time revealed at its extremity a pair of powerful mandibles. These mandibles snapped firm hold of the victim at the base of its wriggling tail. The elbow-shaped lever drew back, till the squirming prize was held close against its captor's face. Then with swift jets from the turbine arrangement of its abdominal gills, the strange monster darted back to a retreat among the weed stems, where it could devour its prey in seclusion.

Under those inexorable jaws the tadpole soon disappeared and for a few minutes the monster rested, working its mandibles to and fro and rubbing them with its front legs before folding back that inscrutable mask over its savage face. Presently a plump minnow, more than an inch long, with a black stripe along its bronze and silver sides, swam down close by the arrow-weed stems. The big eyes of the monster never moved. But, suddenly, out shot the mask once more, revealing the face of doom behind it; and those hooked mandibles fixed themselves in the belly of the minnow. Inexorable as was the grip, it nevertheless for the moment left unimpeded the swimming powers of the victim; and he was a strong swimmer. With lashing tail and beating fins, he dragged his captor out from among the weed stems. For a few seconds there was a vehement struggle. Then the minnow was borne down upon the mud, out in the broad sheen where, a little before, the tadpole had been basking. Clutching ferociously with its six long legs, the conqueror crawled over the prey and bit its backbone in two.

Swift, strong, insatiably ravenous, immeasurably fierce, the larva of the dragon-fly (for such the little monster was) had fair title to be called the wolf of the pool. Its appearance alone was enough to daunt all rivals. Even the great black carnivorous water-beetle, with all its strength and fighting equipment, was careful to give wide berth to that dreadful, quick-darting mask. Had these little wolves been as numerous as they were rapacious, there would soon have been left no life at all in the pool but theirs and that of the frogs. Between these there would have been a long and doubtful struggle, the frogs hunting the larvae among the weed stems, and the larvae devouring the tadpoles on their basking-grounds.

It chanced that the particular larva whose proceedings we have noted was just on the eve of that change which should transport it to the world of air. After eating the minnow it somehow failed to recover its appetite, and remained, all the rest of the day and through the night, clinging to one of the weed stems. Next morning, when the sun was warm on the pool, it crawled slowly up, up, up, till it came out into a new element, and the untried air fanned it dry. Its great round eyes, formerly dull and opaque, had now grown transparent, and were gleaming like live jewels, an indescribable blend of emerald, sapphire, and amethyst. Presently its armour, now for the first time drying in the sun, split apart down the back, and a slender form, adorned with two pairs of crumpled, wet wings, struggled three-quarters of its length from the shell. For a short time it clung motionless, gathering strength. Then, bracing its legs firmly on the edges of the shell, it lifted its tail quite clear, and crawled up the weed a perfect dragon-fly, forgetful of that grim husk it was leaving behind. A few minutes later, the good sun having dried its wings, it went darting and hurtling over the pool, a gemlike, opalescent shining thing, reflected gloriously in the polished mirror beneath.

Little Silk Wing

The first of the twilight over Silverwater. So ethereal were the thin washes of palest orange and apple-green reflection spreading over the surface of the lake, out beyond the fringe of alder bushes, so bubble-like in delicacy the violet tones of the air among the trees, just fading away into the moth-wing brown of dusk, that the Child was afraid to ask even the briefest questions, lest his voice should break the incomparable enchantment. Uncle Andy sat smoking, his eyes withdrawn in a dream. From the other side of the point, quite out of sight, where Bill was washing the dishes after the early camp supper, came a soft clatter of tins. But the homely sound had no power to jar the quiet.

The magic of the hour took it, and transmuted it, and made it a note in the chord of the great stillness. From the pale greenish vault of sky came a long, faint twang as of a silver string, where the swoop of a night hawk struck the tranced air to a moment's vibration. A minute or two later the light splash of a small trout leaping, and then, from the heart of the hemlock wood further down the shore, the mellow *hoo-hoo-hoo-oo* of a brown owl.

The Child was squatting on the mossy turf and staring out, round-eyed, across the water. Suddenly he jumped, clapped both grimy little hands to his face, and piped a shrill "Oh!" A bat's wing had flittered past his nose so close that he might have caught it in his teeth if he had wanted to—*and* been quick enough.

Uncle Andy turned, took his pipe from his mouth with marked deliberation, and eyed the Child severely.

"What on earth's the matter?" he inquired, after a disapproving pause.

"I thought it was trying to bite my nose," explained the Child apologetically.

"There's not very much to bite, you know," said Uncle Andy, in a carping mood at having had his reveries disturbed.

"I know it's pretty little, and turns up—rather," agreed the Child; "but I don't want anything to bite it."

"Nonsense!" said Uncle Andy. "Who'd want to?"

"It was that bat!" declared the Child, pointing to the shadowy form zigzagging over the fringe of bushes at the edge of the water. "He came down and hit me right in the face—almost."

"That bat bite you!" retorted Uncle Andy with a sniff of scorn. "Why, he was doing you the most friendly turn he knew how. No doubt there was a big mosquito just going to bite you, and that little chap there snapped it up in time to save you. There are lots of folk beside bats that get themselves misunderstood just when they are trying hardest to do some good."

"Oh, I see!" murmured the Child politely—which, of course, meant that he did not see at all what Uncle Andy was driving at. "*Why* do bats get themselves misunderstood, Uncle Andy?"

His uncle eyed him narrowly. He was always suspecting the Child of making game of him—than which nothing could be further from the Child's honest and rather matter-of-fact intentions. The question, to be sure, was rather a poser. While he pondered a reply to it—apparently absorbed in the task of relighting his pipe—the Child's attention was diverted. And forever the question of why bats get themselves misunderstood remained unanswered.

The bat chanced at the moment to be zigzagging only a dozen feet or so away, when from the empty air above, as if created on the instant out of nothingness, dropped a noiseless, shadowy shape of wings. It seemed to catch the eccentric little flutterer fairly. But it didn't—for the bat was a marvelous adept at dodging. With a lightning swerve it emerged from under the great wings and darted behind Uncle Andy's head. The baffled owl, not daring to come so near the hated man-creatures, winnowed off in ghostly silence.

At the same moment a tiny, quivering thing, like a dark leaf, floated to the ground. There, instead of lying quiet like a leaf, it fluttered softly.

"What's *that?*" demanded the Child.

"*Hush!*" ordered Uncle Andy in a peremptory whisper.

The shadowy leaf on the ground continued to flutter, as if trying to rise into the air. Presently the bat reappeared and circled over it. A moment more and it dropped, touched the ground for a second with wide, uplifted wings, and then sailed off again on a long, swift, upward curve. The fluttering, shadowy leaf had disappeared.

For once the Child had no questions ready. He had so much to ask about all at once. His eyes like saucers with interrogation, he turned appealingly to his uncle and said nothing.

"That was the little one—one of the two little ones," said Uncle Andy obligingly.

"But what?—why?——"

"You see," went on Uncle Andy, hastening to explain before he could be overwhelmed, "your poor little friend was a mother bat, and she was carrying her two young ones with her, clinging to her neck with their wings, while she was busy hunting gnats and moths and protecting your nose from mosquitoes. When the owl swooped on her, and so nearly caught her, she dodged so violently that one of the little ones was jerked from its hold. Being too young to fly, it could do nothing but flutter to the ground and squat there, beating its wings till the mother came to look for it. How she managed to pick it up again so neatly, I can't say. But you saw for yourself how neat it was, eh?"

The Child nodded his head vigorously and smacked his lips in agreement.

"But why does she carry them around with her that way?" he inquired. "It seems to me awfully dangerous. I don't think *I'd* like it."

He pictured to himself his own substantial mamma swooping erratically through the air, with skirts flying out behind and himself clinging precariously to her neck. And at the thought he felt a sinking sensation at the pit of his stomach.

"Well, you know, you're not a bat," said Uncle Andy sententiously. "If you were you'd probably think it much pleasanter, and far *less* dangerous, than being left at home alone while your mother was out swooping 'round after moths and June bugs.'"

"Why?" demanded the Child promptly.

"Well, you just listen a bit," answered Uncle Andy in his exasperating way. He hated to answer any of the Child's most innocent questions directly if he could get at them in a roundabout way. "Once upon a time"—("Ugh!" thought the Child to himself, "*this* is going to be a fairy story!" But it wasn't). "Once upon a time," went on Uncle Andy slowly, "there was a young bat—a baby bat so small you might have put him into your mother's thimble. He lived high up in the peak of the roof of an old barn down in the meadows beside the golden, rushing waters of the Nashwaak stream, not more than five or six miles from Fredericton. We'll call him Little Silk Wing."

"*I*'ve been to Fredericton!" interjected the Child with an important air.

"Really!" said Uncle Andy. "Well, Little Silk Wing hadn't. And now, who's going to tell this story, you or I?"

"I won't interrupt any more!" said the Child penitently. "But why was he called Little Silk Wing, Uncle Andy?"

His uncle looked at him in despair. Then he answered, with unwonted resignation, "His wings weren't really any silkier than those of his tiny sister. But he got hold of the name *first*, that's all. So it was his!

"When the two were first born they were so tiny as to be quite ridiculous—little shriveled, pale mites, that could do nothing but hang to their mother's breasts, and nurse diligently, and grow. They grew almost at once to the same color as their mother, plumped out till they were so big as to be not quite lost in a thimble and developed a marvelous power of clinging to their mother's body while she went careering through the air in her dizzy evolutions.

But when they were big enough for their weight to be a serious interference with their mother's hunting, then she was forced, most reluctantly, to leave them at home sometimes. She would take them both together into the narrow crevice between the top beam and the slope of the roof, and there they would lie motionless, shrouded in their exquisitely fine, mouse-colored wing membranes, and looking for all the world like two little bits of dry wood. It was not always lonely for them, because there were usually at least two or three grown-up bats hanging by their toes from the edge of a nearby crack, taking brief rest from the toil of their aerial chase. But it was always monotonous, unless they were asleep. For all movement was rigorously forbidden them, as being liable to betray them to some foe."

"Why, what could get at them, away up there?" demanded the Child, to whom the peak of a lead always seemed the remotest, most inaccessible, and most mysterious of spots.

"Wait and see!" answered Uncle Andy, with the air of an oracle. "Well, one night a streak of moonlight, like a long white finger, came in through a crack above and lit up those two tiny huddled shapes in their crevice. It came so suddenly upon them that Little Silk Wing, under the touch of that blue-white radiance, stirred uneasily and half unfolded his wings. The movement caught the great, gleaming eyes cf an immense brown hunting spider who chanced at that moment to be prowling down the underside of the roof. He was one of the kind that does not spin webs, but catches its prey by stealing up and pouncing upon it. He knew that a little bat, when young enough, was no stronger than a big butterfly, and its blood would be quite good enough to suck. Stealthily he crept down into the brightness of that narrow ray, wondering whether the youngster was too big for him to tackle or not. He made up his mind to have a go at it. In fact, he was just gathering his immense, hairy legs beneath him for that fatal pounce of his, when he was himself pounced upon by a flickering shadow, plucked from his place, paralyzed by a bit through the thorax, and borne off to be devoured at leisure by a big bat which had just come in."

"Oh, I see," muttered the Child feelingly. He was himself a good deal afraid of spiders, and he meant that he understood now why it was less dangerous for little bats to go swinging wildly through the twilight clinging to their mother's necks than to stay at home alone.

But Uncle Andy paid no heed to the interruption.

"On the following night," he continued, "Little Silk Wing and his sister found themselves once more alone in the crevice at the end of the beam. They knew nothing of the peril from which they had been saved the night before, so they had learned no lesson. On this night they were restless, for their mother had fluttered away, leaving them both a little hungry. Hunting had been bad, and she had somewhat less milk for them than their growing appetites demanded. When once more that slender finger of moonlight, feeling its way through a chink in the roof, fell upon them in their crevice, it was the little sister this time that stirred and fluttered under its ghostly touch. She stretched one wing clear out upon the beam, and it was with difficulty that she restrained herself from giving vent to one of her infinitesimally thin squeaks, tiny as a bead that would drop through the eye of a needle.

"There was no great prowling spider to catch sight of her tonight. But a very hungry mouse, as it chanced, was just at that moment tip-toeing along the beam, wondering what he could find that would be good to eat. A lump of toasted cheese, or an old grease rag, or a well-starched collar, or a lump of cold suet pudding would have suited him nicely, but inexorable experience had taught him that such delicacies were seldom to be found in the roof of the barn. Under the circumstances, any old moth or beetle or spider, dead or alive, would be better than nothing.

How his little black, beadlike eyes glistened as they fell upon that frail membrane of a wing fluttering on the beam! He darted forward, straight and swift as a weaver's shuttle, seized the delicate wing in his strong white teeth, and dragged the baby bat from her hiding place. Baby as she was, she was game. For one moment she sat up and chattered angry defiance, in a voice like the winding of a watch, but so thin and high-pitched that only a fine ear could have caught it. Then the mouse seized her, bit her tiny neck through, and dragged her off, sprawling limply, along the beam."

The Child nodded vigorously. He needed nothing more to convince him of the superior security of a life of travel and adventure, as compared with the truly appalling perils of staying at home.

"I see you take me!" said Uncle Andy approvingly. "But this, as you will observe, was not Little Silk Wing, but his sister. For Little Silk Wing life became now more interesting. Having only one baby left, his mother was able to carry him with her wherever she went. And she would not have left him alone again for the world, lest the unknown but dreadful fate which had befallen his sister should overtake him also.

He was old enough and wide awake enough by this time to appreciate his advantages. He could feel the thrill of his mother's long, swinging swoops through the dewy coolness of the dusk. He could thrill in sympathy with her excitement of the chase, when she went fluttering up into the thin pallor of the upper air, following inexorably the desperate circlings of some high-flying cockchafer. When she dropped like lead to snap up some sluggish night moth, its wings were not yet quite dry from the chrysalis, as he clung to the swaying grass tops, his tiny eyes sparkled keenly. And when she went zigzagging, with breathless speed and terrifying violence, to evade the noiseless attack of the brown owl, he hung on to her neck with the tenacity of despair and imagined that their last hour had come. But it hadn't, for his mother was clever and expert. She had fooled many owls in her day.

This adventurous life of his, of course, was lived entirely at night. During the day he slept, for the most part, folded in his mother's wing membranes, while she hung by her toes from the edge of a warped board in the warm goldy-brown shadows of the peak of the old barn. Outside, along the high ridge pole, swallows, king birds, jays, and pigeons gathered under the bright blue day to scream, chatter or coo their ideas of life, each according to the speech of its kind. And sometimes a cruel-eyed, hook-beaked, trim, well-bred looking hawk would perch there on the roof—quite alone, let me tell you—and gaze around as if wondering where all the other birds *could* have gone to! And once in a while also a splendid white-headed eagle would come down out of the blue, and wing low over the barn, and scream his thin, terrifying yelp, as if he were hoping there might be something like spring lambs hidden in the barn. But none of these things, affairs of the garish, dazzling, common day, moved in the least the row of contented little bats, all drowsing the useless hours of day away as they hung by their toes in the soft gloom under the roof. They would wake up now and again, to be sure, and squeak, and crowd each other a little. Or perhaps rouse themselves enough to make a long and careful toilet, combing their exquisitely fine fur with their delicate claws, and passing every corner of the elastic silken membrane of their wings daintily between their lips. But as for what went on in the gaudy light on the outer side of the roof, it concerned them not at all.

But Little Silk Wing seems to have been born to illustrate the dangers which beset the life of the stay-at-home. For two days there had been an unwonted disturbance in the deep-grassed meadow that surrounded the barn. There had been the clanking of harness, the long, shrill, vibrant clatter of the scarlet mowing machine, the snorting of horses, and the shouting and laughter of men turning the fresh hay with their forks. Then came carts and children, with shrill laughter and screams of merriment, and the hay was hauled into the barn, load after load, fragrant, crackling with grasshoppers; and presently the mows began to fill up till the men with the pitchforks, sweating over the hot work of stowing the hay, came up beneath the eaves.

Reluctantly and indignantly the bats woke up. Some of them, as the loads came in with noisy children on top, bestirred themselves sufficiently to shake the sleep out of their eyes, unfold their draped wings, flutter down into the daylight, and fly off to the peaceful gloom of the nearest woods.

But the mother of Little Silk Wing was not so easily disturbed. She opened her tiny black beads of eyes as wide as she could, but gave no other sign of having noticed the invaders of the old barn's drowsy peace. She had seen such excitement before, and never known any harm to come of it. And she hated flying out into the full glare of the sun.

But there is such a thing, you know, as being a bit *too* calm and self-possessed. As the hay got higher up in the mow, beyond the eaves, and almost up to the level of the topmost beam, one of the farm hands noticed the little bat hanging under the ridgepole. He was one of those dull fools, not cruel at heart, perhaps, but utterly without imagination, who, if they see something interesting, are apt to kill it just because they don't know any other way to show their interest. He up with the handle of his pitchfork and knocked the poor little mother bat far out into the stubble."

"Oh!" cried the Child. "Didn't it hurt her *dreadfully?*"

"It killed her," replied Uncle Andy simply. "But by chance it didn't hurt Little Silk Wing himself, as he clung desperately to her neck. The children, with cries of sympathy and reprobation, rushed to pick up the little dark body. But the black-and-white dog was ahead of them. He raced in and snatched the queer thing up, gently enough, in his teeth. But he let it drop again at once in huge surprise. It had come apart. All of a sudden it was two bats instead of one. He couldn't understand it at all. And neither could the children. And while they stood staring—the black-and-white dog with his tongue hanging out and his tail forgetting to wag, and the children with their eyes quite round—Little Silk Wing fluttered up into the air, flew hesitatingly this way and that for a moment till he felt sure of himself, and then darted off to the shelter of those woods where he had so often accompanied his mother on her hunting."

The Child heaved a sigh of relief. "I'm so glad he got off," he murmured.

"I thought you would be. That's why he did," said Uncle Andy enigmatically.

Queen Bomba of the Honey-Pots

I

In the hot, honey-scented, murmurous dark of the bees' nest, deep-hidden in the bank beneath the wild-rose thicket, the burly young queen, Bomba of the bumblebees, was seized with a sudden inexplicable restlessness. When she had emerged, two days before, from her cocoon-cell weak on her legs, bedraggled, and dazed by the busy crowding stir of the nest, she had been tenderly fed with thin honey by the great Queen-Mother herself, and cleaned and caressed by two or three of her sturdy little bustling worker-sisters. But as soon as she was strong enough to look after herself, and had found her way to the well-supplied communal honey-pots, she was amiably ignored, as everyone in the nest was working at high pressure. She had dutifully fallen to with the rest, and found her time well occupied in feeding the ever-hungry larvae in their cells. But now this task no longer contented her. For the moment she did not know what she wanted. She went blundering here and there over the combs, shouldering the little workers aside, and paying no heed whatever to the tiny, insatiable mouths in the brood-cells. Then, suddenly, her desires took definite shape. It was change she wanted, and space, and a free wing, and the unknown air. With a deep buzz of decision she rushed to the big waxen honey-pot beside the entrance of the nest, sucked up enough of the thin honey to fill her crop with comfort, then hurriedly crawled along the narrow tunnel which led to the outer world. In her quest for the great adventure she was oblivious to the stream of workers which she passed on the way.

At the exit, half hidden by a tuft of grass, she stopped short, as the first full glare of daylight struck her in the face. For the moment she was half minded to turn back into the familiar dark. But her sturdy spirit forbade any such ignominy. She crept out into the warm grass. Warm scents and soft airs encouraged her. She spread her wings, and stretched them; and at last, lured by the dazzle of sunshine beyond the shadow of the bank, she sprang into the air and went winging off, with a deep droning hum of elation, into the mysterious spaces of green and sheen and bloom.

As she took wing she was accosted by three or four ardent young males of her race—square-built, burly, black-and-orange beaux, hardly half her size but full of energy and enterprise. At this moment, however, their eager wooing left her cold. She was set on exploring the new and wonderful world which had just been revealed to her. Impatiently eluding her wooers she boomed away over the sun-steeped meadow, and pounced down upon a patch of late-flowering purple clover. Here she revelled for an hour or two among the honeyed blossoms, plunging her long tongue to the very bottom the deep and narrow tubes where the nectar lay concealed, and disturbing a host of tiny foraging flies. From the meadow she flew over a tall green hedge, and swung down into the many-colored tangle of an old-fashioned garden, where all the flowers of late summer were holding a riot of bloom. Over this profusion of riches she went quite wild for a time, sampling nectar of a dozen flavours and pollen of many varied hues, squeezing her broad, black-and-yellow head and shoulders into the foxgloves and the snapdragons, rollicking about in the wide radiant bowls of the hollyhock blossoms, rifling the pale blue campanulas, diving bodily into the Canterbury Bells, and giving voice to shrill, squeaking buzzes of excitement and impatience whenever she felt her quarters too restricted. Once a tall being, all in white, came moving slowly down the garden walk, pausing at times to examine or to sniff at a glowing blossom. Bomba circled around the stranger's head several times, in amiable curiosity, and then, attracted by a vivid gleam of scarlet, droned off to the other side of the garden to investigate a row of tall poles draped to their tops with flowering runner-beads.

Late in the afternoon, when the shadows were lengthening across the garden and a strange chill, such as she had never dreamt of in the home nest, began to make the air seem less friendly, Bomba flew off to an ancient brick wall which faced westward and was still bathed in sunshine. This wall was clothed with rambler roses, pink, white, and deep crimson. The mass of bloom was humming with life—with flies of innumerable kinds, with green and bronze beetles, honey-bees, slim, dapper wasps, and workers, drones and big queens of Bomba's own species. She ignored them all alike, happy in her care-free independence. But when the chill in the air grew fresher she forsook the revels, slipped in under the veil of blossom and leaves, and crept drowsily into a crevice in the sun-warmed bricks. Here she slept away the starlit night, and never emerged next day till the sun was high in the blue and the last of the dew was vanishing from the garden world.

As she crawled out upon a crimson rose, and stood basking in the sun, her broad velvet bands of black and gold richly aglow, she was aware of a curiously attractive perfume which was not of the flower. It was somehow more living and vital, and of more personal significance to herself. It excited her strangely. Presently she became aware that it emanated from an attractive drone of her species, who was hovering close above her, humming persuasively. Of more compliant mood today than when first she left the nest, she rose into the air to meet this scented wooer; and the two soared away slowly together, on their mating flight, over the gay-hued patterns of the garden.

Her lover, however, and her interest in lovers, being very soon forgotten, Bomba passed the brief remnant of the summer in careless vagrancy. This was the one time of holiday that her life, predestined to toil, would ever afford. For the present she had nothing to do but feast through the hours of sun, and doze away the hours of dark or storm in the shelter of her cranny in the brick wall, and all the time, though she knew it not, she was laying up strength and substance to last her through her long winter's sleep beneath the snow.

As the honey-bearing blossoms passed away with the passing summer, Bomba began to realize that a sinister change was approaching, and the instinct inherited from a million generations of ancestors warned her that her cranny in the brick wall would soon be an insufficient shelter. Long and earnest search at last yielded her a site that seemed suitable for her winter's retreat. On a dry knoll of sandy loam stood a spreading beech tree, and in the light soil beneath one of its roots she proceeded to dig her burrow. She did not, as might have been expected, choose the sunny side of the tree, but rather, in her prevision, the shadowed north, in order that the early, deceiving warmth of the following spring might not awaken her too soon and lure her forth to her doom in a world not yet ready for her.

Not being a very expert digger as compared with some of her remote cousins, she spent several arduous days in tunnelling a narrow tube about four inches in depth. The end of this tunnel she enlarged to a circular chamber wherein she could curl up comfortably. Here, for the next week or two, she spent the chill nights and the wet or lowering days, only coming forth when the noon sun tempted her. But when the few remaining late flowers were all rifled of their honey, and the dancing flies were all gone, and the bedraggled garden looked sorrowful and neglected, and even at high noon the air had a menacing nip in its caress, she felt an irresistible drowsiness creeping over her. Half asleep already, she crawled into her dry, warm burrow, and forthwith sank into a slumber too deep for dreams. The days grew shorter, the nights longer and darker, frosts slew the final valiant blossoms, and at last the snow came, silently, and buried meadow, grove, and garden far from sight—almost, it would seem, from memory. Wild storms swept over the white, enshrouded earth, and savage cold scourged the unsheltered fields; but Bomba, in her snug chamber beneath the beech-roots, slept untroubled through it all, carrying secure in her fertilized ovaries the heritage of the future of her race.

II

Not only was the snow all gone, but spring was firmly established in the land, before the growing warmth awakened Bomba, and she crept forth from her chamber to renew her acquaintance with the sun. Crocus and narcissus and polyanthus starred the brown garden beds;

orange-gold dandelions made gay the young grass of the meadows, the willows along the meadow brook were all a cloud of creamy lemon catkins; and the grey old sugar-maple which overhung the garden wall had burst into a film of aerial rose.

It was, above all, the creamy fragrant willow blooms which attracted Bomba for the moment. She would revel among them in the noon-day glow, her heavy, booming note rising above the soft hum of the myriad lesser bees, and small wasps, and many-tinted flies which held riot in the scented pollen. But she was still drowsy; and every day, after gorging herself luxuriously, she would hurry back to her deep chamber under the beech-roots, and sleep till the sun was once more nearing his height. But when spring forgot its caprices and melted into summer, she was seized with a new and imperious impulse, the impulse to found a colony and assume the sovereignty which she was born for. Her narrow cell grew distasteful to her, and she fell to searching the open, grassy slopes and bushy hillocks for more spacious quarters. After a long quest she found, in a steep and tangled fence-corner, just what she wanted. It was a forsaken burrow of the little, striped ground squirrel.

The burrow was roomy and dry, and the entrance to it was by a narrow tunnel about two feet long. The only fault Bomba could find with it was that it had a back door, another tunnel to afford its former occupants a means of exit in case of undesirable visitors. Bomba had no need of a back door, which meant draughts, so in cleaning up the nest she packed the litter into this entrance and pretty well stopped it up, intending to make it quite draught-proof later on, when she should find time to plaster it with leaf-bud gum and wax.

Meanwhile, in spite of her ceaseless activity, she was secreting thin morsels of wax from the scales of her under-body—a coarse, dark, yellowish wax, very unlike the delicate white secretion of the hive bees. This wax she presently scraped off and collected, kneaded it together, chewed it, and tempered it with her saliva. Then, close beside the inner doorway of the nest she began to build what looked like a large, round, shallow cell, with extremely thin but amazingly tough walls. It was not an ordinary cell, however, but a honey pot, a temporary thing for holding day-by-day supplies; for Bomba knew that her business among the blossoms was liable to be interrupted at any moment by storm or rain, and she must have a store of food indoors, in order not to be delayed in her urgent task of home-building. Into this honey-pot, as soon as it was deep enough, she disgorged what was left of honey in her crop, and then bustled forth, impatient to begin her foraging for the new nest.

But for all her impatience, Bomba's first care, on emerging from the darkness of her tunnel, was to locate herself. She had had trouble enough to find the new home site. She was not going to let herself lose it. With her head towards the almost invisible entrance she rose on the wing and hovered slowly about, in ever-widening circles, for several minutes. Not until she had her directions fixed securely and every landmark noted did she swing away on her great business of gathering supplies.

Unlike her far-off cousin, the hive bee, who is so specialized, so automatic in all her actions, that she seems unable ever to think of more than one thing at a time, Bomba could think of everything at once and seized upon opportunity as it came up. She was no purist in method. When the hive bee goes out to gather pollen, she quite ignores honey, she even ignores every kind of pollen except the one which she has started to collect; and when she has her mind set on honey, the most alluring display of pollen leaves her utterly uninterested. Bomba, on the other hand, was out for all she could get. If one blossom offered her honey, she accepted it eagerly, sucking it up and storing it in her honey sac. If the next flower had been already rifled of its nectar, but was rich in pollen, she would seize upon that with equal zest, and stuff it into the capacious pollen baskets on her thighs. Nor did she care what particular brand of pollen it might be. Red, orange, yellow, or creamy buff, it was all the same to her; so that her thighs were soon decorated with vivid, streaky protuberances of the precious spoil. As soon as she felt herself freighted, within and without, to her full capacity, she flew straight back to the nest, circled about the entrance to make sure of it, and then hurried in to unload. Her honey she disgorged into the honey-pot by the door; the pollen she stripped from her thighs and deposited on a smooth spot in the centre of the nest, treating it, as she did so, with a minute proportion of something of the nature of formic acid from her own glands to keep it sweet. Then she hastened forth again for another load, and this fragrant toil engrossed her till nearly sunset, for she was intent on getting in as big a store as possible while daylight lasted.

But the fall of dusk, the coming out of the evening star—a sudden gleam of silver in the pure green-violet sky—meant no relaxation to the impatient Bomba. The poet sings to Hesperus as:

> Star that bringest home the bee
> And set'st the weary labourer free,

but it brought not Bomba home to rest, by any means. Of rest and sleep she had had enough already; and, to the work on which she was now feverishly bent, darkness was no hindrance. In the depth of the nest it was always dark; but all her senses were so subtly acute that this mattered not at all.

And now, kneading up a stiff paste of pollen moistened with honey, she proceeded to build a low, circular platform, or pedestal, of the mixture, in the centre of the floor. On this savoury foundation she modelled a spacious cell of wax. In the bottom of this cell she laid her first eggs, a baker's dozen of them, and then, sealing the top with a thin waxen film, she began to brood them, solicitously as a mother thrush. For four days she stuck to her task, only leaving it for brief intervals to snatch a mouthful of honey; and then the eggs hatched out into a bunch of hungry grubs, which fell straightway to satisfying their hunger by devouring the pollen-paste floor on which they squirmed. Now Bomba's duties grew more exacting. She had to rush the work of gathering honey and pollen; for the little grubs in the cell grew swiftly and their appetites with them. She opened the waxen covering of the cell and pumped in continual rations of the nourishing paste. And between whiles she continued to brood the little family, that the warmth of her great velvety body might hasten their development. Soon they grew so big that the cell was crowded and they all had to stand up on their tails in order to find room, and in this position Bomba had to feed them individually, thrusting the food into each little greedy mouth in turn. In about seven days, however, they had reached full growth, and then their appetites all ceased simultaneously. Each spun itself a tough, perpendicular, silken-paper, yellow-brown cocoon, independent, but firmly attached to those of its neighbours—shut itself up in it, and went to sleep to await the great final change.

The group of cocoons, all stiffly erect and knitted together, now needing no longer their waxen envelope, Bomba stripped it off and used the previous wax to build other and smaller cells encircling the base of the cocoon bundle. In each of these, as she completed it, at intervals of two and three days, she laid five or six more eggs and sealed them up to hatch. She also had to collect more and more honey, more and more pollen, and to build higher the walls of the great honey-pot beside the door as the nectared store increased. When not at any of these tasks she spent her time, not less arduously, in brooding the cocoons, stretching her furry black-and-yellow body to warm them all, like a sitting hen who has been given a bigger clutch than she can properly cover.

Within the nest these days were just one round of uneventful toil; but outside, upon her foraging expeditions among the flowers of field and garden, Bomba's life was not without its risks and its adventures. On account of her great size and strength, and the power of her long (though not very venomous) sting, she had fewer foes to dread than most of her lesser cousins; but, having the sole responsibility of the home, for the present, on her shoulders, she was bound to be careful, though by nature unsuspicious. The biggest and fiercest of northern spiders were of no concern to her, for none would venture within range of that darting flame, her sting, and she could wreck their toughest webs without an effort. But some of the bigger insect-eating birds were a peril against which she had to be vigilant. And some of the hunting mice and shrews that infested the meadow were very dangerous, because they knew how to pounce upon her and seize her by the broad back, in such a way that her sting could not reach them.

For the most part, however, the insect-hunters were inclined to leave her alone, respecting her almost as much as they did that most vicious and venomous fighter, the great black hornet.

On one of these mornings, while Bomba's first brood were yet in their cocoons, and, Bomba was out on one of her hurried foragings, a prowling shrew-mouse stumbled upon the entrance of the nest. He was hungry, and the smell that came from the burrow was appetizing. He knew enough about the wild bee, however, to dampen any tendency to rashness. He stood motionless, and listened intently. Keen as were his ears, he could not detect a sound from within. There was no rustle of wings—no bustle of busy feet over the combs—no warning hum. He judged, rightly enough, that the colony was just being started, and that its queen and foundress was out gathering supplies. He decided to slip in, snatch a few mouthfuls of rich and satisfying brood-comb, and get away before the owner's return.

But he had miscalculated. Just as his tawny hind-quarters were disappearing into the burrow, Bomba returned. Swooping downward like a flash of flame, she sank her long sting deep into the tender flesh between marauder's thighs. The terrible weapon seared like fire. With a squeal of anguish the shrew doubled back convulsively, then sprang at his assailant. But Bomba was already out of reach, circling over him with a deep, angry hum, and obviously ready to strike again.

The shrew was courageous, but his courage failed him now. The pain of his wound was intolerable. He darted away in a panic, to hide himself under the grass and lick his wound till the anguish should be eased. And Bomba, never vindictive, was satisfied with her victory. She crept into the burrow in anxious haste to assure herself her treasure had not been tampered with.

On the eleventh day from the commencement of their chrysalis sleep the perfect workers began to break the tops of their cocoons and crawl forth, very frail, damp, and dishevelled. Bomba guided them all, by ones and twos, to the great honey-pot, where they slaked their hunger, then gathered them back to her cocoon couch to be warmed by her body and helped with their first, much needed toilets. For the next day or so she mothered them tenderly in the intervals of her other duties—and the duty of keeping the honey-pot supplied, needless to say, was a heavy one. But by the end of that time the youngsters had reached their full strength, and all her care was rewarded. She had now a dozen sturdy, sprightly, glossy young workers, less than half her size, but keen and diligent to share with her the swiftly multiplying labours of the nest. The youngsters eagerly buzzed forth to collect honey and pollen, and fell to mixing bee-bread, feeding the new batch of larvae, constructing fresh brood-cells, and replenishing the big communal honey-pot, with the instinctive skill which was their heritage of a million generations. They also reinforced the tops of their old cocoons with wax, and turned these into storage cells that no precious space or labour should be wasted.

III

The colony being now fairly established, it grew with amazing speed. Every two or three days a new batch of eggs hatched out into hungry larvae, a new detachment of velvety, black-and-yellow little workers emerged from their cocoons to swell the happy industry of the nest. To them all Bomba was both queen and mother. Her rule was absolute, unquestioned; but for all her royalty she, unlike the sequestered queen of the hive bees, took full share in all tasks of the community, besides performing her own peculiar duty of laying eggs. Now, however, she began to leave more of the dangerous outdoor work, the gathering of supplies, to her subjects, and spent more of her time in the homework of the nest. But she could not forget the lure of the sunshine or the riot of bloom which now clothed garden and meadow with colour. Once or twice a day she would go booming forth to levy toll of her favourite flowers.

One day, when she had her head buried deep in the fragrant calyx of a honeysuckle, the Lady of the Garden stood close by and watched her at her work. Presently the Lady put forth a slender finger and, very cautiously and delicately, stroked the black-and-gold velvet of

Bomba's back. The touch was light as dandelion down, and conveyed no menace to Bomba's sensitive nerves. She gave a shrill little squeak of protest, and went on sucking up the honey with redoubled speed, probably thinking that the intruder was after a share of it. The Lady laughed, and drew back a step or two,. still watching and wondering if the great bee was going to resent the liberty which had been taken with her. Nothing was further from Bomba's thought. She withdrew her head, having drained all the honey, and hummed over to the next blossom.

At this moment a hungry shrike—a bird fitly known as "the butcher-bird"—who had his nest in a tree beyond the garden wall, swooped down and made a dash at the unsuspecting Bomba, just as she sank her head into the calyx. It was the moment of fate for her—and consequently, for the little community at home in the burrow as well. But the Lady, quicker than thought, gave a sharp cry and struck at the audacious bird with her hand. The shrike, startled, missed his aim, merely brushed the blossom roughly with a wing tip, and flew up into the nearest tree. The Lady indignantly hurled a handful of gravel at him—which, strangely enough, almost hit him—and drove him from the garden. She hated him heartily, ever since she had discovered the thorn bush on whose spikes he impaled the butterflies, grasshoppers, and little birds who were his victims, when he had captured more than he could eat. As for Bomba, somewhat flustered by her narrow escape, she darted straight away to the safe shelter of the nest, without waiting to complete her honeyed load. For the nest was indeed a safe shelter now—with a hundred ready and fiery stings to guard it from all intruders.

By the time the hay was gathered in and the hot noons were growing drowsily shrill with the noise of the grasshoppers and cicadas, Bomba's swarm had grown powerful and her little citadel in the burrow nearly filled its earthen hiding-place. Though built apparently at haphazard, it was now an elaborate structure, tier upon tier of coarse, irregular comb all centred about the original bunch of cocoons. Throughout it was traversed by galleries so spacious that even Bomba's bulky form could reach every cell comfortably—the little workers building not only for their own puny stature but for hers. As to the character and contents of the cells there was rather a lack of system, but in general there was a tendency to keep the brood cells near the centre, surrounded by the pollen cells, for storing thick honey, and a few scattered honey-pots for thin, watery day-to-day supplies, towards the circumference. The great communal honey-pot beside the entrance had long ago been abandoned, and its waxen walls used up in new construction.

About this time, when the rich, heavy days were shortening and the ripeness of later summer had come upon the lazy air, Bomba, at the height of her prosperity, began to take thought for the future of her race. She, and she alone, had premonition of the bitter season that was to come. She began to lay two new kinds of eggs, one kind, in ordinary worker cells, to produce males or drones instead of workers, the other kind, laid in large cells, destined to hatch into big larvae which should ultimately be transformed into great and splendid queens like herself.

With this change in her activities Bomba suddenly found herself strictly confined to the nest for a time. She was confronted by an entirely new and inexplicable anxiety. As soon as she began laying the drone and queen eggs some of the workers—who were themselves all imperfectly developed females, and not without certain feminine instincts—were seized with a strange fratricidal jealousy. From time to time they would make murderous raids upon these new kinds of eggs, seeking to tear them to pieces. Bomba angrily beat off all these attacks, but she dared not leave the nest even for the briefest turn in the sunshine. She had to be ceaselessly on guard, night and day. But as soon as the eggs were hatched the mothering instincts of the workers triumphed over their jealousy, and they began tending the new larvae with all care. A few, their thwarted sex-instincts partially aroused, even began to emulate Bomba and laid some eggs for themselves. These eggs, however, never having been fertilized by a mating, were incapable of producing either workers or queens. All that hatched from them, for some inscrutable reason known only to Mother Nature herself, were small drones. These disappointed little females were doing their best in producing mates for others, though at no possible profit to themselves.

All these drones of Bomba's tribe, though scarcely larger than the workers, were fine, independent, capable fellows, far superior to those greedy and lazy spongers the drones of the hive-bee. As soon as they were grown up they promptly left the nest, to forage for themselves and to seek amorous adventure through the last bright weeks of the fleeting summer. They were quite capable of looking after themselves, and it was not for them to loaf about at home and eat up the stores which others had collected.

Bomba's care was now all for her young queens—who took much longer than the workers or the drones to reach maturity. Each as it came forth from its big cocoon she tended lovingly, and saw it at length fly forth, leaded with honey, never to return. By the time the last young queen had left the nest Bomba was visibly growing old. Worn with her labours, she was weary and bedraggled, and her velvety garb had a somewhat moth-eaten look. She laid a few more worker eggs; and then stopped, as there was no need of raising fresh young bees just to be killed by the autumn frosts. The colony now dwindled apace. Many of the workers, having no more young to tend at home, forsook the nest and revelled away their closing days among the late asters and zinnias and dahlias of the garden. Others, more indolent or more toil-worn, fell to eating up the stored honey in the cells, to crawl forth finally for a last, listless flight, and fall into the grass when the worn-out little engine of their being came to a stop.

To Bomba the now almost deserted nest grew suddenly hateful. It was all the creation of her own tremendous energy and life-force, but she had no more use for it. The old fire flickered up again, though feebly, in her nerves. Once more, after all her toils, she would roam free. She crawled out into the glow of the afternoon sun and soared briskly over the garden wall—turning her back upon the nest forever.

Drawn by the blaze of a bed of flame-coloured late nasturtiums she quite lost her head for half an hour or so, dipping into one gorgeous bloom after another, as if to make the most of the fleeting joy. But presently her elation flagged. She felt heavy with sleep, and clung to the blossom she was on as if she were dazed. Soon she lost her hold, and went fluttering to the ground. The air had suddenly turned cold. Too drowsy to fly she crawled in among the pale-green stalks, and nestled down there till she was almost hidden. It was an inadequate shelter, but to her it seemed sufficient for the moment. She would hunt up a better one when she again felt ready to fly. Soon she dropped to sleep. The sleep passed into a deep coma. The sun went down, and with twilight an invisible shroud of damp cold settled upon the garden. At its touch the last faint spark of Bomba's life flickered out, painlessly. But she had lived to the full; and she left behind her a score of royal and fertile daughters, to carry on, when spring should come again, the ancient, fine traditions of her race.

Mrs. Gammit and the Porcupines

"I hain't come to borry yer gun, Mr. Barron, but to ax yer advice."

Mrs. Gammit's rare appearances were always abrupt, like her speech; and it was without surprise—though he had not seen her for a month or more—that Joe Barron turned to greet her.

"It's at yer sarvice, jest as the gun would be ef ye wanted it, Mrs. Gammit—*an'* welcome! But come in an' set down an' git cooled off a mite. 'Tain't no place to talk, out here in the bilin' sun."

Mrs. Gammit seated herself on the end of the bench, just inside the kitchen door, twitched off her limp, pink cotton sunbonnet, and wiped her flushed face with the sleeve of her calico waist. Quite unsubdued by the heat and moisture of the noon-day sun, under which she had tramped nine miles through the forest, her short, stiff, grey hair stood up in irregular tufts above her weather-beaten forehead. Her host, sitting sidewise on the edge of the table so that he could swing one leg freely and spit cleanly through the open window, bit off a contemplative squid of "blackjack" tobacco, and waited for her to unfold the problems that troubled her.

Mrs. Gammit's rugged features were modelled to fit an expression of vigorous, if not belligerent, self-confidence. She knew her capabilities, well-tried in some sixty odd years of unprotected spinsterhood. Merit alone, not matrimony, it was, that had crowned this unsullied spinsterhood with the honorary title of "Mrs." Her massive and energetic nose was usually carried somewhat high, in a not unjustifiable scorn of such foolish circumstance as might seek to thwart her will.

But to-day these strenuous features found themselves surprised by an expression of doubt, of bewilderment, almost one might say of humility. At her little clearing in the heart of the great wilderness things had been happening which, to her amazement, she could not understand. Hitherto she had found an explanation, clear at least to herself, for everything that befell her in these silent backwoods which other folks seemed to find so absurdly mysterious. Armed with her self-confidence she had been able, hitherto, to deal with every situation that had challenged her, and in a manner quite satisfactory to herself, however the eternal verities may have smiled at it. But now, at last, she was finding herself baffled.

Joe Barron waited with the patience of the backwoodsman and the Indian, to whom, as to Nature herself, time seems no object, though they always somehow manage to be on time. Mrs. Gammit continued to fan her hot face with her sunbonnet, and to ponder her problems, while the lines deepened between her eyes. A big black and yellow wasp buzzed angrily against the window-pane, bewildered because it could not get through the transparent barrier. A little grey hen, with large, drooping comb vividly scarlet, hopped on to the doorsill, eyed Mrs. Gammit with surprise and disapprobation, and ran away to warn the rest of the flock that there was a woman round the place. That, as they all knew by inheritance from the "shooings" which their forefathers had suffered, meant that they would no longer be allowed in the kitchen to pick up crumbs.

At last Mrs. Gammit spoke—but with difficulty, for it came hard to her to ask advice of any one.

"I sp'ose now, mebbe, Mr. Barron, you know more about the woods critters'n what I do?" she inquired, hopefully but doubtfully.

The woodsman lifted his eyebrows in some surprise at the question.

"Well, now, if I don't I'd *oughter*," said he, "seein' as how I've kinder lived round amongst 'em all my life. If I know *anything*, it's the backwoods an' all what pertains to that same!"

"Yes, you'd *oughter* know more about them than I do!" assented Mrs. Gammit, with a touch of severity which seemed to add "and see that you do!" Then she shut her mouth firmly and fell to fanning herself again, her thoughts apparently far away.

"I hope 'tain't no *serious* trouble ye're in!" ventured her host presently, with the amiable intention of helping her to deliver her soul of its burden.

But, manlike, he struck the wrong note.

"Do you suppose," snapped Mrs. Gammit, "I'd be traipsin' over here nine mile thro' the hot woods to ax yer advice, Mr. Barron if *'twarn't* serious?" And she began to regret that she had come. Men never did understand anything, anyway.

At this sudden acerbity the woodsman stroked his chin with his hand, to hide the ghost of a smile which flickered over his lean mouth.

"Jest like a woman, to git riled over nawthin'!" he thought. "Sounds kinder nice an' homey, too!" But aloud, being always patient with the sex, he said coaxingly—

"Then it's right proud I am that ye should come to me about it, Mrs. Gammit. I reckon I kin help you out, mebbe. What's wrong?"

With a burst of relief Mrs. Gammit declared her sorrow.

"It's the aigs," said she, passionately, "Fer nigh on a month, now, I've been alosin' of 'em as fast as the hens kin git 'em laid. An' all I kin do, I cain't find out what's atakin' 'em."

Having reached the point of asking advice, an expression of pathetic hopefulness came into her weather-beaten face. Under quite other conditions it might almost have been possible for Mrs. Gammit to learn to lean on a man, if he were careful not to disagree with her.

"Oh! Aigs!" said the woodsman, relaxing slightly the tension of his sympathy. "Well, now, let's try an' git right to the root of the trouble. Air ye plumb sure, in the first place, that the hens is really *layin'* them aigs what ye don't git?"

Mrs. Gammit stiffened.

"Do I look like an eejut?" she demanded.

"Not one leetle mite, you don't!" assented her host, promptly and cordially.

"I was beginning to think mebbe I did!" persisted the injured lady.

"Everybody knows," protested the woodsman, "as how what you don't know, Mrs. Gammit, ain't hardly wuth knowin'."

"O' course, that's puttin' it a leetle too strong, Mr. Barron," she answered, much mollified. "But I do reckon as how I've got *some* horse sense. Well, I *thought* as how them 'ere hens *might* 'ave stopped layin' on the suddint; so I up an' watched 'em. Land's sakes, but they was alayin' fine. Whenever I kin take time to stan' right by an' *watch* 'em lay, I git all the aigs I know what to do with. But when I *don't* watch 'em, *clost*—nary an aig. Ye ain't agoin' to persuade me a hen kin jest quit layin' when she's a mind ter, waitin' tell ye pass her the compliment o' holdin' out yer hand fer the aig!"

"There's lots o' hens that pervarted they'll turn round an' *eat* their own aigs!" suggested the woodsman, spitting thoughtfully through the open window. The cat, coiled in the sun on a log outside, sprang up angrily, glared with green eyes at the offending window, and scurried away to cleanse her defiled coat.

"Them's not *my* poultry!" said Mrs. Gammit with decision. "I thought o' that, too. An' I watched 'em on the sly. But they hain't a one of 'em got no sech onnateral tricks. When they're through layin', they jest hop off an' run away acacklin', as they should." And she shook her head heavily, as one almost despairing of enlightenment. "No, ef ye ain't got no more idees to suggest than that, I might as well be goin'."

"Oh, I was jest kinder clearin' out the underbrush, so's to git a square good look at the situation," explained Barron. "Now, I kin till ye somethin' about it. Firstly, it's a weasel, bein' so sly, an' quick, an' audashus! Ten to one, it's a weasel; an' ye've got to trap it. Secondly, if 'tain't a weasel, it's a fox, an' a *mighty* cute fox, as ye're goin' to have some trouble in aketchin'. An' thirdly—an' lastly —if 'tain't neither weasel nor fox, it's jest bound to be an extra cunnin' skunk, what's takin' the trouble to be keerful. Generally speakin', skunks ain't keerful, because they don't have to be, nobody wantin' much to fool with 'em. But onc't in a while ye'll come acros't one that's as sly as a weasel."

"Oh, 'tain't none o' them!" said Mrs. Gammit, in a tone which conveyed a poor opinion of her host's sagacity and woodcraft. "I've suspicioned the weasels, an' the foxes, an' the woodchucks, but hain't found a sign o' any one of 'em round the place. An' *as* fer *skunks*—well, I reckon, I've got a nose on my face." And to emphasize the fact, she sniffed scornfully.

"*To* be sure! An' a fine, handsome nose it is, Mrs. Gammit!" replied the woodsman, diplomatically. "But what you *don't* appear to know about skunks is that when they're up to mischief is jest the time when you don't smell 'em. Ye got to bear that in mind!"

Mrs. Gammit looked at him with suspicion.

"Be that really so?" demanded she, sternly.

"True's gospel!" answered Barron. "A skunk ain't got no smell unless he's a mind to."

"Well," said she, "I guess it ain't no skunk, anyhow. I kind o' feel it in my bones 'tain't no skunk, smell or no smell."

The woodsman looked puzzled. He had not imagined her capable of such unreasoning obstinacy. He began to wonder if he had overrated her intelligence.

"Then I give it up, Mrs. Gammit," said he, with an air of having lost all interest in the problem.

But that did not suit his visitor at all. Her manner became more conciliatory. Leaning forward, with an almost coaxing look on her face, she murmured—

"I've had an *idee* as how it *might* be—mind, I don't say it *is*, but jest it *might* be———" and she paused dramatically.

"Might be what?" inquired Barron, with reviving interest.

"Porkypines!" propounded Mrs. Gammit, with a sudden smile of triumph.

Joe Barron neither spoke nor smiled. But in his silence there was something that made Mrs. Gammit uneasy.

"Why *not* porkypines?" she demanded, her face once more growing severe.

"It *might* be porkypines as took them aigs o' yourn, Mrs. Gammit, an' it *might* be *bumbly-bees!*" responded Barron. "But 'tain't likely!"

Mrs. Gammit snorted at the sarcasm.

"Mebbe," she sneered, "ye kin tell me *why* it's so impossible it could be porkypines. I seen a big porkypine back o' the barn, only yestiddy. An' that's more'n kin be said o' yer weasels, an' foxes, an' skunks, what ye're so sure about, Mr. Barron."

"A porkypine ain't necess*air*ly after aigs jest because he's back of a barn," said the woodsman. "An' anyways, a porkypine don't eat aigs. He hain't got the right kind o' teeth fer them kind o' vittles. He's *got* to have something he kin gnaw on, somethin' substantial an' solid—the which he prefers is a young branch o' good tough spruce, though it *do* make his meat kinder strong. No, Mrs. Gammit, it ain't no porkypine what's stealin' yer aigs, take my word fer it. An' the more I think o' it the surer I be that it's a weasel. When a weasel learns to suck aigs, he gits powerful cute. Ye'll have to be right smart, I'm telling ye, to trap him."

During this argument of Barron's his obstinate and offended listener had become quite convinced of the justice of her own conclusions. The sarcasm had settled it. She *knew*, now, that she had been right all along in her suspicion of the porcupines. And with this certainty her indignation suddenly disappeared. It is *such* a comfort to be certain. So now, instead of flinging his ignorance in his face, she pretended to be convinced—remembering that she needed his advice as to how to trap the presumptuous porcupine.

"Well, Mr. Barron," said she, with the air of one who would take defeat gracefully, "supposin' ye're right—an' ye'd *oughter* know—how would ye go about *ketchin'* them weasels?"

Pleased at this sudden return to sweet reasonableness, the woodsman once more grew interested.

"I reckon we kin fix *that!*" said he, confidently and cordially. "I'll give ye three of my little mink traps. There's holes, I reckon, under the back an' sides o' the shed, or barn, or wherever it is that the hens have their nests?"

"Nat'rally!" responded Mrs. Gammit. "The thieves ain't agoin' to come in by the front doors, right under my nose, be they?"

"Of course," assented the woodsman. "Well, you jest set them 'ere traps in three o' them holes, well under the sills an' out o' the way. Don't go fer to *bait* 'em, mind, or Mr. Weasel 'll git to suspicionin' somethin', right off. Jest sprinkle bits of straw, an' hayseed, an' sech rubbish over 'em, so it all looks no ways out o' the ordinary. You do this right, Mrs. Gammit; an' first thing ye know ye'll have yer thief. I'll git the traps right now, an' show ye how to set 'em."

And as Mrs. Gammit walked away with the three steel traps under her arm, she muttered to herself—

"Yes, Joe Barron, an' I'll show ye the thief. An' he'll have quills on him, sech as no *weasel* ain't never had on him, I reckon."

On her return, Mrs. Gammit was greeted by the sound of high excitement among the poultry. They were all cackling wildly, and craning their necks to stare into the shed as if they had just seen a ghost there. Mrs. Gammit ran in to discover what all the fuss was about. The place was empty; but a smashed egg lay just outside one of the nests, and a generous tuft of fresh feathers showed her that there had been a tussle of some kind. Indignant but curious, Mrs. Gammit picked up the feathers, and examined them with discriminating eyes to see which hen had suffered the loss.

"Lands sakes!" she exclaimed presently, "ef 'tain't the old rooster! He's made a fight fer that 'ere aig! Lucky he didn't git stuck full o' quills!"

Then, for perhaps the hundredth time, she ran fiercely and noisily behind the barn, in the hope of surprising the enemy. Of course she surprised nothing which Nature had endowed with even the merest apology for eyes and ears; and a cat-bird in the choke-cherry bushes squawked at her derisively. Stealth was one of the things which Mrs. Gammit did not easily achieve. Staring defiantly about her, her eyes fell upon a dark, bunchy creature in the top of an old hemlock at the other side of the fence. Seemingly quite indifferent to her vehement existence, and engrossed in its own affairs, it was crawling out upon a high branch and gnawing, in a casual way, at the young twigs as it went.

"Ah, ha! What did I tell ye? I knowed all along as how it was a porkypine!" exclaimed Mrs. Gammit, triumphantly, as if Joe Barron could hear her across eight miles of woods. Then, as she eyed the imperturbable animal on the limb above her, her face flushed with quick rage, and snatching up a stone about the size of her fist she hurled it at him with all her strength.

In a calmer moment she would never have done this—not because it was rude, but because she had a conviction, based on her own experience, that a stone would hit anything rather than what it was aimed at. And in the present instance she found no reason to change her views on the subject. The stone did not hit the porcupine. It did not, even for one moment, distract his attention from the hemlock twigs. Instead of that, it struck a low branch, on the other side of the tree, and bounced back briskly upon Mrs. Gammit's toes.

With a hoarse squeak of surprise and pain the good lady jumped backwards, and hopped for some seconds on one foot while she gripped the other with both hands. It was a sharp and disconcerting blow. As the pain subsided a concentrated fury took its place. The porcupine was now staring down at her, in mild wonder at her inexplicable gyrations. She glared up at him, and the tufts of gray hair about her sunbonnet seemed to rise and stand rigid.

"Ye think ye're smart!" she muttered through her set teeth. "But I'll fix ye fer that! Jest you wait!" And turning on her heel she stalked back to the house. The big, brown teapot was on the back of the stove, where it had stood since breakfast, with a brew rust-red and bitter-strong enough to tan a moose-hide. Not until she had reheated it and consumed five cups, sweetened with molasses, did she recover any measure of self-complacency.

That same evening, when the last of the sunset was fading in pale violet over the stump pasture and her two cow-bells were *tonk-tonking* softly along the edge of the dim alder swamp, Mrs. Gammit stealthily placed the traps according to the woodsman's directions. Between the massive logs which formed the foundations of the barn and shed, there were openings numerous enough, and some of them spacious enough, almost, to admit a bear—a very small, emanciated bear. Selecting three of these, which somehow seemed to her fancy particularly adapted to catch a porcupine's taste, she set the traps, tied them, and covered them lightly with fine rubbish so that, as she murmured to herself when all was done, "everythin' looked as nat'ral as nawthing'." Then, when her evening chores were finished, she betook herself to her slumbers, in calm confidence that in the morning she would find one or more porcupines in the trap.

Having a clear conscience and a fine appetite, in spite of the potency of her tea Mrs. Gammit slept soundly. Nevertheless, along toward dawn, in that hour when dream and fact confuse themselves, her nightcapped ears became aware of a strange sound in the yard. She snorted impatiently and sat up in bed. Could some beneficent creature of the night be out there sawing wood for her? It sounded like it. But she rejected the idea at once. Rubbing her eyes with both fists, she crept to the window and looked out.

There was a round moon in the sky, shining over the roof of the barn, and the yard was full of a white, witchy radiance. In the middle of it crouched two big porcupines, gnawing assiduously at a small wooden tub. The noise of their busy teeth on the hard wood rang loud upon the stillness, and a low *tonk-a-tonk* of cow-bells came from the pasture as the cows lifted their heads to listen.

The tub was a perfectly good tub, and Mrs. Gammit was indignant at seeing it eaten. It had contained salt herrings; and she intended, after getting the flavour of fish scoured out of it, to use it for packing her winter's butter. She did not know that it was for the sake of its salty flavour that the porcupines were gnawing at it, but leaped to the conclusion that their sole object was to annoy and persecute herself.

"Shoo! Shoo!" she cried, snatching off her nightcap and flapping it at them frantically. But the animals were too busy to even look up at her. The only sign they gave of having heard her was to raise their quills straight on end so that their size apparently doubled itself all at once.

Mrs. Gammit felt herself wronged. As she turned and ran downstairs she muttered, "First it's me aigs—an' now it's me little tub—an' Lordy knows what it's goin' to be next!" Then her dauntless spirit flamed up again, and she snapped, "But there ain't agoin' to be no next!" and cast her eyes about her for the broom.

Of course, at this moment, when it was most needed, that usually exemplary article was not where it ought to have been—standing beside the dresser. Having no time to look for it, Mrs. Gammit snatched up the potato-masher, and rushed forth into the moonlight with a gurgling yell, resolved to save the tub.

She was a formidable figure as she charged down the yard, and at ordinary times the porcupines might have given way. But when a porcupine has found something it really likes to eat, its courage is superb. These two porcupines found the herring-tub delicious beyond anything they had ever tasted. Reluctantly they stopped gnawing for a moment, and turned their little twinkling eyes upon Mrs. Gammit in sullen defiance.

Now this was by no means what she had expected, and the ferocity of her attack slackened. Had it been a lynx, or even a bear, her courage would probably not have failed her. Had it been a man, a desperado with knife in hand and murder in his eyes, she would have flown upon him in contemptuous fury. But porcupines were different. They were mysterious to her. She believed firmly that they could shoot their quills, like arrows, to a distance of ten feet. She had a swift vision of herself stuck full of quills, like a pincushion. At a distance of eleven feet she stopped abruptly, and hurled the potato-masher with a deadly energy which carried it clean over the barn. Then the porcupines resumed their feasting, while she stared at them helplessly. Two large tears of rage brimmed her eyes, and rolled down her battered cheeks; and backing off a few paces she sat down upon the saw-horse to consider the situation.

But never would Mrs. Gammit have been what she was had she been capable of acknowledging defeat. In a very few moments her resourceful wits reasserted themselves.

"Queer!" she mused. "One don't never kinder seem to hit what one aims at! But one always hits *somethin'!* Leastways, *I* do! If I jest fling enough things, an' keep on aflingin', I might hit a porkypine jest as well as anything else. There ain't nawthin' onnateral about a porkypine, to keep one from hitt'n' him, I reckon."

The wood-pile was close by; and the wood, which she had sawed and split for the kitchen stove, was of just the handy size. She was careful, now, not to take aim, but imagined herself anxious to establish a new wood-pile, in haste, just about where that sound of insolent gnawing was disturbing the night. In a moment a shower of sizable firewood was dropping all about the herring-tub.

The effect was instantaneous. The gnawing stopped, and the porcupines glanced about uneasily. A stick fell plump upon the bottom of the tub, staving it in. The porcupines back away and eyed it with grieved suspicion. Another stick struck it on the side, so that it bounced like a jumping, live thing, and hit one of the porcupines sharply, rolling him over on his back. Instantly his valiant quills went down quite flat; and as he wriggled to his feet with a squeak of alarm, he looked all at once little and lean and dark, like a wet hen. Mrs. Gammit smiled grimly.

"Ye ain't feelin' quite so sassy now, be ye?" she muttered; and the sticks flew the faster from her energetic hands. Not many of them, to be sure, went at all in the direction she wished, but enough were dropping about the herring-tub to make the porcupines remember that they had business elsewhere. The one that had been struck had no longer any regard for his dignity, but made himself as small as possible and scurried off like a scared rat. The other, unvanquished but indignant, withdrew slowly, with every quill on end. The sticks fell all about him; but Mrs. Gammit, in the excitement of her triumph, was now forgetting herself so far as to take aim, therefore never a missile touched him. And presently, without haste, he disappeared behind the barn.

With something almost like admiration Mrs. Gammit eyed his departure.

"Well, seein' as I hain't scairt ye *much*," she muttered dryly, "mebbe ye'll obleege me by coming back an' gittin' into my trap. But ye ain't agoin' to hev no more o' my good herrin'-tub, ye ain't." And she strode down the yard to get the tub. It was no longer a good tub, for the porcupines had gnawed two big holes in the sides, and Mrs. Gammit's own missiles had broken in the bottom. But she obstinately bore the poor relics into the kitchen. Firewood they might become, but not food for the enemy.

No more that night was the good woman's sleep disturbed, and she slept later than usual. As she was getting up, conscience-stricken at the sound of the cows in the pasture lowing to be milked, she heard a squeaking and fluttering under the barn, and rushed out half dressed to see what was the matter. She had no doubt that one of the audacious porcupines had got himself into a trap.

But no, it was neither porcupine, fox, nor weasel. To her consternation, it was her old red top-knot hen, which now lay flat upon the trap, with outstretched wings, exhausted by its convulsive floppings. She picked it up, loosed the deadly grip upon its leg, and slammed the offending trap across the barn with such violence that it bounced up and fell into the swill-barrel. Her feelings thus a little relieved, she examined Red Top-knot's leg with care. It was hopelessly shattered and mangled.

"Ye cain't never scratch with *that* ag'in, ye cain't!" muttered Mrs. Gammit, compassionately. "Poor dear, ther ain't nawthin' fer it but to make vittles of ye now! Too bad! Too bad! Ye was always sech a fine layer an' a right smart setter!" And carrying the victim to the block on which she was wont to split kindling wood, she gently but firmly chopped her head off.

Half an hour later, as Mrs. Gammit returned from the pasture with a brimming pail of milk, again she heard a commotion under the barn. But she would not hurry, lest she should spill the milk. "Whatever it be, it'll be there when I git there!" she muttered philosophically; and kept on to the cool cellar with her milk. But as soon as she had deposited the pail she turned and fairly ran in her eagerness. The speckled hen was cackling vain-gloriously; and as Mrs. Gammit passed the row of nests in the shed she saw a white egg shining. But she did not stop to secure it.

As she entered the barn, a little yellowish brown animal, with a sharp, triangular nose and savage eyes like drops of fire, ran at her with such fury that for an instant she drew back. Then, with a roar of indignation at its audacity, she rushed forward and kicked at it. The kick struck empty air; but the substantial dimensions of the foot seemed to daunt the daring little beast, and it slipped away like a darting flame beneath the sill of the barn. The next moment, as she stooped to look at the nearest of the two traps, another slim yellow creature, larger than the first, leaped up, with a vicious cry, and almost reached her face. But, fortunately for her, it was held fast by both hind legs in the trap, and fell back impotent.

Startled and enraged, Mrs. Gammit kicked at it, where it lay darting and twisting like a snake. Naturally, she missed it; but it did not miss her. With unerring aim it caught the toe of her heavy cowhide shoe, and fixed its teeth in the tough leather. Utterly taken by surprise, Mrs. Gammit tried to jump backwards. But instead of that, she fell flat on her back, with a yell. Her sturdy heels flew up in the air, while her petticoats flopped back in her face, bewildering her. The weasel, however, had maintained his dogged grip upon the toe of her shoe; so something *had* to give. That something was the cord which anchored the trap. It broke under the sudden strain. Trap and weasel together went flying over Mrs. Gammit's prostrate head. They brought up with a stupefying slam against the wall of the pig-pen, making the pig squeal apprehensively.

Disconcerted and mortified, Mrs. Gammit scrambled to her feet, shook her petticoats into shape, and glanced about to see if the wilderness in general had observed her indiscretion. Apparently, nothing had noticed it. Then, with an air of relief, she glanced down at her vicious little antagonist. The weasel lay stunned, apparently dead. But she was not going to trust appearances. Picking trap and victim up together, on the end of a pitchfork, she carried them out and dropped them into the barrel of rain water at the corner of the house. Half-revived by the shock, the yellow body wriggled for a moment or two at the bottom of the barrel. As she watched it, a doubt passed through Mrs. Gammit's mind. Could Joe Barron have been right? *Was* it weasels, after all, that were taking her eggs? But she dismissed the idea at once. Joe Barron didn't know everything! And there, indisputably, were the porcupines, bothering her all the time, with unheard-of impudence. Weasels, indeed!

"'Twa'n't *you* I was after," she muttered obstinately, apostrophizing the now motionless form in the rain-barrel. "It was them dratted porkypines, as comes after my aigs. But *ye're* a bad lot, too, an' I'm right glad to have got ye where ye won't be up to no mischief."

All athrill with excitement, Mrs. Gammit hurried through her morning's chores, and allowed herself no breakfast except half a dozen violent cups of tea "with sweetenin'." Then, satisfied that the weasel in the rain-barrel was by this time securely and permanently dead, she fished it out, and reset the trap in its place under the barn. The other trap she discovered in the swill-barrel, after a long search. Relieved to find it unbroken, she cleaned it carefully and put it away to be returned, in due time, to its owner. She would not set it again —and, indeed, she would have liked to smash it to bits, as a sacrifice to the memory of poor Red Top-knot.

"I hain't got no manner o' use fer a porkypine trap what'll go out o' its way to ketch hens," she grumbled.

The silent summer forenoon, after this, wore away without event. Mrs. Gammit, working in her garden behind the house, with the hot, sweet scent of the flowering buckwheat-field in her nostrils and the drowsy hum of bees in her ears, would throw down her hoe about once in every half-hour and run into the barn to look hopefully at the traps. But nothing came to disturb them. Neither did anything come to disturb the hens, who attended so well to business that at noon Mrs. Gammit had seven fresh eggs to carry in. When night came, and neither weasels nor porcupines had given any further sign of their existence, Mrs. Gammit was puzzled. She was one of those impetuous women who expect everything to happen all at once. When milking was over, and her solitary, congenial supper, she sat down on the kitchen doorstep and considered the situation very carefully.

What she had set herself out to do, after the interview with Joe Barron, was to catch a porcupine in one of his traps, and thus, according to her peculiar method of reasoning, convince the confident woodsman that porcupines *did* eat eggs! As for the episode of the weasel, she resolved that she would not say anything to him about it, lest he should twist it into a confirmation of his own views. As for those seven eggs, so happily spared to her, she argued that the capture of the weasel, with all its attendant excitement, had served as a warning to the porcupines and put them on their guard. Well, she would give them something else to think about. She was now all impatience, and felt unwilling to await the developments of the morrow, which, after all, might refuse to develop! With a sudden resolution she arose, fetched the gnawed and battered remains of the herring-tub from their concealment behind the kitchen door, and propped them up against the side of the house, directly beneath her bedroom window.

At first her purpose in this was not quite clear to herself. But the memory of her triumph of the previous night was tingling in her veins, and she only knew she wanted to lure the porcupines back, that she might do *something* to them. And first, being a woman, that something occurred to her in connexion with hot water. How conclusive it would be to wait till the porcupines were absorbed in their consumption of the herring-tub, and then pour scalding water down upon them. After all, it was more important that she should vanquish her enemies than prove to a mere man that they really were her enemies. What did she care, anyway, what that Joe Barron thought? Then, once more, a doubt assailed her. What if he were right? Not that she would admit it, for one moment. But just supposing! Was she going to pour hot water on those porcupines, and scald all the bristles off their backs, if they really *didn't* come after her eggs? Mrs. Gammit was essentially just and kind-hearted, and she came to the conclusion that the scheme might be too cruel.

"Ef it be you uns as takes the aigs," she murmured thoughtfully, "a kittle o' bilin' water to yer backs ain't none too bad fer ye! But ef it be *only* my old herrin'-tub ye're after, then bilin' water's too ha'sh!"

In the end, the weapon she decided upon was the big tin pepper-pot, well loaded.

Through the twilight, while the yard was all in shadow, Mrs. Gammit sat patient and motionless beside her open window. The moon rose, seeming to climb with effort out of the tangle of far-off tree-tops. The faint, rhythmic breathing of the wilderness, which, to the sensitive ear, never ceases even in the most profound calm, took on the night change, the whisper of mystery, the furtive suggestion of menace which the daylight lacks. Sitting there in ambush, Mrs.

Gammit felt it all, and her eager face grew still and pale and solemn like a statue's. The moonlight crept down the roofs of the barn and shed and house, then down the walls, till only the ground was in shadow. And at last, through this lower stratum of obscurity, Mrs. Gammit saw two squat, sturdy shapes approaching leisurely from behind the barn.

She held her breath. Yes, it was undoubtedly the porcupines. Undaunted by the memory of their previous discomfiture, they came straight across the yard, and up to the house, and fell at once to their feasting on the herring-tub. The noise of their enthusiastic gnawing echoed strangely across the attentive air.

Very gently, with almost imperceptible motion, Mrs. Gammit slid her right hand, armed with the pepper-pot, over the edge of the window-sill. The porcupines, enraptured with the flavour of the herring-tub, never looked up. Mrs. Gammit was just about to turn the pepper-pot over, when she saw a third dim shape approaching, and stayed her hand. It was bigger than a porcupine. She kept very still, breathing noiselessly through parted lips. Then the moonlight reached the ground, the shadows vanished, and she saw a big wildcat stealing up to find out what the porcupines were eating.

Seeing the feasters so confident and noisy, yet undisturbed, the usually cautious wildcat seemed to think there could be no danger near. Had Mrs. Gammit stirred a muscle, he would have marked her; but in her movelessness her head and hand passed for some harmless natural phenomenon. The wildcat crept softly up, and as he drew near, the porcupines raised their quills threateningly, till nothing could be seen of their bodies but their blunt snouts still busy on the herring-tub. At a distance of about six feet the big cat stopped, and crouched, glaring with wide, pale eyes, and sniffing eagerly. Mrs. Gammit was amazed that the porcupines did not at once discharge a volley at him and fill him full of quills for his intrusion.

The wildcat knew too much about porcupines to dream of attacking them. It was what they were eating that interested him. They seemed to enjoy it so much. He crept a few inches nearer, and caught a whiff of the herring-tub. Yes, it was certainly fish. A true cat, he doted on fish, even salt fish. He made another cautious advance, hoping that the porcupines might retire discreetly. But instead of that they merely stopped gnawing, put their noses between their forelegs, squatted flat, and presented an unbroken array of needle points to his dangerous approach.

The big cat stopped, quite baffled, his little short tail, not more than three inches long, twitching with anger. He could not see that the tub was empty; but he could smell it, and he drew in his breath with noisy sniffling. It filled him with rage to be so baffled; for he knew it would be fatal to go any nearer, and so expose himself to a deadly slap from the armed tails of the porcupines.

Just what he would have attempted, however, in his eagerness, will never be known. For at this point, Mrs. Gammit's impatience overcame her curiosity. With a gentle motion of her wrist she turned the pepper-pot over, and softly shook it. The eyes of the wildcat were fixed upon that wonderful, unattainable herring-tub, and he saw nothing else. But Mrs. Gammit in the vivid moonlight saw a fine cloud of pepper sinking downwards slowly on the moveless air.

Suddenly the wildcat pawed at his nose, drew back, and grew rigid with what seemed an effort to restrain some deep emotion. The next moment he gave vent to a loud, convulsive sneeze, and began to spit savagely. He appeared to be not only very angry, but surprised as well. When he fell to clawing frantically at his eyes and nose with both paws, Mrs. Gammit almost strangled with the effort to keep from laughing. But she held herself in, and continued to shake down the pungent shower. A moment more, and the wildcat, after an explosion of sneezes which almost made him stand on his head, gave utterance to a yowl of consternation, and turned to flee. As he bounded across the yard he evidently did not see just where he was going, for he ran head first into the wheelbarrow, which straightway upset and kicked him. For an instant he clawed at it wildly, mistaking it for a living assailant. Then he recovered his wits a little, and scurried away across the pasture, sneezing and spitting as he went.

Meanwhile the porcupines, with their noses to the ground and their eyes covered, had been escaping the insidious attack of the pepper. But at last it reached them. Mrs. Gammit saw a curious shiver pass over the array of quills.

Now it was contrary to all the most rigid laws of the porcupine kind to uncoil themselves in the face of danger. At the same time, it was impossible to sneeze in so constrained an attitude. Their effort was heroic, but self-control at last gave way. As it were with a snap, one of the globes of quills straightened itself out, and sneezed and sneezed and sneezed. Then the other went through the same spasmodic process, while Mrs. Gammit, leaning half-way out of the window, squealed and choked with delight. But the porcupines were obstinate, and would not run away. Very slowly they turned and retired down the yard, halting every few feet to sneeze. With tears streaming down her cheeks Mrs. Gammit watched their retreat, till suddenly some of the vagrant pepper was wafted back to her own nostrils, and she herself was shaken with a mighty sneeze. This checked her mirth on the instant. Her face grew grave, and drawing back with a mortified air she slammed the window down.

"Might 'a' knowed I'd be aketchin' cold," she muttered, "settin' in a draught this time o' night."

Not until she had thoroughly mastered the tickling in her nostrils did she glance forth again. Then the porcupines were gone, and not even an echo of their far-off sneezes reached her ears.

In the days that followed, neither weasel, wildcat, nor porcupine came to Mrs. Gammit's clearing, and the daily harvest of strictly fresh eggs was unfailing. At the end of a week, the good lady felt justified in returning the traps to Joe Barron, and letting him know how mistaken he had been.

"There, Mr. Barron," said she, handing him the three traps, "I'm obleeged to you, an' there's yer traps. But there's one of 'em ain't no good."

"Which one be it?" asked the woodsman as he took them.

"I've marked it with a bit of string," replied Mrs. Gammit.

"What's the matter with it? I don't see nawthin' wrong with it!" said Barron, examining it critically.

"'Tain't no good! You take my word fer it! That's all I've got to say!" persisted Mrs. Gammit.

"Oh, well, seein' as it's you sez so, Mrs. Gammit, that's enough," agreed the woodsman, civilly. "But the other is all right, eh? What did they ketch?"

"Well, they ketched a big weasel!" said Mrs. Gammit, eyeing him with challenge.

A broad smile went over Barron's face.

"I knowed it," he exclaimed. "I knowed as how it was a weasel."

"An' *I* knowed as how ye'd say jest them very words," retorted Mrs. Gammit. "But ye don't know everythin', Joe Barron. It wa'n't no weasel as was takin' them there aigs!"

"What were it then?" demanded the woodsman, incredulously.

"It was two big porkypines an' a monstrous big wildcat," answered Mrs. Gammit in triumph.

"Did ye ketch 'em at it?" asked the woodsman, with a faint note of sarcasm in his voice. But the sarcasm glanced off Mrs. Gammit's armour. She regarded the question as a quite legitimate one.

"No, I kain't say as I did, *exackly*," she replied. "But they come anosin' round, an' to teach 'em a lesson to keep their noses out o' other people's hens' nests I shook a little pepper over 'em. I tell ye, they took to the woods, asneezin' that bad I thought ye might 'a' heard 'em all the way over here. Ye'd 'ave bust yerself laffin', ef ye could 'a' seed 'em rootin'. An' since then, Mr. Barron, I git all the aigs I want. Don't ye talk to me o' *weasels*—the skinny little rats. *They* ain't wuth noticin', no more'n a chipmunk."

The Vagrants of the Barren

With thick smoke in his throat and the roar of flame in his ears, Pete Noël awoke, shaking as if in the grip of a nightmare. He sat straight up in his bunk. Instantly he felt his face scorching. The whole cabin was ablaze. Leaping from his bunk, and dragging the blankets with him, he sprang to the door, tore it open, and rushed out into the snow.

But being a woodsman, and alert in every sense like the creatures of the wild themselves, his wits were awake almost before his body was, and his instincts were even quicker than his wits. The desolation and the savage cold of the wilderness had admonished him even in that terrifying moment. As he leaped out in desperate flight, he had snatched with him not only the blankets, but his rifle and cartridge-belt from where they stood by the head of the bunk, and also his larrigans and great blanket coat from where they lay by its foot. He had been sleeping, according to custom, almost fully clothed.

Outside in the snow he stood, blinking through scorched and smarting lids at the destruction of his shack. For a second or two he stared down at the things he clutched in his arms, and wondered how he had come to think of them in time. Then, realizing with a pang that he needed something more than clothes and a rifle, he flung them down on the snow and made a dash for the cabin, in the hope of rescuing a hunk of bacon or a loaf of his substantial woodsman's bread. But before he could reach the door a licking flame shot out and hurled him back, half blinded. Grabbing up a double handful of snow, he buried his face in it to ease the smart. Then he shook himself, coolly carried the treasures he had saved back to a safe distance from the flames, and sat down on the blankets to put on his larrigans.

His feet, clothed only in a single pair of thick socks, were almost frozen, while the rest of his body was roasting in the fierce heat of the conflagration. It wanted about two hours of dawn. There was not a breath of air stirring, and the flames shot straight up, murky red and clear yellow intertwisting, with here and there a sudden leaping tongue of violet white. Outside the radius of the heat the tall woods snapped sharply in the intense cold. It was so cold, indeed, that as the man stood watching the ruin of his little, lonely home, shielding his face from the blaze now with one hand then with the other, his back seemed turning to ice.

The man who lives alone in the great solitude of the forest has every chance to become a philosopher. Pete Noël was a philosopher. Instead of dwelling upon the misfortunes which had smitten him, he chose to consider his good luck in having got out of the shack alive. Putting on his coat, he noted with satisfaction that its spacious pockets contained matches, tobacco, his pipe, his heavy clasp-knife, and his mittens. He was a hundred miles from the nearest settlement, fifty or sixty from the nearest lumber-camp. He had no food. The snow was four feet deep, and soft. And his trusty snow-shoes, which would have made these distances and these difficulties of small account to him, were helping feed the blaze. Nevertheless, he thought, things might have been much worse. What if he had escaped in his bare feet? This thought reminded him of how cold his feet were at this moment. Well the old shack had been a good one, and sheltered him well enough. Now that it would shelter him no longer, it should at least be made to contribute something more to his comfort. Piling his blankets carefully under the shelter of a broad stump, he sat down upon them. Then he filled and lighted his pipe, leaned back luxuriously, and stretched out his feet to the blaze. It would be time enough for him to "get a move on" when the shack was quite burned down. The shack was home as long as it lasted.

When the first mystic greyness, hard like steel and transparent like glass, began to reveal strange vistas among the ancient trees, the fire died down. The shack was a heap of ashes and pulsating, scarlet embers, with here and there a flickering, half-burned timber, and the red-hot wreck of the tiny stove sticking up in the ruins. As soon as the ruins were cool enough to approach, Pete picked up a green pole, and began poking earnestly among them. He had all sorts of vague hopes. He particularly wanted his axe, a tin kettle, and something to eat. The axe was nowhere to be found, at least in such a search as could then be made. The tins, obviously, had all gone to pieces or melted. But he did, at least, scratch out a black, charred lump about the size of his fist, which gave forth an appetizing smell. When the burnt outside had been carefully scraped off, it proved to be the remnant of a side of bacon. Peter fell to his breakfast with about as much ceremony as might have sufficed a hungry wolf, the deprivation of a roof-tree having already taken him back appreciably nearer to the elemental brute. Having devoured his burnt bacon, and quenched his thirst by squeezing some half-melted snow into a cup of birch-bark, he rolled his blankets into a handy pack, squared his shoulders, and took the trail for Conroy's Camp, fifty miles southwestward.

It was now that Pete Noël began to realize the perils that confronted him. Without his snowshoes, he found himself almost helpless. Along the trail the snow was from three to four feet deep, and soft. There had been no thaws and no hard winds to pack it down. After floundering ahead for four or five hundred yards he would have to stop and rest, half reclining. In spite of the ferocious cold, he was soon drenched with sweat. After a couple of hours of such work, he found himself consumed with thirst. He had nothing to melt the snow in; and, needless to say, he knew better than to ease his need by eating the snow itself. But he hit upon a plan which filled him with self-gratulation. Lighting a tiny fire beside the trail, under the shelter of a huge hemlock, he took off his red cotton neckerchief, filled it with snow, and held it to the flames. As the snow began to melt, he squeezed the water from it in a liberal stream. But, alas! the stream was of a colour that was not enticing. He realized, with a little qualm, that it had not occurred to him to wash that handkerchief since—well, he was unwilling to say when. For all the insistence of his thirst, therefore, he continued melting the snow and squeezing it out, till the resulting stream ran reasonably clear. Then patiently he drank, and afterward smoked three pipefuls of his rank, black tobacco as substitute for the square meal which his stomach was craving.

All through the biting silent day he floundered resolutely on, every now and then drawing his belt a little tighter, and all the while keeping a hungry watch for game of some kind. What he hoped for was rabbit, partridge, or even a fat porcupine; but he would have made a shift to stomach even the wiry muscles of a mink, and count himself fortunate. By sunset he came out on the edge of a vast barren, glorious in washes of thin gold and desolate purple under the touch of the fading west. Along to eastward ran a low ridge, years ago licked by fire, and now crested with a sparse line of ghostly rampikes, their lean, naked tops appealing to the inexorable sky. This was the head of the Big Barren. With deep disgust, and something like a qualm of apprehension, Pete Noël reflected that he had made only fifteen miles in that long day of effort. And he was ravenously hungry. Well, he was too tired to go farther that night; and in default of a meal, the best thing he could do was sleep. First, however, he unlaced his larrigans, and with the thongs made shift to set a clumsy snare in a rabbit track a few paces back among the spruces. Then, close under the lee of a black wall of fir-trees standing out beyond the forest skirts, he clawed himself a deep trench in the snow. In one end of this trench he built a little fire, of broken deadwood and green birch saplings laboriously hacked into short lengths with his clasp-knife. A supply of this firewood, dry and green mixed, he piled beside the trench within reach. The bottom of the trench, to within a couple of feet of the fire, he lined six inches deep with spruce-boughs, making a dry, elastic bed.

By the time these preparations were completed, the sharp-starred winter night had settled down upon the solitude. In all the vast there was no sound but the occasional snap, hollow and startling, of some great tree overstrung by the frost, and the intimate little whisper and hiss of Pete's fire down in the trench. Disposing a good bunch of boughs under his head, Pete lighted his pipe, rolled himself in his blankets, and lay down with his feet to the fire.

There at the bottom of his trench, comforted by pipe and fire, hidden away from the emptiness of the enormous, voiceless world outside, Peter Noël looked up at the icy stars, and at the top of the frowning black rampart of the fir-trees, touched grimly with red flashes from his fire. He knew well—none better than he—the savage and implacable sternness of the wild. He knew how dreadful the silent adversary against whom he had been called, all unprepared, to pit his craft. Thee was no blinking the imminence of his peril. Hitherto he had always managed to work, more or less, *with* nature, and so had come to regard the elemental forces as friendly. Now they had turned upon him altogether and without warning. His anger rose as he realized that he was at bay. The indomitable man-spirit awoke with the anger. Sitting up suddenly, over the edge of the trench his deep eyes looked out upon the shadowy spaces of the night with challenge and defiance. Against whatever odds, he declared to himself, he was master. Having made his proclamation in that look, Pete Noël lay down again and went to sleep.

After the fashion of winter campers and of woodsmen generally, he awoke every hour or so to replenish the fire; but toward morning he sank into the heavy sleep of fatigue. When he aroused himself from this, the fire was stone grey, the sky overhead was whitish, flecked with pink streamers, and rose-pink lights flushed delicately the green wall of the fir-trees leaning above him. The edges of the blankets around his face were rigid and thick with ice from his breathing. Breaking them away roughly, he sat up, cursed himself for having let the fire out, then, with his eyes just above the edge of the trench, peered forth across the shining waste. As he did so, he instinctively shrank back into concealment. An eager light flamed into his eyes, and he blessed his luck that the fire had gone out. Along the crest of the ridge, among the rampikes, silhouetted dark and large against the sunrise, moved a great herd of caribou, feeding as they went.

Crouching low in his trench, Pete hurriedly did up his blankets, fixed the pack on his back, then crawled through the snow into the shelter of the fir-woods. As soon as he was out of sight, he arose, recovered the thongs of his larrigans from the futile snare, and made his way back on the trail as fast as he could flounder. That one glance over the edge of his trench had told his trained eye all he needed to know about the situation.

The caribou, most restless, capricious, and far-wandering of all the wilderness kindreds, were drifting south on one of their apparently aimless migrations. They were travelling on the ridge, because as Pete instantly inferred, the snow there had been partly blown away, partly packed, by the unbroken winds. They were far out of gunshot. But he was going to trail them down even through that deep snow. By tireless persistence and craft he would do it, if he had to do it on his hands and knees.

Such wind as there was, a light but bitter air drawing irregularly down out of the north-west, blew directly from the man to the herd, which was too far off, however, to catch the ominous taint and take alarm. Pete's first care was to work around behind the herd till this danger should be quite eliminated. For a time his hunger was forgotten in the interest of the hunt; but presently, as he toiled his slow way through the deep of the forest, it grew too insistent to be ignored. He paused to strip bark from such seedlings of balsam fir as he chanced upon, scraping off and devouring the thin, sweetish pulp that lies between the bark and the mature wood. He gathered, also, the spicy tips of the birch-buds, chewing them up by handfuls and spitting out the residue of hard husks. And in this way he managed at least to soothe down his appetite from angry protest to a kind of doubtful expectancy.

At last, after a couple of hours' hard floundering, the woods thinned, the ground sloped upward, and he came out upon the flank of the ridge, a long way behind the herd, indeed, but well around the wind. In the trail of the herd the snow was broken up, and not more than a foot and a half in depth. On a likely-looking hillock he scraped it away carefully with his feet, till he reached the ground; and here he found what he expected—a few crimson berries of the wintergreen, frozen, but plump and sweetfleshed. Half a handful of these served for the moment to cajole his hunger, and he pressed briskly but warily along the ridge, availing himself of the shelter of every rampike in his path. At last, catching sight of the hindmost stragglers of the herd, still far out of range, he crouched like a cat, and crossed over the crest of the ridge for better concealment.

On the eastern slope the ridge carried numerous thickets of underbrush. From one to another of these Pete crept swiftly, at a rate which should bring him, in perhaps an hour, abreast of the leisurely moving herd. In an hour, then, he crawled up to the crest again, under cover of a low patch of juniper scrub. Confidently, he peered through the scrub, his rifle ready. But his face grew black with bitter disappointment. The capricious beasts had gone. Seized by one of their incomprehensible vagaries—Pete was certain that he had not alarmed them—they were now far out on the white level, labouring heavily southward.

Pete set his jaws resolutely. Hunger and cold, each the mightier from their alliance, were now assailing him savagely. His first impulse was to throw off all concealment and rush straight down the broad-trodden trail. But on second thought he decided that he would lose more than he would gain by such tactics. Hampered though they were by the deep, soft snow, he knew that, once frightened, they could travel through it much faster than they were now moving, and very much faster than he could hope to follow. Assuredly, patience was his game. Slipping furtively from rampike to rampike, now creeping, now worming his way like a snake, he made good time down to the very edge of the level. Then, concealment no more possible, and the rear of the herd still beyond gunshot, he emerged boldly from the covert of a clump of saplings and started in pursuit. At the sight of him, every antlered head went up in the air for one moment of wondering alarm; then, through a rolling white cloud the herd fled onward at a speed which Pete, with all his knowledge of their powers, had not imagined possible in such a state of the snow. Sullen, but not discouraged, he plodded after them.

Noël was now fairly obsessed with the one idea of overtaking the herd. Every other thought, sense, or faculty was dully occupied with his hunger and his effort to keep from thinking of it. Hour after hour he plodded on, following the wide, chaotic trail across the white silence of the barren. There was nothing to lift his eyes for, so he kept them automatically occupied in saving his strength by picking the easiest steps through the ploughed snow. He did not notice at all that the sun no longer sparkled over the waste. He did not notice that the sky had turned from hard blue to ghostly pallor. He did not notice that the wind, now blowing in his teeth, had greatly increased in force. Suddenly, however, he was aroused by a swirl of fine snow driven so fiercely that it crossed his façe like a lash. Lifting his eyes from the trail, he saw that the plain all about him was blotted from sight by a streaming rout of snow-clouds. The wind was already whining its strange derisive menace in his face. The blizzard had him.

As the full fury of the storm swooped upon him, enwrapping him, and clutching at his breath, for an instant Pete Noël quailed. This was a new adversary, with whom he had not braced his nerves to grapple. But it was for an instant only. Then his weary spirit lifted itself, and he looked grimly into the eye of the storm. The cold, the storm, the hunger, he would face them all down, and win out yet. Lowering his head, and pulling a flap of his blanket coat across his mouth to make breathing easier, he plunged straight forward with what seemed like a new lease of vigour.

Had the woods been near, or had he taken note of the weather in time, Pete would have made for the shelter of the forest at once. But he knew that, when last he looked, the track of the herd had been straight down the middle of the ever-widening barren. By now he must be a good two miles from the nearest cover; and he knew well enough that, in the bewilderment of the storm, which blunted even such woodcraft as his, and blurred not only his vision, but every other sense as well, he could never find his way. His only hope was to keep to the trail of the caribou. The beasts would either lie down or circle to the woods. In such a storm as this, as he knew well enough, no animal but man himself could hunt, or follow up the trail. There was no one but man who could confront such a storm undaunted. The caribou would forget both their cunning and the knowledge that they were being hunted. He would come upon them, or they would lead him to shelter. With an obstinate pride in his superiority to the other creatures of the wilderness, he scowled defiantly at the storm, and because he was overwrought with hunger and fatigue, he muttered to himself as he went, cursing the elements that assailed him so relentlessly.

For hours he floundered on doggedly, keeping the trail by feeling rather than by sight, so thick were the cutting swirls of snow. As the drift heaped denser and denser about his legs, the terrible effort, so long sustained began to tell on him, till his progress became only a snail's pace. Little by little, in the obstinate effort to conserve strength and vitality, his faculties all withdrew into themselves, and concentrated themselves upon the one purpose—to keep going onward. He began to feel the lure of just giving up. He began to think of the warmth and rest he could get, the release from the mad chaos of the wind, by the simple expedient of burrowing deep into the deep snow. He knew well enough that simple trick of the partridge, when frost and storm grow too ferocious for it. But his wiser spirit would not let him delude himself. Had he had a full stomach, and food in his pockets, he might, perhaps, safely have emulated this cunning trick of the partridge. But now, starving, weary, his vitality at the last ebb, he knew that if he should yield to the lure of the snow, he would be seen no more till the spring sun should reveal him, a thing of horror to the returning vireos and blackbirds, on the open, greening face of the barren. No, he would not burrow to escape the wind. He laughed aloud as he thought upon the madness of it; and went butting and plunging on into the storm, indomitable.

Suddenly, however, he stopped short, with a great sinking in his heart. He felt cautiously this way and that, first with his feet, fumbling through the deep snow, and then with his hands. At last he turned his back abruptly to the wind, cowered down with his head between his arms to shut out the devilish whistling and whining, and tried to think how or when it had happened. He had lost the trail of the herd!

All his faculties stung to keen wakefulness by this appalling knowledge, he understood how it happened, but not where. The drifts had filled the trail, till it was utterly blotted off the face of the plain; then he had kept straight on, guided by the pressure of the wind. But the caribou, meanwhile, had swerved, and moved off in another direction. Which direction? He had to acknowledge to himself that he had no clue to judge by, so whimsical were these antlered vagrants of the barren. Well, he thought doggedly, let them go! He would get along without them. Staggering to his feet, he faced the gale again, and thought hard, striving to remember what the direction of the wind had been when last he observed it, and at the same time to recall the lay of the heavy-timbered forest that skirted this barren on two sides.

At length he made up his mind where the nearest point of woods must be. He saw it in his mind's eye, a great promontory of black firs jutting out into the waste. He turned, calculating warily, till the wind came whipping full upon his left cheek. Sure that he was now facing his one possible refuge, he again struggled forward. And as he went, he pictured to himself the whole caribou herd, now half foundered in the drift, labouring toward the same retreat. Once more, crushing back hunger and faintness, he summoned up his spirit, and vowed that if the beasts could fight their way to cover, he could. Then his woodcraft should force the forest to render him something in the way of food that would suffice to keep life in his veins.

For perhaps half an hour this defiant and unvanquishable spirit kept Pete Noël going. But as the brief northern day began to wane, and a shadow to darken behind the thick white gloom of the storm, his forces, his tough, corded muscles and his tempered nerves, again began to falter. He caught himself stumbling, and seeking excuse for delay in getting up. In spite of every effort of his will, he saw visions—thick, protecting woods close at one side or the other, or a snug log camp, half buried in the drifts, but with warm light flooding from its windows. Indignantly he would shake himself back into sanity, and the delectable visions would vanish. But while they lasted they were confusing, and presently when he aroused himself from one that was of particularly heart-breaking vividness, he found that he had let his rifle drop! It was gone hopelessly. The shock steadied him for some minutes. Well, he had his knife. After all, that was the more important of the two. He ploughed onward, once more keenly awake, and grappling with his fate.

The shadows thickened rapidly; and at last, bending with the insane riot of the storm, began to make strange, monstrous shapes. Unravelling these illusions, and exorcising them, kept Pete Noël occupied. But suddenly one of these monstrous shapes neglected to vanish. He was just about to throw himself upon it, in half delirious antagonism, when it lurched upward with a snort, and struggled away from him. In an instant Pete was alive in every faculty, stung with an ecstasy of hope. Leaping, floundering, squirming, he followed, open knife in hand. Again and yet again the foundered beast, a big caribou bull, buried halfway up the flank, eluded him. Then, as his savage scramble at last overtook it, the bull managed to turn half about, and thrust him violently in the left shoulder with an antler-point. Unheeding the hurt, Noël clutched the antler with his left hand, and forced it inexorably back. The next moment his knife was drawn with practised skill across the beast's throat.

Like most of our eastern woodsmen, Pete Noël was even finicky about his food, and took all his meat cooked to a brown. He loathed underdone flesh. Now, however, he was an elemental creature, battling with the elements for his life. And he knew, moreover, that of all possible restoratives, the best was at his hand. He drove his blade again, this time to the bull's heart. As the wild life sighed itself out, and vanished, Pete crouched down like an animal, and drank the warm, red fluid streaming from the victim's throat. As he did so, the ebbed tide of warmth, power, and mastery flooded back into his own veins. He drank his fill; then, burrowing half beneath the massive body, he lay down close against it to rest and consider.

Assured now of food to sustain him on the journey, assured of his own ability to master all other obstacles that might seek to withstand him, Pete Noël made up his mind to sleep, wrapping himself in his blankets under the shelter of the dead bull. Then the old hunter's instinct began to stir. All about him, in every momentary lull of the wind, were snortings and heavy breathings. He had wandered into the midst of the exhausted herd. Here was a chance to recoup himself, in some small part, for the loss of his cabin and supplies. He could kill a few of the helpless animals, hide them in the snow, and take the bearings of the spot as soon as the weather cleared. By and by he could get a team from the nearest settlement, and haul out the frozen meat for private sale when the game warden chanced to have his eyes shut.

Getting out his knife again, he crept stealthily toward the nearest heavy breathing. Before he could detect the beast in that tumultuous gloom, he was upon it. His outstretched left hand fell upon a wildly heaving flank. The frightened animal arose with a gasping snort, and tried to escape; but, utterly exhausted, it sank down again almost immediately, resigned to this unknown doom which stole upon it out of the tempest and the dark. Pete's hand was on it again the moment it was still. He felt it quiver and shrink beneath his touch. Instinctively he began to stroke and rub the still hair as he slipped his treacherous hand forward along the heaving flank. The heavings grew quieter, the frightened snortings ceased. The exhausted animal seemed to feel a reassurance in that strong, quiet touch.

When Pete's hand had reached the unresisting beast's neck, he began to feel a qualm of misgiving. His knife was in the other hand, ready for use there in the howling dark; but somehow he could not at once bring himself to use it. It would be a betrayal. Yet he had suffered a grievous loss, and here, given into his grasp by fate, was the compensation. He hesitated, arguing with himself impatiently. But even as he did so, he kept stroking that firm, warm, living neck; and through the contact there in the savage darkness, a sympathy passed between the man and the beast. He could not help it. The poor beasts and he were in the same predicament, together holding the battlements of life against the blind and brutal madness of storm. Moreover, the herd had saved him. The debt was on his side. The caress which had been so traitorous grew honest and kind. With a shamefaced grin Pete shut his knife, and slipped it back into his pocket.

With both hands, now, he stroked the tranquil caribou, rubbing it behind the ears and at the base of the antlers, which seemed to give it satisfaction. Once when his hand strayed down the long muzzle, the animal gave a terrified start and snort at the dreaded man smell so violently invading its nostrils. But Pete kept on soothingly and firmly; and again the beast grew calm. At length Pete decided that his best place for the night, or until the storm should lift, would be by the warmth of this imprisoned and peaceable animal. Digging down into the snow beyond the clutches of the wind, he rolled himself in his blankets, crouched close against the caribou's flank, and went confidently to sleep.

Aware of living companionship, Noël slept soundly through the clamour of the storm. At last a movement against his side disturbed him. He woke to feel that his strange bedfellow had struggled up and withdrawn. The storm was over. The sky above his upturned face was sharp with stars. All about him was laboured movement, with heavy shuffling, coughing, and snorting. Forgetful of their customary noiselessness, the caribou were breaking gladly from their imprisonment. Presently Pete was alone. The cold was still and of snapping intensity; but he, deep in his hollow, and wrapped in his blankets, was warm. Still drowsy, he muffled his face and went to sleep again, for another hour.

When he roused himself a second time he was wide awake and refreshed. It was just past the edge of dawn. The cold gripped like a vice. Faint mystic hues seemed frozen for ever into the ineffable crystal of the air. Pete stood up, and looked eastward along the tumbled trail of the herd. Not half a mile away stood the forest, black and vast, the trail leading straight into it. Then, a little farther down toward the right he saw something that made his heart leap exultantly. Rising straight up, a lavender and silver lily against the pallid saffron of the east, soared a slender smoke. That smoke, his trained eyes told him, came from a camp chimney; and he realized that the lumbermen had moved up to him from the far-off head of the Ottanoonsis.

The Ledge on Bald Face

That one stark naked side of the mountain which gave it its name of Old Bald Face fronted full south. Scorched by sun and scourged by storm throughout the centuries, it was bleached to an ashen pallor that gleamed startlingly across the leagues of sombre, green-purple wilderness outspread below. From the base of the tremendous bald steep stretched off the interminable leagues of cedar swamp, only to be traversed in dry weather or in frost. All the region behind the mountain face was an impenetrable jumble of gorges, pinnacles, and chasms, with black woods clinging in crevice and ravine and struggling up desperately towards the light.

In the time of spring and autumn floods, when the cedar swamps were impenetrable to all save mink, otter, and musk-rat, the only way from the western plateau to the group of lakes that formed the source of the Ottanoonsis, on the east, was by a high, nerve-testing trail across the wind-swept brow of Old Bald Face. The trail followed a curious ledge, sometimes wide enough to have accommodated an ox-wagon, at other times so narrow and so perilous that even the sure-eyed caribou went warily in traversing it.

The only inhabitants of Bald Face were the eagles, three pairs of them, who had their nests, widely separated from each other in haughty isolation, on jutting shoulders and pinnacles accessible to no one without wings. Though the ledge-path at its highest point was far above the nests, and commanded a clear view of one of them, the eagles had learned to know that those who traversed the pass were not troubling themselves about eagles' nests. They had also observed another thing—of interest to them only because their keen eyes and suspicious brains were wont to note and consider everything that came within their purview—and that was that the scanty traffic by the pass had its more or less regular times and seasons. In seasons of drought or hard frost it vanished altogether. In seasons of flood it increased the longer the floods lasted. And whenever there was any passing at all, the movement was from east to west in the morning, from west to east in the afternoon.

This fact may have been due to some sort of dimly recognised convention among the wild kindreds, arrived at in some subtle way to avoid unnecessary—and necessarily deadly—misunderstanding and struggle. For the creatures of the wild seldom fight for fighting's sake. They fight for food, or, in the mating season, they fight in order that the best and strongest may carry off the prizes.

But mere purposeless risk and slaughter they instinctively strive to avoid. The airy ledge across Bald Face, therefore, was not a place where the boldest of the wild kindred—the bear or the bull-moose, to say nothing of lesser champions—would wilfully invite the doubtful combat. If, therefore, it had been somehow arrived at that there should be no disastrous meetings, no face-to-face struggles for the right of way, at a spot where dreadful death was inevitable for one or both of the combatants, that would have been in no way inconsistent with the accepted laws and customs of the wilderness. On the other hand, it is possible that this alternate easterly and westerly drift of the wild creatures—a scanty affair enough at best of times—across the front of Bald Face was determined in the first place, on clear days, by their desire not to have the sun in their eyes in making the difficult passage, and afterwards hardened into custom. It was certainly better to have the sun behind one in treading the knife-edge pass above the eagles.

Joe Peddler found it troublesome enough that strong, searching glare from the unclouded sun of early morning full in his eyes as he worked over toward the Ottanoonsis lakes. He had never attempted the crossing of Old Bald Face before, and he had always regarded with some scorn the stories told by Indians of the perils of that passage. But already, though he had accomplished but a small portion of his journey, and was still far from the worst of the pass, he had been forced to the conclusion that report had not exaggerated the difficulties of his venture. However, he was steady of head and sure of foot, and the higher he went in that exquisitely clear, crisp air, the more pleased he felt with himself. His great lungs drank deep of the tonic wind which surged against him rhythmically, and seemed to him to come unbroken from the outermost edges of the world. His eyes widened and filled themselves, even as his lungs, with the ample panorama that unfolded before them. He imagined—for the woodsman, dwelling so much alone, is apt to indulge some strange imaginings—that he could feel his very spirit enlarging, as if to take full measure of these splendid breadths of sunlit, wind-washed space.

Presently, with a pleasant thrill, he observed that just ahead of him the ledge went round an abrupt shoulder of the rock-face at a point where there was a practically sheer drop of many hundreds of feet into what appeared a feather-soft carpet of tree-tops. He looked shrewdly to the security of his footing as he approached, and also to the roughnesses of the rock above the ledge, in case a sudden violent gust should chance to assail him just at the turn. He felt that at such a spot it would be so easy—indeed, quite natural—to be whisked off by the sportive wind, whirled out into space, and dropped into that green carpet so far below.

In his flexible oil-tanned "larrigans" of thick cow-hide, Peddler moved noiselessly as a wild-cat, even over the bare stone of the ledge. He was like a grey shadow drifting slowly across the bleached face of the precipice. As he drew near the bend of the trail, of which not more than eight or ten paces were now visible to him, he felt every nerve grow tense with exhilarating expectation. Yet, even so, what happened was the utterly unexpected.

Around the bend before him, stepping daintily on her fine hooves, came a young doe. She completely blocked the trail just on that dizzy edge.

Peddler stopped short, tried to squeeze himself to the rock like a limpet, and clutched with fingers of iron at a tiny projection.

The doe, for one second, seemed petrified with amazement. It was contrary to all tradition that she should be confronted on that trail. Then, her amazement instantly dissolving into sheer madness of panic, she wheeled about violently to flee. But there was no room for even her lithe body to make the turn. The inexorable rock-face bounced her off, and with an agonised bleat, legs sprawling and great eyes starting from their sockets, she went sailing down into the abyss.

With a heart thumping in sympathy, Peddler leaned outward and followed that dreadful flight, till she reached that treacherously soft-looking carpet of tree-tops and was engulfed by it. A muffled crash came up to Peddler's ears.

"Poor leetle beggar!" he muttered. "I wish't I hadn't scared her so. But I'd a sight rather it was her than me!"

Peddler's exhilaration was now considerably damped. He crept cautiously to the dizzy turn of the ledge and peered around. The thought upon which his brain dwelt with unpleasant insistence was that if it had been a surly old bull-moose or a bear which had confronted him so unexpectedly, instead of that nervous little doe, he might now be lying beneath that deceitful green carpet in a state of dilapidation which he did not care to contemplate.

Beyond the turn the trail was clear to his view for perhaps a couple of hundred yards. It climbed steeply through a deep re-entrant, a mighty perpendicular corrugation of the rock-face, and then disappeared again around another jutting bastion. He hurried on rather feverishly, not liking that second interruption to his view, and regretting, for the first time, that he had no weapon with him but his long hunting-knife. He had left his rifle behind him as a useless burden to his climbing. No game was now in season, no skins in condition to be worth the shooting, and he had food enough for the journey in his light pack. He had not contemplated the possibility of any beast, even bear or bull-moose, daring to face him, because he knew that, except in mating-time, the boldest of them would give a man wide berth. But, as he now reflected, here on this narrow ledge even a buck or a lynx would become dangerous, finding itself suddenly at bay.

The steepness of the rise in the trail at this point almost drove Peddler to helping himself with his hands. As he neared the next turn, he was surprised to note, far out to his right, a soaring eagle, perhaps a hundred feet below him. He was surprised, too, by the fact that the eagle was paying no attention to him whatever, in spite of his invasion of the great bird's aerial domain. Instinctively he inferred that the eagle's nest must be in some quite inaccessible spot at safe distance from the ledge. He paused to observe from above, and thus fairly near at hand, the slow flapping of those wide wings, as they employed the wind to serve the majesty of their flight. While he was studying this, another deduction from the bird's indifference to his presence flashed upon his mind. There must be a fairly abundant traffic of the wild creatures across this pass, or the eagle would not be so indifferent to his presence. At this thought he lost his interest in problems of flight, and hurried forward again, anxious to see what might be beyond the next turn of the trail.

His curiosity was gratified all too abruptly for his satisfaction. He reached the turn, craned his head around it, and came face to face with an immense black bear.

The bear was not a dozen feet away. At sight of Peddler's gaunt dark face and sharp blue eyes appearing thus abruptly and without visible support around the rock, he shrank back upon his haunches with a startled "woof."

As for Peddler, he was equally startled, but he had too much discretion and self-control to show it. Never moving a muscle, and keeping his body out of sight so that his face seemed to be suspended in mid-air, he held the great beast's eyes with a calm, unwinking gaze.

The bear was plainly disconcerted. After a few seconds he glanced back over his shoulder, and seemed to contemplate a strategic movement to the rear. As the ledge at this point was sufficiently wide for him to turn with due care, Peddler expected now to see him do so. But what Peddler did not know was that dim but cogent "law of the ledge," which forbade all those who travelled by it to turn and retrace their steps, or to pass in the wrong direction at the wrong time. He did not know what the bear knew namely—that if that perturbed beast *should* turn, he was sure to be met and opposed by other wayfarers, and thus to find himself caught between two fires.

Watching steadily, Peddler was unpleasantly surprised to see the perturbation in the bear's eyes slowly change into savage resentment —resentment at being balked in this inalienable right to an unopposed passage over the ledge. To the bear's mind that grim, confronting face was a violation of the law which he himself obeyed loyally and without question. To be sure, it was the face of man, and therefore to be dreaded. It was also mysterious, and therefore still more to be dreaded. But the sense of bitter injustice, with the realisation that he was at bay and taken at a disadvantage, filled him with a frightened rage which swamped all other emotion. Then he came on.

His advance was slow and cautious by reason of the difficulty of the path and his dread lest that staring, motionless face should pounce upon him just at the perilous turn and hurl him over the brink. But Peddler knew that his bluff was called, and that his only chance was to avoid the encounter. He might have fled by the way he had come, knowing that he would have every advantage in speed on that narrow trail. But before venturing up to the turn he had noted a number of little projections and crevices in the perpendicular wall above him. Clutching at them with fingers of steel and unerring toes, he swarmed upwards as nimbly as a climbing cat. He was a dozen feet up before the bear came crawling and peering around the turn.

Elated at having so well extricated himself from so dubious a situation, Peddler gazed down upon his opponent and laughed mockingly. The sound of that confident laughter from straight above his head seemed to daunt the bear and thoroughly damp his rage. He crouched low, and scurried past growling. As he hurried along the trail at a rash pace, he kept casting anxious glances over his shoulder, as if he feared the man were going to chase him. Peddler lowered himself from his friendly perch and continued his journey, cursing himself more than ever for having been such a fool as not to bring his rifle.

In the course of the next half-hour he gained the highest point of the ledge, which here was so broken and precarious that he had little attention to spare for the unparalleled sweep and splendour of the view. He was conscious, however, all the time, of the whirling eagles, now far below him, and his veins thrilled with intense exhilaration. His apprehensions had all vanished under the stimulus of that tonic atmosphere. He was on the constant watch, however, scanning not only the trail ahead—which was now never visible for more than a hundred yards or so at a time—and also the face of the rock above him, to see if it could be scaled in an emergency.

He had no expectation of an emergency, because he knew nothing of the law of the ledge. Having already met a doe and a bear, he naturally inferred that he would not be likely to meet any other of the elusive kindreds of the wild, even in a whole week of forest faring. The shy and wary beasts are not given to thrusting themselves upon man's dangerous notice, and it was hard enough to find them, with all his woodcraft, even when he was out to look for them. He was, therefore, so surprised that he could hardly believe his eyes when, on rounding another corrugation of the rock-face, he saw another bear coming to meet him.

"Gee!" muttered Peddler to himself. "Who's been lettin' loose the menagerie? Or hev I got the nightmare, mebbe?"

The bear was about fifty yards distant—a smaller one than its predecessor, and much younger also, as was obvious to Peddler's initiated eye by the trim glossiness of its coat. It halted the instant it caught sight of Peddler. But Peddler, for his part, kept right on, without showing the least sign of hesitation or surprise. This bear, surely, would give way before him. The beast hesitated, however. It was manifestly afraid of the man. It backed a few paces, whimpering in a worried fashion, then stopped, staring up the rock-wall above it, as if seeking escape in that impossible direction.

"If ye're so skeered o' me as ye look," demanded Peddler, in a crisp voice, "why in h—ll don't ye turn an' vamoose, 'stead o' backin' an' fillin' that way? Ye can't git up that there rock, 'less ye're a fly."

The ledge at that point was a comparatively wide and easy path; and the bear at length, as if decided by the easy confidence of Peddler's tones, turned and retreated. But it went off with such reluctance, whimpering anxiously the while, that Peddler was forced to the conclusion there must be something coming up the trail which it was dreading to meet. At this idea Peddler was delighted, and hurried on as closely as possible at the retreating animal's heels. The bear, he reflected, would serve him as an excellent advance guard, protecting him perfectly from surprise, and perhaps, if necessary, clearing the way for him. He chuckled to himself as he realised the situation, and the bear, catching the incomprehensible sound, glanced nervously over its shoulder and hastened its retreat as well as the difficulties of the path would allow.

The trail was now descending rapidly, though irregularly, towards the eastern plateau. The descent was broken by here and there a stretch of comparatively level going, here and there a sharp though brief rise, and at one point the ledge was cut across by a crevice some four feet in width. As a jump, of course, it was nothing to Peddler; but in spite of himself he took it with some trepidation, for the chasm looked infinitely deep, and the footing on the other side narrow and precarious. The bear, however, had seemed to take it quite carelessly, almost in its stride, and Peddler, not to be outdone, assumed a similar indifference.

It was not long, however, before the enigma of the bear's reluctance to retrace its steps was solved. The bear, with Peddler some forty or fifty paces behind, was approaching one of those short steep rises which broke the general descent. From the other side of the rise came a series of heavy breathings and windy grunts.

"Moose, by gum!" exclaimed Peddler. "Now, I'd like to know if *all* the critters hev took it into their heads to cross Old Bald Face to-day!"

The bear heard the gruntlings also, and halted unhappily, glancing back at Peddler.

"Git on with it!" ordered Peddler sharply. And the bear, dreading man more than moose, got on.

The next moment a long, dark, ominous head, with massive, overhanging lip and small angry eyes, appeared over the rise. Behind this formidable head laboured up the mighty humped shoulders and then the whole towering form of a moose-bull. Close behind him followed two young cows and a yearling calf.

"Huh! I guess there's goin' to be some row!" muttered Peddler, and cast his eyes up the rock-face, to look for a point of refuge in case his champion should get the worst of it.

At sight of the bear the two cows and the yearling halted, and stood staring, with big ears thrust forward anxiously, at the foe that barred their path. But the arrogant old bull kept straight on, though slowly, and with the wariness of the practised duellist. At this season of the year his forehead wore no antlers, indeed, but in his great knife-edged fore-hooves he possessed terrible weapons which he could wield with deadly dexterity. Marking the confidence of his advance, Peddler grew solicitous for his own champion, and stood motionless, dreading to distract the bear's attention.

But the bear, though frankly afraid to face man, whom he did not understand, had no such misgivings in regard to moose. He knew how to fight moose, and he had made more than one good meal, in his day, on moose calf. He was game for the encounter. Reassured to see that the man was not coming any nearer, and possibly even sensing instinctively that the man was on his side in this matter, he crouched close against the rock and waited, with one huge paw upraised, like a boxer on guard, for the advancing bull to attack.

He had not long to wait.

The bull drew near very slowly, and with his head held high as if intending to ignore his opponent. Peddler, watching intently, felt some surprise at this attitude, even though he knew that the deadliest weapon of a moose was its fore-hooves. He was wondering, indeed, if the majestic beast expected to press past the bear without a battle, and if the bear, on his part, would consent to this highly reasonable arrangement. Then like a flash, without the slightest warning, the bull whipped up one great hoof to the height of his shoulder and struck at his crouching adversary.

The blow was lightning swift, and with such power behind it that, had it reached its mark, it would have settled the whole matter then and there. But the bear's parry was equally swift. His mighty forearm fended the stroke so that it hissed down harmlessly past his head and clattered on the stone floor of the trail. At the same instant, before the bull could recover himself for another such pile-driving blow, the bear, who had been gathered up like a coiled spring, elongated his body with all the force of his gigantic hindquarters, thrusting himself irresistibly between his adversary and the face of the rock, and heaving outwards.

These were tactics for which the great bull had no precedent in all his previous battles. He was thrown off his balance and shouldered clean over the brink. By a terrific effort he turned, captured a footing upon the edge with his fore-hooves, and struggled frantically to drag himself up again upon the ledge. But the bear's paw struck him a crashing buffet straight between the wildly staring eyes. He fell backwards, turning clean over, and went bouncing, in tremendous sprawling curves, down into the abyss.

Upon the defeat of their leader the two cows and the calf turned instantly—which the ledge at this point was wide enough to permit—and fled back down the trail at a pace which seemed to threaten their own destruction. The bear followed more prudently, with no apparent thought of trying to overtake them. And Peddler kept on behind him, taking care, however, after this exhibition of his champion's powers, not to press him too closely.

The fleeing herd soon disappeared from view. It seemed to have effectually cleared the trail before it, for the curious procession of the bear and Peddler encountered no further obstacles.

After about an hour the lower slopes of the mountain were reached. The ledge widened and presently broke up, with trails leading off here and there among the foothills. At the first of these that appeared to offer concealment the bear turned aside and vanished into a dense grove of spruce with a haste which seemed to Peddler highly amusing in a beast of such capacity and courage. He was content, however, to be so easily quit of his dangerous advance guard.

"A durn good thing for me," he mused, "that that there b'ar never got up the nerve to call my bluff, or I might 'a' been layin' now where that unlucky old bull-moose is layin', with a lot o' flies crawlin' over me."

And as he trudged along the now easy and ordinary trail, he registered two discreet resolutions—first, that never again would he cross Old Bald Face without his gun *and* his axe; and second, that never again would he cross Old Bald Face at all, unless he jolly well had to.

Textual Note

The sources[1] of the copy texts for the stories are as follows:

"Mothers of the North" from *Neighbours Unknown* (New York: Macmillan, 1911).

"A Master of Supply" from *Hoof and Claw* (New York: Macmillan, 1914).

"The Keepers of the Nest" from *Feet of the Furtive* (London: Ward, Lock, 1912).

"By the Winter Tide" from *The Watchers of the Trails* (Boston: Page, 1904).

"The Little Homeless One" from *Wisdom of the Wilderness* (New York: Dent, 1923).

"The Lord of the Air" from *The Kindred of the Wild* (Boston: Page, 1902).

"The Keeper of the Water Gate" from *The Watchers of the Trails.*

"The King of the Mamozekel" from *The Kindred of the Wild.*

"The Little Wolf of the Pool" from *The Watchers of the Trails.*

"Little Silk Wing" from *The Children of the Wild* (New York: Macmillan, 1913).

"Queen Bomba of the Honey-Pots" from *They Who Walk the Wild* (New York: Macmillan, 1924).

"Mrs Gammit and the Porcupines" from *The Backwoodsmen* (New York: Macmillan, 1911).

"Vagrants of the Barren," from *The Backwoodsmen.*

"The Ledge on Bald Face" from *The Secret Trails* (New York: Macmillan, 1916)

---

[1] Following Donald Conway's strong argument that the American published collections of Roberts' work best reflect his authorial intentions, I have where possible used these for the sources of the copy texts. See Donald Conway, "Actaeon or Odysseus: The Bibliographer's Roberts," in *The Proceedings of the Sir Charles G.D. Roberts Symposium*, ed. by Carrie MacMillan (Halifax: Centre for Canadian Studies, Mount Allison University / Nimbus, 1984), 5-16.

Selective Bibliography

Note: The most comprehensive bibliography of Roberts is contained in Glenn Clever, ed., *The Charles G.D. Roberts Symposium* (Ottawa, 1984), and prepared by John Coldwell Adams.

i) Selected Titles from Roberts' Own Collections of Animal Stories

Earth's Enigmas. Boston: Lamson Wolffe, 1896.
The Kindred of the Wild: A Book of Animal Life. Boston: Page, 1902.
The Watchers of the Trails: A Book of Animal Life. Boston: Page, 1904.
The Haunters of the Silences: A Book of Animal Life. Boston: Page, 1907.
The Backwoodsmen. New York: Macmillan, 1911.
Feet of the Furtive. London: Ward, Lock, 1912.
Hoof and Claw. New York: Macmillan, 1914.
The Secret Trails. New York: Macmillan, 1916.
Wisdom of the Wilderness. New York: Macmillan, 1923.

ii) Other Selections of Roberts' Animal Stories

Bennett, E.H., ed. *Forest Folk*. Toronto: Ryerson, 1949.
Lucas, Alec. *The Last Barrier and Other Stories*. Toronto: McClelland & Stewart, 1958.
Gold, Joseph, ed. *King of Beasts and Other Stories*. Toronto: Ryerson, 1967.
Eyes of the Wilderness. Copyright Joan Roberts. Illustrated by Brian Carter. Toronto: McGraw-Hill Ryerson, 1980.
Adams, John Coldwell, ed. *The Lure of the Wild: the*

last three animal stories by Sir Charles G.D. Roberts. Ottawa: Borealis, 1980.

iii) Animal Stories by Other Authors for Comparison

Kipling, Rudyard. *The Jungle Book*. [1894] London: Macmillan, 1950.

———. *The Second Jungle Book* [1895] London: Macmillan, 1950.

Seton, Ernest Thompson. *Selected Animal Stories of Ernest Thompson Seton*. Edited by Patricia Morley. Ottawa: Ottawa University Press, 1977. *Available in paperback.

Whitaker, Muriel, ed. *Great Canadian Animal Stories*. Edmonton: Hurtig, 1978.

iv) Critical Discussions of the Animal Stories

a) The Nature Fakir Controversy

Burroughs, John. "Real and Sham Natural History," *Atlantic Monthly* XCI (March 1903), 198-309.

———. "Mr. Roberts' *Red Fox*," *Outing* XLVIII (July 1906), 512a-512b.

———. *Ways of Nature* (Being Vol XI of *The Complete Writings of John Burroughs*). London: Wise, 1924.

Roberts, Charles G.D., "Prefatory Note" to *The Watchers of the Trails*. Boston: Page, 1904.

Clark, Edward B., "Roosevelt on Nature Fakirs," *Everybody's Magazine* XVI (June 1907), 770-4.

Roosevelt, Theodore, "Nature Fakers," *Everybody's Magazine* VII (Sept 1907), 423-7.

MacLulich, T.D., "The Animal Story and the Nature Faker Controversy," *Essays on Canadian Writing*, No. 33 (Fall 1986), 112-24.

b) Early Discussions (before 1965)

Anon., "The Animal Story," *Edinburgh Review* CCXIV (July 1911), 94-118.

Roberts, Charles G.D., "Ernest Thompson Seton," *The Bookman, London*, 45 (1913), 147-9.

Poirier, Michael, "The Animal Story in Canadian Literature," *Queen's Quarterly* XXXIV (Winter 1927), 198-312; 398-419.

Lucas, A., "Introduction" to *The Last Barrier and Other Stories*. Toronto: McClelland & Stewart, 1958.

Magee, W.H., "The Animal Story: A Challenge in Technique," *Dalhousie Review* XLIV (1964), 156-64.

c) Recent Discussions (since 1964)

Gold, Joseph, "The Precious Speck of Life," *Canadian Literature*, No. 26 (Aut 1965), 22-32.

Lucas, Alec, "Nature Writers and the Animal Story," in *Literary History of Canada*. Toronto: University of Toronto Press, 1965. Also in 2nd Edition of this, Vol I. Toronto: University of Toronto Press, 1976.

Keith, W.J., "Stories of Wild Life," in *Charles G.D. Roberts*. Toronto: Copp Clark, 1969.

Polk, James, "Lives of the Hunted," *Canadian Literature*, No. 53 (Summer 1972), 51-9.

Murray, Tim, "In the Ancient Wood," *Journal of Canadian Fiction*, No. 15 (1975), 158-60. (On *The Heart of the Ancient Wood*, but illuminating on Roberts' attitude to romantic idealism.)

MacDonald, Robert H., "The Revolt against Instinct: The Animal Stories of Seton and Roberts," *Canadian Literature*, No. 84 (Spring 1980), 18-29. (A return to the nature fakir controversy in contemporary terms.)

Ware, Martin. *Canadian Romanticism in Transition: Divergent Perspectives in an Era of Upheaval*. Unpublished Ph.D. Thesis, Dalhousie University, 1980. (Contains a discussion of the evolution of Roberts' vision, including his Darwinian ideas, as writer, and particularly as poet.)

Cogswell, Fred. *Sir Charles G.D. Roberts and his Works*. Toronto: ECW Press, 1983. Also in *Canadian Writers and their Works: Poetry Series*, vol 2. Ed. by Robert Lecker et al. Toronto: ECW Press, 1983, 186-232.

Clever, Glenn. *The Sir Charles G.D. Roberts Symposium: Reappraisals: Canadian Writers: 10*. Ottawa: University of Ottawa Press, 1984.

Macmillan, Carrie. *The Proceedings of the Sir Charles G.D. Roberts Symposium*: Mount Allison University. Sackville & Halifax: Centre for Canadian Studies Mt A & Nimbus, 1984.

Conway, C. Donald. *Sufficient Vision: A Reading of the Poetry and Prose Fiction of Charles G.D. Roberts*. Unpublished Ph.D. Thesis. University of New Brunswick, 1985.

Whalen, Terry, "Charles G.D. Roberts," in *Canadian Writers and their Works: Fiction Series*, Vol 2. Ed. by Robert Lecker et al. Toronto: ECW Press, 1989.

v) Biographical Studies of Roberts

Roberts, Lloyd. *The Book of Roberts*. Toronto: Ryerson, 1923.

Pomeroy, Elsie. *Sir Charles G.D. Roberts: A Biography*. Toronto: Ryerson, 1943.

Polk, James. *Wilderness Writers: Ernest Thompson Seton, Charles G.D. Roberts, Grey Owl*. Toronto: Clarke Irwin, 1972.

Adams, John Coldwell. *Sir Charles God Damn: The*

Life of Charles G.D. Roberts.Toronto: University of Toronto Pres, 1986.

Boone, Laurel, ed. *The Collected Letters of Sir Charles G.D. Roberts*. Fredericton: Goose Lane, 1989.

vi) Scientific Discussions of the Kinship of Man and Animals

Ewer, R.F. *Ethology of Mammals*. London: Elek, 1973.

Griffin, Donald R. *Animal Thinking*. Cambridge: Harvard University Press, 1984.

———. *The Limits of Animal Awareness*. 2nd Edition. New York: Rockefeller University Press, 1981.

Lorenz, Konrad. *Animal and Human Behaviour*. Vol II Cambridge: Harvard University Press, 1971.

Tolman, E.C. *Purposive Behavior in Man and Animals*. New York: Appleton Century, 1932.

Québec, Canada
1997